Daughters of Disaster

Carol Dare

Carol Albrecht Dare

Daughters of Disaster

by

Carol Albrecht Dare

Copyright 2015 by Carol Albrecht Dare

All rights reserved.

ISBN: 1512271071

ISBN 13: 9781512271072

Art by Fran Stuck

Juniper Books may be purchased through booksellers or by contacting

Carol Dare
Juniper Books
1843 Lexington Circle, S.E.
Salem, OR 97306
503-623-3184
cdare14@yahoo.com

Author's note

Except for historical figures, the characters in this book are imaginary. A colored regiment, with a renowned band, served with distinction as part of the French Fourth Army, earning numerous citations during World War I. The historical events are correct, but I have taken occasional minor liberties with geography and the details of their performances in order to make a coherent story.

Comments about Carol Albrecht Dare's book *When the World Wept*, historical fiction during the Great Depression and World War II

Friend and Family stories and "letters in her personal collection from family members in the military forces make the characters come alive." Phyllis A. Costanti

"...represented well what average families might have gone through. I learned a lot from all the facts and details about the war." Jessie Figueroa

"...interesting and delightful World War II story filled with the sights and sounds of the period. You hear children laugh, feel Oregon breezes, and smell clean desert air. You feel the stresses of war on the characters." L. Gaither

...true to life story inspired by actual experiences of a Dallas, Oregon, nurse during World War II. Fran Stuck

"...like a stepping stone back in time. ...little details give this book an authentic tone ...effects of WWII on daily life for the average American. Appealing characters..." JJ Oregon

"...I enjoyed Oregon history during WWII. In addition, ...the book provided a look backwards at family values and national pride...." Norma Ninomiya

<u>Dedicated to my children</u>

Crystal Ann Wittich

Loyd Lee White

Victor Lee Wachsmuth

Main Characters

The Hoffman Families:
 1. John (born 1860) married Pamela
    Children:
    Jack
    Thelma
    Frank
    Leah
    Eric
    Barbara
    Samuel

 2. Thomas (born 1862) married Blanche Spencer
    Children:
    Julia
    Amy
    Tom
    Alex
    Diane

 3. Robert (born 1865) married Catherine
    Children:
    Bob
    Rachel

The Spencer characters:
The Spencer Sisters:
 Blanche
 Elizabeth

The Spencer Brothers (3rd cousins of Elizabeth and Blanche)
 Hiram
 Phil

Other important characters:
 Sonia Kirkendall
 Vicky Kirkendall (daughter of Sonia)
 Drew Robinson married Frances
 Matthew McCall
Scott Morris and Vince Morris, brothers

Chapter One

December, 1904

Elizabeth Spencer, Plainville's oldest spinster at twenty-eight, planned to make a home for her five nieces and nephews if her sister died. But she had not counted on Blanche.

Her three nieces greeted her at the door of their American farmhouse style home. Elizabeth's shirtwaist, jacket, and long flannel skirt were slightly damp from the rain. "I left as soon as I heard," she said, removing her hat.

"I'm sorry you had to cut your Omaha assignment short, but she's been asking for you." Julia, the oldest niece at eighteen, led her through the hallway, covered with a long braided rug, to their sick mother's bedroom. The other two girls followed.

"Would you like a cup of coffee?" Amy offered.

Elizabeth shook her head, her eyes lighting on Diane, the youngest, who looked terrified. Though the three sisters shared the same coffee-colored hair and blue eyes, Diane's face displayed a small pink birthmark near the right temple as well as especially handsome, intelligent eyes framed by long lashes.

The girls left the two women alone. Elizabeth sat beside her sister's bed, and heard with dismay the plans Blanche had made for her children. "You can't do that, Blanche!"

"It's for the best. You're too young to be saddled with five children." Blanche spoke in a thin, but determined voice from her bed.

"But I want them. I could have had five of my own by now. Are you sure Dr. Williams knows what he is talking about?"

"I've seen two doctors. There's no way around it. I have an inoperable tumor. I'll soon be gone."

"Oh, my dear sister." Elizabeth took her hand. "You've been like a mother to me too. Still, I don't want to see my nieces and nephews farmed out to just anybody. Why can't they live with me?"

"They're going to live with people I know and respect. Julia will earn her keep at the hotel. The owner, as you know, is a dear friend of mine. Hannah Baker will give Julia a job as soon as she learns the work."

"The others are much too young to do that. Let them live with me."

"Amy is sixteen. She is to live at the Schafer farm. Mrs. Schafer has been poorly for a long time. With only young children of her own, she can use the help."

"But why not let your children stay with me? "

"Unmarried? With you going off for private nursing? Dashing off all the time to work for the Red Cross? And writing for the paper? You enjoy what you do. The children would interfere with that."

"I could give it up." Elizabeth tried to control her tears. She hadn't counted on this at all.

"Tom will go to the Gephart family. They're short of sons. He can learn how to farm."

"Oh, Blanche, he's only fifteen, and I don't think he's very interested in farming. He likes adventure."

"Alex will live with Reverend Rice and his wife. He can help with chores. Now that he's fourteen, he's old enough to learn the blacksmith trade with his uncle John here in town."

"If he can't live with me, a home with John Hoffman would be best. The man would be a good influence."

"With seven children of their own, he and Pamela don't have room for more, but he can teach Alex his trade a few hours a day."

"And little Diane? Surely she can live with me." Elizabeth held her breath.

Blanche winced.

"Is the pain worse?"

"Yes, today it is. Robert and Catherine Hoffman have agreed to have Diane."

"Not that cold-hearted mercenary. Is he going to teach her banking?" Elizabeth could not hide the sarcasm in her voice. Robert showed little respect for working women, and he never hired them. He dominated every conversation. Even Robert's wife, naturally talkative, barely got in a word when Robert was around.

"It'll be some time before my youngest can learn a trade. She's only thirteen."

"I could teach her mine."

"Writing? She might have no interest in it. It's best she go with her other uncle. It's all in my will. You're to keep this house. When the children are grown, maybe you can provide a home for them here in town if necessary."

"Well, of course. I could provide a home for them now if you'd let me." *Please let me. They need me and I need them. I've always wanted children.*

"It wouldn't work. Still, I trust you to step in if things don't work out for them."

"Yes, I understand." Elizabeth sighed in resignation. "Have you heard from their father?"

"Of course not. Thomas ran off to Omaha with that woman. Though he settled money on each of them when they reach twenty-one, his children are of no further concern to him."

Elizabeth was silent. Had Thomas Hoffman heard Blanche was dying? Surely his brothers here in Plainville, John and Robert, would have let him know that his former wife was gravely ill.

Yet, even if he wanted the children, could they be happy with him in Omaha? Elizabeth knew nothing of his new wife. At least here in Plainville, the children were among familiar surroundings. She would be able to visit them and make sure they were safe.

Blanche said in a weak voice, "I'm tired now, Lizzy. Let me rest. I've worked hard to find good homes for the children, places where they could learn to make a living."

"I'm sure you have. You've been a thoughtful mother. Sleep now, Blanche. I'll look in on you later." She tucked the quilt around her sister.

◆ ◆ ◆

Diane, listening at her mother's bedroom door, dashed out of the hallway. She was terrified of losing her mama. If only she'd been a better daughter. Then Mama would be well.

Of the three brothers, Uncle John, the blacksmith, was the oldest. Thomas, her papa, was in the middle. He lived in Omaha.

Robert was the youngest. The thought of living with Uncle Robert filled her with dread. He was a stiff, cold man. He and Uncle John were vastly different. Robert was tall, smooth, imposing.

Uncle John, shorter and slightly stocky, was cheerful and friendly. His house rang with laughter and song. Robert's was intimidating, despite Aunt Catherine's efforts to be welcoming.

◆ ◆ ◆

Elizabeth left the house filled with sadness. She had realized for some time that Blanche was not well. But she had clung to the hope that Dr. Williams would be able to cure her. That hope was gone.

The gray sky matched her wretched spirits. Cold wind stung her eyes and whipped around her as she tramped swiftly, but she would never be able to escape the devastating news she had just received. Her long skirts barely escaped brushing the mud on the road, but her sturdy shoes became caked.

She passed the dry goods store owned by Rex Jenkins, a widower, who gave her a bright smile. She returned a wave from a customer, hitching his horse in front, but she hurried on to avoid a visit. Several men waited their turn in the barber shop. Robert Hoffman pushed through the door of the bank. Shopkeepers along Main Street opened their doors. A few horses hitched to farm wagons were tethered to posts.

When she passed the last building on the edge of Plainville, she gazed out over the empty prairie, muddy and dark. Some people called the plains lonely, but she'd never felt it so before. Now, already missing her sister, she found it desolate. Blanche was the only close relative she had left, except for the children.

Usually she greeted the month of December with pleasure and jubilation. Not today. She wept bitter tears.

Why couldn't Blanche see that the children belonged with her? Especially galling was the idea of Diane living with Robert Hoffman. It was a mystery as to why Blanche didn't see Robert for the grasping, aloof man he was. His son, Bob, unsociable and impolite, would be no companion either.

Despite her meager income, she knew she could provide for the children. After all, Blanche had managed on her small savings and by taking in occasional boarders, not much more than she could make nursing and writing articles. And there was plenty of room in the large house she would inherit.

She'd lost Warren shortly after her graduation from nursing school. The children filled the void he left in her life when she returned to Plainville. Her only chance to be a mother, to have a family with her, had now evaporated.

Still, she could not defy her sister's wishes. Now they would be scattered, unable to see each other, to live as brothers and sisters. How would they adjust to their new surroundings?

She straightened. She would have to be brave for all of them. She resolved that she would try to fill the empty place left by their mother in the lives of her nieces and nephews, and provide love and support whenever she could.

◆ ◆ ◆

Elizabeth's best friends were Frances and Drew Robinson. The couple had located in Plainville a few years ago from Lincoln where they had attended the university. Together, the energetic couple published the *Plainville Gazette,* and lived in rooms behind the newspaper office. As Elizabeth shared many of their beliefs and interests, they quickly befriended her.

Frances Robinson, her beautiful, delicate features showing concern, said, "what is it, Elizabeth? You're very quiet."

Looking up, Elizabeth shook herself. "I'm not a very good dinner guest, am I? I'm thinking about Blanche. I wish she would let me raise the children. I love them very much."

"Of course you do." Frances took her hand in sympathy. "Still, you should give her credit for thinking of you. Five children at your age all alone would be a tremendous burden as well as a financial one."

"But for little Diane to live with Robert Hoffman, just because he is her father's brother. It's not right." She moved crisp potatoes about her plate. "And his son, Bob, is unfriendly, aggressive. Besides, I could manage. If your good husband were to let me go, I could always make a living nursing."

Drew spoke up. "Let you go? Ridiculous. Your articles for the *Gazette* are immensely popular."

Elizabeth rewarded him with a smile. "Thank you. I'm just thinking of all the possibilities. What's coming over the wires these days?"

"There's news about young Teddy Roosevelt mostly. Our new President seems even more confident since he won election on his own."

"The Supreme Court decision supporting his position against trust monopolies must have been rewarding," Frances said.

"There's fighting in Chicago," Drew said, helping himself to more roast beef. "Has the Red Cross gotten in touch with you, Elizabeth?"

"No, they must have enough volunteers nearby. I would have liked to visit Hull House. I read that Jane Addams is doing marvelous work in a settlement house in the slums."

Drew chuckled. "Well, I wouldn't worry about missing the Chicago mess. There's bound to be a catastrophe somewhere else before too long. You'll be wanted."

"You're laughing at me." Elizabeth looked slightly hurt.

"Not really. I'm teasing. Frances and I admire your dedication." He gave her a fond look.

Elizabeth, good-natured, smiled. She knew that Frances, the closest friend she had ever had, would take Blanche's place in her heart.

Chapter Two

After her mother's funeral, Diane stood in the ornately decorated living room in the large Queen Anne style house situated on a slight rise overlooking the town. Uncle Robert, Catherine and their two children, Bob and Rachel, stared at her.

Uncle Robert smoothed his mustache. "She's a quiet little thing, isn't she? Too bad her father is irresponsible."

It stung Diane to hear Uncle Robert speak of her papa that way.

Aunt Catherine fidgeted. "I'm sure she'll be no trouble at all. In the attic room she'll have complete privacy." She smiled at Diane. "There's a large window for light and air. Are you feeling all right, dear?"

Diane nodded. *I'm frightened and sad and lonely for my mother and my family. I stole candy from the General Store. Mama died. It's my fault.*

"Now it's time for you to practice your piano, Rachel." Catherine looked beseechingly at Robert. "Shall we have music lessons for Diane?"

"That won't be necessary. I doubt she has any musical talent."

Even though his harsh assessment hurt her, Diane breathed a sigh of relief. She had no desire to spend her time practicing the piano.

Catherine, resigned, said, "Bob, go practice your horn. Diane, would you like to help me with supper?"

Robert lit a cigar and settled down in the parlor to read the paper until the meal was served.

In the kitchen, Catherine floured pork chops. "Rachel and Bob have to practice their music every day. There's to be a musical program this spring, you know. Perhaps you're lucky not to be taking lessons."

As Diane washed and cut up cabbage and potatoes, Catherine chatted. "I hope you don't mind the attic room. It's really quite spacious. Robert thought it might suit you."

"I don't mind."

"It was a lovely funeral. Elizabeth, tall, stately, looked so sad and pale in that black outfit. It's strange she never married. I wonder what kind of a living she makes writing for the newspaper. When she went off to Galveston to help out after the big hurricane, she was gone several weeks. I suppose she was paid well for her newspaper article about her experience. It's a good thing she has the house. She's going to need it, being an old maid and all."

Diane, slicing bread, looked up. "It was Grandpa Spencer's house."

"Yes, of course. And there were only the two girls. He probably arranged for both of them to have it. Dr. Spencer was such a good man, going out in the middle of the night to see a sick patient. He served the whole county."

Catherine chatted on. Robert and sleep were probably the only things that could quiet Catherine. But Diane couldn't be sure about sleep. If Catherine had not been such a well-meaning woman, she would have been called a busybody.

During the meal, Catherine let Robert do most of the talking. He listed several chores he wanted Bob to do that week, noted that he had a meeting at the Masonic Lodge that evening, mentioned people he had chatted with at the funeral.

"Brother John and Pamela and that bunch of theirs use a lot of space, almost a whole pew. I wish Pamela would clamp down on the younger ones. They fidgeted and whispered at times during the service." His face showed his distaste.

Catherine fluttered about, pouring coffee, serving fresh bread. "I'm sure Pamela has a time looking after so many. Little Samuel is only seven."

"Some families are even bigger than theirs," Rachel piped up. "The Mullers have ten children."

"Yes, well, the Mullers live on a farm where there's plenty of room," Robert said. "At John's house here in town, they're crowded."

Bob helped himself to a second piece of pie. "Uncle John's raising onions this year on his land down by the river."

"A part-time farmer." Robert sighed. "I suppose he makes a little off of it, what with all those youngsters to help." Diane saw that Uncle Robert found it embarrassing that his brother still felt it necessary to farm.

"Oh, yes," Catherine said, "Jack is a big strapping fellow, and the next one, the one they call Friendly Frank because he's always smiling, is a good worker too."

After dinner, Rachel and Diane dried the dishes as Catherine washed them and chatted about the funeral.

"That was an odd hat Hannah was wearing. Feathers sticking straight up. It's difficult to see around a hat like that. She and George are doing well with the hotel, what with the railroad coming here, and more settlers coming all the time. Julia will have a good job there. Poor Mrs. Schafer could barely walk into the church. It's such a tragedy. She's so young. Dear little Amy's going to have quite a responsibility, taking on her care and the small children too. I'm surprised Mrs. Smith came to the funeral. That hussy. She carried on with a few men after the service. They say she's having an affair with someone."

Diane raised an eyebrow. "What's 'carrying on?'"

"Oh, teasing and laughing." Catherine handed Diane a plate.

Diane wondered. Teasing and laughing? Were those bad things?

Rachel rolled her eyes, causing Diane to grin. Apparently, she wasn't the only one who wondered.

After the chores were done, Diane escaped to her room to read *Rebecca of Sunnybrook Farm*. It was difficult to concentrate, but she needed the diversion. Next, she wanted to read *The Red Badge of Courage*, a new book Aunt Elizabeth had given her. She looked forward to school where she could see Alex and Uncle John's children.

When they ate Sunday dinner at Uncle John's house, her cousins always welcomed her and bombarded her with questions and comments. The redheads, Eric, her age at thirteen, and Barbara, at eleven, dragged her off to look at their dried butterflies, homemade toys, and borrowed books.

The last few days had torn at her heart. With her mother gone, it seemed nobody wanted her. After she finally turned the kerosene lamp off, she cried herself to sleep.

♦ ♦ ♦

On Saturdays, Plainville swarmed with farm families who came in to do their banking and shopping. They left their orders at the general store and then went visiting and trading. Before they headed home, they picked up their orders.

Town dwellers often joined the crowds on Main Street to buy fresh farm products and to visit with their country friends. Aunt Catherine's order would be delivered Saturday afternoon. Since she stopped to gossip with everyone, her trips downtown took up most of the morning.

At school recess on Friday, Alex told Diane that their sister, Amy, would be coming to town Saturday with Mr. and Mrs. Schafer when they shopped for supplies. If Diane walked to the hotel in the evening, she could see Amy and visit with the three Hoffman siblings while the Schafers and their children attended a Grange meeting in town.

Excited, Diane decided to slip out and meet her two sisters at the hotel Saturday night.

As luck would have it, Uncle Robert left the house after dinner, so she told Catherine about the visit, and sped the few blocks to the downtown hotel.

Her sisters hugged her in delight. At a corner table of the dining room, the four siblings laughed and joked, pleased to be together after days apart.

They reported on their new lives. Julia basked in the attention she received at the hotel where people were always coming and going. Hannah and George Baker doted on her and taught her all they knew about the hotel business. Julia was the child they never had.

"All the customers are polite and friendly," Julia said. "They like Hannah's food, but most would like more fresh vegetables."

Out in the country, Amy adored the small children in her charge, though Mrs. Schafer was too sick to be much company.

Alex found life with Reverend Rice quiet (Reverend was often in his study working on his sermon), but John Hoffman's blacksmith shop was always fascinating. The conversation could get racy when several men stood around gossiping and jesting as they waited under an old elm tree for their horses to be shod.

In the past, his mother had not allowed him to hang around the shop, thinking him too young for the blacksmith training or the ribald language. Now, Uncle John welcomed him there. His cousins often worked with him as they ran and fetched to help the blacksmith.

If iron was in short supply, Uncle John sent Alex and his three older sons, Jack, Frank and Eric, out on the Overland Trail to gather scraps of it left along the way by the pioneer trains. When they had gathered all they could carry in the wagon and headed back to town, they took turns running races on stretches of the trail.

The four siblings at the hotel were still talking, comparing notes, when the Schafers came by in the farm wagon to pick up Amy. Reluctant to leave, Diane sensed that it would be a mistake to be gone too long.

As she left the hotel, she bumped into Uncle Robert outside.

"What the Sam Hill are you doing downtown on Saturday night?" Robert's loud bellow could be heard all over the block.

Chapter Three

Diane stood still. "I'm just visiting my sisters, Uncle Robert," she said quietly.

"This is no place for a young girl."

There's no need to get upset, Uncle Robert."

"Don't be sassy. Get on home with you. And don't let me catch you here at night again."

Diane walked off, her back straight.

For a whole week, every time he saw her, Uncle Robert glared. His frowning mustache made him look especially forbidding.

After that, to avoid repercussions, she seldom ventured beyond the school and their home by herself. Still, she wondered what Uncle Robert did downtown so late. Could it be that he had a secret of some kind, and feared being found out if he ran into her? Otherwise, his reaction seemed out of proportion to anything she'd done.

◆ ◆ ◆

Life settled into a routine at the Robert Hoffman home. Every day after school, Diane helped with chores and worked with Aunt Catherine to prepare the evening meal while her cousins practiced their music.

The only chore that Diane actually detested was fetching potatoes from the outside root cellar because spiders lived there. She suspected other creatures hovered in the corners.

At the dinner table, Uncle Robert railed against President Roosevelt, novels, the younger generation, and horseless carriages. "The dirty things spit oil, fire, and smoke, and frighten the horses," he said.

By contrast, Catherine treated Diane kindly, if absentmindedly. She chatted about everybody in town as she worked with the girl, but Robert seldom spoke to Diane. He seemed to resent her being there, though she knew he had agreed to the arrangement with her mother.

Julia said he saw himself as a pillar in the community. He couldn't refuse to take in one of his brother's children, since Thomas had more or less abandoned them. Julia once told Diane that Uncle Robert's ambition was to be the richest and most envied man in Plainville. His own father had been a blacksmith, and he worked to rise above manual labor.

Diane sought to please Uncle Robert by working hard at home and school. But when she brought home a nearly perfect school report, he merely glanced at it and grunted.

As for her cousins, sixteen-year-old Bob ignored Diane, while Rachel, her own age, was helpful, but not overly-friendly. They shared few interests. Rachel concentrated on her music and tended to keep to herself. Diane spent what little spare time she had reading.

The only thing to look forward to was summer and the Independence Day picnic. She knew her brothers, sisters, and cousins would be there along with the entire community. She'd see her friend Matthew as well.

♦ ♦ ♦

The dreary days at Uncle Robert's house were broken up by lively Sunday dinners after church once a month at Uncle John Hoffman's house. Aunt Catherine, Rachel, and Diane baked pies and cakes to bring along. Diane figured wryly that Uncle Robert and Bob contributed their good natures.

Uncle John liked to tease his nieces and nephews by pretending he didn't know them. "Who are these good-looking young people? Are they ours, Pamela? I thought we only had seven."

The children protested. They laughed, and rushed to Uncle John for a hug.

If the weather was bad, Diane played cards and checkers with her cousins while dinner was prepared by Aunt Pamela and the older girls.

To accommodate everyone, Aunt Pamela, her plump, motherly figure pointing and directing, set the boys to extending their already long dining table into the living area with extra boards over sawhorses.

Julia and Alex joined the monthly dinner. Pamela felt it was important to gather as family now and then. All fifteen of them would squeeze together, with the two youngest, redheaded Barbara and little Samuel, sitting on apple boxes. Diane sat beside Eric, called Eric the Red after the Viking explorer, because of his freckles and carrot-red hair.

Uncle John often told them about the early days of the settlement, when some settlers were forced to use dogs pulling hand cultivators if their horses got sick or died. As the only blacksmith, he made all the breaking plows for the new settlers.

He warned the children about the blizzard of 1886 and the bigger one of 1888, which killed school children who got lost in the snow on their way home from school.

He liked to relate the latest antics of "The katzenjammer Kids," his favorite Sunday comic strip from the *Denver Post*. He also brought news from the community.

"They say Mrs. Schafer won't recover. People insist she's getting worse all the time."

Aunt Pamela fussed. "What about Amy, your niece? If Mrs. Schafer dies what will she do?"

"Hans will still need someone to look after the house and the children. I imagine she'll stay on."

Uncle John turned to farming. "We'll miss Jack for the spring plowing here in the garden and down by the river, but he's wanted to be a soldier ever since Teddy Roosevelt led his rough riders up San Juan Hill in the Spanish-American war. Just as well he joined up. I'm glad the soil by the river is not as hard as that Nebraska marble that the farmers find out on the plains."

"At least they have Nebraska coal for fuel," Uncle Robert said, in a rare form of jocularity. He was referring to dried cow manure, often burned for fuel. "We usually have to make do with real, honest-to-goodness coal and wood."

After the girls washed the dishes, everyone gathered around the prized Steinway piano to sing, accompanied by Aunt Pamela, one of her daughters, or Rachel. Because Robert did not care to sing, he and Catherine left with the three children after only a few songs.

At the end of every visit, Diane wished she lived with such a happy family. Uncle Robert's home seemed bleak by comparison. Sometimes she dreamed about her early life with her loving parents. Papa used to sing songs to them and tell stories. If she had been a better daughter, perhaps he would not have left.

Chapter Four

One evening, Diane was allowed to join her Aunt Elizabeth, Julia, and Alex at her old home for supper. Elizabeth embraced all three of her young relatives, asked about their school work, and made sure they were progressing in their lessons.

At the dinner table, Julia said, "I hope we get to see Tom at the Independence Day picnic." She munched on a cookie Elizabeth had baked for them. "All the farmers come. Surely the Gepharts will bring Tom."

Elizabeth watched Diane. "How do you like living with Robert and Catherine?"

Diane looked away. "Aunt Catherine's nice. Rachel and I dry the dishes, but she and Bob have to practice their music lessons, so I help Aunt Catherine with the meals and cleaning."

Elizabeth frowned. They were not treating Diane the same as their own children. "Would you like piano lessons?"

"Not really. I'd rather read *David Copperfield*."

Elizabeth saw some logic in that. She decided to say nothing to Robert for now. "Try keeping a journal about your reading, Diane. That way you'll learn from it."

Elizabeth told the children about national and world news, believing it important that they be well-informed. She took the *Omaha Bee* and the Sunday *Denver Post.* She subscribed to the *Saturday Evening Post* and *Collier's* and exchanged other magazines with friends. As a writer for the local *Gazette,* she got additional news from outside the area as it came over the wire in the newspaper office.

When the children asked, Elizabeth told them about her Red Cross stint during the Galveston Hurricane five years earlier.

"A huge tidal wave pushed the sea level fifteen feet above normal and flooded most of the city, drowning hundreds of people. Others were killed inside smashed buildings. The wind howled, and it rained all night. Electricity was out and telephone lines were down. People were on their own, in the dark, in flood water, and the howling wind.

The children shivered at the tale, better than a ghost story.

"There were some amazing rescues. In one incident, a convent was flooded to the second floor. Resourceful nuns saved hundreds of drifting, helpless people by drawing them into the sturdy brick building with poles and ropes.

"When the Red Cross arrived, we set up tents for the grieving homeless and cooked food for them, while they tried to get their lives back in order. They were in shock over the deaths of their relatives and friends, and some of them were injured. I worked in the first aid tent.

"Clara Barton organized the effort. Despite her great age, she worked tirelessly.

"Afterward, the people decided to build a seawall to protect against hurricanes."

Elizabeth didn't mention the most horrid events in Galveston; the burning of thousands of bodies, the looting, and the immediate shooting of suspected looters by authorities.

"I also helped out in the mining fields in Colorado during a labor dispute a couple of years ago. But that's another story. It's time for all of you to get home. I promised you'd be home before dark."

Diane kissed her aunt good-bye. "Aunt Elizabeth, when I get older I want to help people just like you do."

Flattered, Elizabeth chuckled. "I hope you do, Diane. I hope you do."

♦ ♦ ♦

Sonia Kirkendall hid a yawn as she tried to listen to the Sunday sermon. It was impossible to pay attention, she decided. She eyed the benches in front of her and watched the John Hoffman family. How she envied Pamela with her strong, handsome lads seated on one side of her.

Sonia could see herself walking down the street between two stalwart boys. She imagined them fetching her coat, opening doors, helping her into and out of the wagon, tending to her every need.

Why couldn't she have helpful sons? She had always wanted boys. Vicky was useful, but not the help that sons would have been. Vicky always favored her papa anyway. And Lowell treated his daughter like the Queen of Sheba.

What was she going to do about her husband? He was no use to her. There had to be a way to get rid of him.

Chapter Five

Hiram Spencer watched snow falling rapidly outside the train window. "If this keeps up," he said to his younger brother, "we'll never get to Plainville before dark."

Phil, waking from a nap, peered out. "How far away are we?"

"The conductor says about two miles."

The other male passengers stared out the windows, afraid of being delayed before they reached their destinations. The coach became colder every minute. To their dismay, the train slowed to a crawl, and finally stopped.

"We'll freeze to death in this railroad car," said a man named Kirkendall.

The conductor tried to calm him. "We have extra blankets, Sir."

"Is there any hope of the train starting?"

"We can't get through," the conductor told them. "But the railroad has locomotives equipped with plows. They'll be sending those out."

Hiram listened. Two miles. I can walk and send some wagons out to rescue the passengers. Otherwise, we might be here for hours. "I'll walk to Plainville and send out some help," he said.

The conductor frowned. "You'll be walking through deep snow."

"I've walked through snow before."

"It could be dangerous," a passenger said. "Men have become lost and frozen in a blizzard such as this."

"We could freeze in this railroad car too."

Phil got up. "I'm going with you."

Hiram winced. A sickly child, Phil often caught winter head colds and fevers. Though he appeared healthy enough, his frame was somewhat slight, compared to his brother's muscular body.

"It's better that two of you go," another passenger said.

Hiram conceded, reluctantly. "You're probably right. Let's get started, Phil." The boys grabbed their long coats, donned caps and gloves, and set off with their small traveling bags slung over their backs.

"Keep to the tracks," the conductor yelled after them, "or you'll get lost."

The youths, wearing boots, tramped through the knee-high snow in the direction of Plainville. Hiram judged they had gone a mile when they began to pant from the exertion.

"Will horses be able to get through?" Phil wondered aloud.

"If the snow doesn't get too much deeper, they should be able to make it."

"The road's nearby. Would it be easier to walk over it?"

"No. We best stay on the railroad tracks. I can feel them under my boots. On the road, we could easily miss the edge and wander off."

Each step became a major effort. The cold wind blew through their thick winter coats, and the flakes kept coming down, hindering visibility. Phil fell behind. Hiram worried that he was wearing out.

In relief, Hiram at last eyed the outlines of the town buildings. Light streamed out from windows, a welcoming sight. They knocked on the door of the first house they saw.

The householder, Rex Jenkins, pulled them inside to warm up. "My God, where did you come from? Don't you realize there's a blizzard raging?"

When they told him about the stalled train, he said, "I can hitch up my horses and take the sled, but we're going to need more than one. I'll head downtown to find someone else. Why didn't the others walk with you?"

"A couple of them were quite old," Hiram said. "I don't think they would have been able to make it. Maybe none of them could. We're the youngest of the lot."

"It's a miracle you made it. You're brave. The snow's still falling."

"We'll ride downtown with you. There's nothing else we can do. We need to get a room for the night."

At the hotel, a group of men, journalist Drew Robinson among them, sat drinking coffee in the dining room. When they heard about the passengers trapped in the cold train along with the engineer and other trainmen in the blizzard, two men offered to hitch up horses and a sled to help bring them to safety.

"There's been traffic on the road since the first snow fell. We should be able to follow it." Drew said as he joined Mr. Jenkins in his sled. The other men blanketed horses and followed Jenkins.

When the rescuers had gone, Hiram turned to the young hotel maid. "We need a room and a hot meal. I'm wondering if your hotel is going to have space for all the passengers on the train. There are about ten or twelve in all."

Julia Hoffman smiled at the two young men in front of her and ushered them into the dining room. "We're serving roast beef, potatoes, beets and rolls this evening. I'll reserve a room for you. Do any of the passengers live here in Plainville?"

"Mr. Kirkendall said he did. I don't know about any of the others." Hiram and Phil took a table.

"Well, he won't need a room. He lives about a mile out of town. They'll be able to drop him off as they come in. Aunt Elizabeth takes in people overnight if we fill up. After we get your food, I'll run and warn her to be ready. People have shoveled the snow off the town walks and she only lives a few blocks away. In fact, almost everything in Plainville is a few blocks away. But we're growing. Settlers move to Plainville all the time. Are you two settling here?" she said, with a hopeful look.

"No," Hiram said, with little enthusiasm. "We're headed west."

Julia set the table for them as the brothers removed their wraps. "The ice harvest starts soon on the river. They could use extra hands."

Hiram's ears perked up. "We are getting short of money, Phil. Maybe we should stay for the ice harvest."

Julia sashayed off to reserve their room and get their food as Hiram watched.

"If you want to hang around here, that's fine with me," Phil said in a teasing way. "But don't try to pretend it's just for the work. I can detect an infatuation as well as the next guy."

"Nonsense," Hiram said, reddening slightly. "We want to see the country. We don't have time for women."

When Julia arrived with their plates, Hiram said, "Wait until I finish. You shouldn't walk around in the dark alone. I'll go with you."

Julia gave him a large smile, and pulled up a chair. "Why sure. I'll be glad for the company."

Later, Phil mentioned to his brother that he'd never seen him finish a meal so fast in his life. When they returned from their walk, rosy-cheeked and energized, Hiram and Julia laughed and talked until Julia had to get back to work.

Because of the snow, trains were stalled on the tracks for days. The weight of it brought down the telegraph wires. When all the men from the stalled train arrived in town, they filled the hotel.

Two elderly gentlemen were taken ill and stayed at Elizabeth's house so that she could nurse them. They soon recovered and left when the blizzard died down.

Desperate to leave, one passenger hired a dray and driver to take him to Lincoln.

Mr. Kirkendall also suffered from exposure. He was cared for by his wife, Sonia. Within a few days, he was dead. As Mr. Kirkendall was a young man, the town was shocked by his sudden death.

Chapter Six

Elizabeth answered the door and found two young men on her porch. They took off their caps. "We've just come from the hotel," the taller one said. "Your niece thought you might be willing to board us for less than we'd have to pay at the hotel."

"This isn't a boarding house. I take in lodgers only when the hotel is full."

"I realize that, but we're here for the ice harvest down at the river. Once the ice house is full, we're going farther west. We can give you references. In fact, we believe we're distant cousins of yours. I'm Hiram Spencer, and this is my brother Phil. We're from Indiana."

"My father came from Indiana." Intrigued, Elizabeth invited them in. "Would you like some coffee?"

Phil stood with his cap in his hand. "That would taste mighty fine."

"Come into the kitchen. We can talk while I put the pot on."

When they were all seated at the kitchen table with steaming cups of coffee before them, Elizabeth examined them carefully. They were polite, handsome boys, still in their teens. She noticed a slight resemblance to her father.

"I have a couple of problems with your boarding here. First, I often have to travel in my role as a volunteer Red Cross nurse and to help out with illnesses and home deliveries. I can be called at any time. Then you'd be out of a room. Second, I'm not much of a cook. Being unmarried, I don't get much practice."

"Well, Miss Spencer, if you have to leave, we'll just move back into the hotel," Hiram said. "We don't have a lot of baggage to bother about. And we're not real picky about food. We tend to gobble up everything we're served."

Elizabeth chuckled. They discussed prices. Then she served them warm apple pie. "You can sample the pie. If it meets with your approval, you can move in tonight."

They grinned in anticipation. The pie disappeared. "Let's go tell Julia and move our stuff in," Hiram said to Phil.

"I'll get your rooms ready." Elizabeth saw them out the door. As she closed it, she smiled. What a piece of luck. A little extra money wouldn't hurt at all. And she would have relatives with her, young people about the house.

♦ ♦ ♦

An announcement in the *Plainville Gazette* indicated that the ice harvest would begin on the 10th of January. That morning, Elizabeth urged Robert to let Diane come with her to watch the ice harvest.

"It'll be a good education for her." She stood in Robert's living room, her face strained. Diane guessed that she disliked asking Uncle Robert if she could go.

"Diane should be working with Catherine. There's laundry to do today." Robert was dressed for work at the bank. He brushed a speck off his suit vest.

Catherine broke in. "Oh, that can wait. There's no hurry. No hurry at all. We can always do it later. Rachel and Bob will be going, so it's just as well--"

"Thank you, Catherine," Elizabeth said. "I'm glad everyone in town will see that Robert allows the three children a bit of time to learn about their community."

"Oh, all right," Robert growled. "But they all have to be home before dinner."

Elizabeth and the three youngsters, along with several other townspeople, tromped off to the river to watch the annual project.

The ice auger measured the ice at two feet deep, well above the one foot required for harvesting. The ice had been scored into blocks with the help of work horses, to help guide the saw.

First, working from the riverbank near the boxcar on the tracks, Hiram and Phil cut a channel to pull the ice through. They sawed the ice into thirty-pound blocks with large ice saws, one of them at each end.

As they cut up chunks of ice, making the channel longer, men guided the horse along the bank. It pulled the ice through the lengthening waterway to the ramp leading to the boxcar. The men guided the blocks to the boxcar by pushing and using pike poles, and then lifting them inside with huge ice tongs.

Some of the ice was shipped off to Omaha or eastern cities where no pure water source existed. But an ample supply of the Plainville ice was stored in the partially underground icehouse, filled with sawdust for insulation. It was located next to the butcher shop to keep meat and butter cold for many months in Plainville. Individual families bought iceboxes from Sears and Roebuck Company to hold blocks of ice. An iceman, the butcher's son, delivered the ice blocks on a regular schedule.

"They're using our horse," Diane's friend, Matthew, told the others. "Buster is young and strong. I love that horse."

The young people slid around on the opposite end of the ice pond and shouted back and forth, their voices clear in the still, cold air. Some of the older children had brought ice skates."

"Isn't Hiram skillful with the sawing?" Julia said, watching him in earnest, her eyes sparkling. She laced up a pair of skates loaned to her by Hannah Baker. "Diane, you can use these skates after I've had a few turns."

Suddenly, the sound of an enormous splash came from the bank. Men were screaming and shouting orders. There was a flurry of activity. Buster had fallen into the icy water as he walked along the sloping bank pulling a heavy chunk of ice.

Chapter Seven

Diane looked at Matthew's horrified face. "Don't worry, Matthew. They'll pull Buster out of the water." Diane stood beside him in sympathy, feeling his deep concern for the horse. She patted his arm to console him.

"It's so cold in the water. Poor Buster."

Men were roping the fallen horse to other horses in order to pull him out. After several attempts and much commotion, the dripping animal was pulled from the freezing river.

"I'll help rub him down." Matthew hastened off. Later, he told Diane it had taken hours of rubbing to warm the beast.

"Poor Buster," Diane said. "I'm glad he's all right."

The accident delayed the ice harvest for over a day, as the men cared for the horses and hurried to store all the cut blocks in the icehouse in case the weather turned warm and melted them. But neither Julia Hoffman nor Hiram Spencer regretted the extra time. They visited in the hotel dining room several hours each evening.

♦ ♦ ♦

At school, Diane noticed that Vicky Kirkendall seldom joined the other children to visit or play. During recess, she leaned against the side of the building and watched the others play baseball or hopscotch, her long blond hair blowing in the wind, her face sad.

In the past, Vicky had been an especially cheerful girl, quick with jokes, often making fun of herself for the amusement of others. People said she had developed the habit at home to get her mother's attention. Sonia Kirkendall was known to be an indifferent mother.

One day Diane, conquering her own shyness, walked over and leaned against the wall beside her. "Don't you like to play?"

"I just don't feel like it right now. I miss my papa."

Diane's stomach lurched. "I think I know how you feel. My mama died right after Christmas."

Vicky threw her a glance. "I'm so sorry. I remember now. Our teacher told us about it."

"Let's walk around the outside of the playground. We can play a guessing game I know. Maybe it will get your mind off of him."

"Okay. I'll try it."

Both girls concentrated on the game. It helped Vicky forget how much she missed her papa. She felt close to Diane, who had also lost a parent.

The next recess they talked about the Independence Day Celebration. Vicky said, "I have twenty cents to spend. How much do you have?"

Embarrassed, Diane said, "I don't have any." Diane wished she had money to see the moving pictures and ride the carrousel at the event. She knew Uncle Robert would not give her any.

"Let's meet there anyway. I'll pay your way on the carrousel."

As Diane walked home from school that afternoon with Eric the Red, Uncle John and Aunt Pamela called out a greeting to her from the tidy rows of vegetables in their garden. Diane stopped for a few minutes to visit.

Uncle John looked up from thinning his carrots. "We'll have a good harvest of vegetables this year."

Suddenly, Diane remembered the hotel guests who wanted more fresh vegetables. She had an idea. "Do you have more than you need?"

John considered. "We probably do, even as big as this family is."

"Maybe Eric and I could sell the extra for you at the hotel. You could pay us with some of the profits. We need money for the Independence Day Celebration."

From her small plot, Aunt Pamela said, "I'd gladly let you sell some of my cabbages if they were ready. I always have a good crop."

Uncle John snorted. He refused to bother with cabbage. It was too much trouble, he said. They always attracted pests. Now he considered Eric and Diane, smoothing his salt and pepper mustache.

"All right. You two can pick some radishes, celery, onions, early lettuce, sweet peas and whatever else is ready on Saturday after Eric picks enough for our family for a few days. You can wash them up nice and sell them. Carry them in the wheelbarrow. How about a profit of 20 percent?"

Excited by the opportunity, the cousins arrived at the hotel early Saturday morning with their baskets of cleaned, just-picked vegetables. Hannah Baker was pleased. She bought all the produce they had. "You're wise to get here so early. None of the farmers have been around yet, not even Sonia Kirkendall."

Julia beamed with pride. "Diane and Eric are the early birds who catch the worms."

"You two have more variety than anyone else," Hannah Baker said as she began to shell the peas in the hotel kitchen.

From then on, every Saturday, Diane and Eric sold the surplus vegetables from John Hoffman's garden to the Bakers. Their coins began to add up.

Sonia Kirkendall was upset that she now had an early morning competitor for her produce.

Those lucky Hoffmans. They're into everything: John with his blacksmith business, Robert with the bank. Related to Elizabeth Spencer with friends at the newspaper, and now my markets. Pamela even has the boys, all those hearty boys, to harvest the vegetables. Well, maybe I'll have sons now too. I suspect Lowell couldn't give me more children. We'll see if I'm right about that.

Sonia discovered that she need not have worried. Mrs. Smith at the general store took all her produce. But Sonia refused to give up her anger.

Chapter Eight

On the Fourth of July, Diane was awakened at five in the morning by a "Boom! Boom! Boom!" She knew the men were striking gunpowder on the anvil in Uncle John's blacksmith shop. There would be fireworks in the evening.

It seemed she had looked forward to this day for ages. It gave her a chance to escape the constant drudgery at Uncle Robert's house, and a chance to see school friends while Robert and Catherine mingled with the adults.

All morning, wagons and carts rumpled past the house, stirring up dust. Finally, despite the heat, Aunt Catherine closed the windows facing the street to keep the dust out.

She chatted as she prepared for the noon meal. "Such a shame about Mr. Kirkendall. And him so young too. What will Sonia do with that farm? She can't continue to handle it on her own, and she has no boys. Just Vicky. Of course, Cal Jones works for her, but it's not like it's his own crop or anything. It's good the rented house is close enough for Vicky to go to the town school. You two have become friends. Sonia's always been a little strange. But she seems to be recovering from her husband's death. Fact is, some are calling her the merry widow."

Catherine hesitated, as though she was considering the matter. Then she said in a slightly dry voice. "They say she danced with everyone at the country barn dance last week."

Bob kept hauling in wood to keep the kitchen stove burning, while Uncle Robert wandered in and out, fretting about the preparations. He studied a speech he had been asked to make during the ceremonies in the park.

Catherine fried chicken and the girls mixed up potato salad. They placed the food in the center of the table along with bread and cheese. Then

Catherine covered the food with a wire rack, and spread a clean cloth over everything. The cloth did not touch the food. It just kept the flies off. Their meal would be ready to eat when they returned from the parade.

As the family walked the few blocks downtown, they watched the special trains arriving at the depot from two directions. People poured out, excited about the festivities. Some had come from one hundred miles away.

People lined Main Street, waiting for the show. Here and there firecrackers popped, but when the parade started, everyone watched.

Decorated wagons carried old Mr. Muller, dressed up as Uncle Sam, and blond-haired Lila Park as Miss Liberty. As the high school band played "The Star-Spangled Banner," George Washington stood in a wagon, crossing the Delaware River, his red cape flying. When the stand-in raised his foot to rest on the side of the wagon, the crowds cheered.

After their meal at home, Diane, wearing her new, pink dimity dress which swirled around her sturdy calves (a final project of her mother's), walked to the park with Uncle Robert and his family. The town band greeted people when they arrived.

Everyone settled down to listen to the speeches. Mr. McCall spoke first. He reminded his audience of the original thirteen colonies and their fight for liberty and justice. He read the Declaration of Independence, the Preamble to the Constitution and the first ten Amendments.

Next, Robert Hoffman praised the stalwart settlers and business people who had founded the small Nebraska community. He spoke of their pioneer spirit and of their visions for the future.

"They came to settle a railroad town in 1886," he said, "and stayed to farm the land and raise their young. Drew Robinson's predecessor printed the first newspaper in John Hoffman's blacksmith shop, the first building in the town.

"Our dear, departed Mr. Smith started the general store, and sometimes hauled supplies from the Omaha trains himself. Hannah and George Baker built a two-room house and rented out half of it. Then they added more rooms and now run a fine hotel.

"Stanley Owens set up a barber shop and he's still running it, old as he is." Mr. Owens raised his skinny arm. Everyone clapped.

"Mr. McCall was a young lawyer, who took a chance on a struggling community. Dr. Spencer treated patients all over the county, often in the dead of night.

"Rex Jenkins built a dry goods store and became our esteemed mayor."

Uncle Robert named the founders of all the businesses in town.

"And I started a bank," he concluded. "Modesty prevents me from saying more. Thank the settlers and have a fine day."

At the conclusion of the speeches, Diane visited with Matthew McCall. He was two years older than she, but they had become friends. Before Blanche's death, Matthew had come to her house with his papa, who discussed legal matters with Blanche.

While the adults talked business, she and Matthew talked about school and horses in the kitchen over cookies and milk.

At the picnic, Matthew said, "Diane, what do you hear from Tom? I never see him anymore since he's going to the country school."

"We don't see my brother much either, Matthew, now that he's out on the farm. Still, he should be here with the Gepharts today."

"Good. Maybe I'll see him." Proper as always, he indicated his companion. "Diane, meet Scott Morris. He's visiting us from Omaha. Our papas were friends there. Scott, this is Diane Hoffman."

Scott was taller than Matthew, with silken sandy hair and green eyes. "Hoffman? Your name is Hoffman?"

"Yes...." *Why was he frowning at her? Perhaps he frowned at everybody. Matthew was just the opposite--the friendliest and most popular boy in school.*

"It's nice to meet you, Scott." Diane smiled, dimples showing. "Excuse me. There's Tom now." She hastened away, glad to escape Scott's probing eyes.

Matthew turned to Scott. "Do you know somebody named Hoffman?"

Scott snarled. "I sure do. Thomas Hoffman, an executive with the railroad, cheated my papa out of some valuable land he claimed belonged to the company. In court, the bribed judge supported Hoffman and the railroad."

Scott supposed Diane to be a spoiled daughter of wealthy Thomas Hoffman. Because of his father's treatment at the hands of Thomas, he knew he'd find it difficult to be friendly. His admiration for the energetic girl with the long dark curls warred with his hostility toward her father. But it was obvious to him that Matthew was taken with her.

"I'm sorry. There are Hoffmans in Plainville," Matthew said. "I don't know if any are related to an Omaha Hoffman. There's to be a three-legged race. Are you game to sign up for it?"

"I certainly am. Lead the way."

"Diane," Tom greeted his youngest sister with open arms. "I'm glad to see you."

"It's been so long, Tom." She hadn't seen him since their mother's funeral. Delighted, Diane gave him a peck on the cheek. "How do you like it out there with the Gepharts?"

"Not much. I have to do all the work. Old Gephart thinks I should work sixteen hours a day. He won't even let me go to school most of the time. I can't wait until I'm old enough to leave."

"Oh, Tom, you're only fifteen. How would you take care of yourself if you left? Maybe we could talk to Uncle Robert. He might let you come live with us."

"Are you kidding? That selfish old man doesn't like kids. Haven't you noticed? He has about as much heart as a codfish. Besides, I'd have trouble getting along with Bob."

"Well...."

"Old Moneybags wouldn't welcome me. And Gephart wouldn't let me go. I'm doing all his work. I'll just leave the first chance I get." He told her more about his mistreatment at the farm, and Diane shared her discontent at Uncle Robert's house. Finally, he went off to pitch horseshoes with Alex.

Her brothers planned to get a baseball game together later. Her eyes became moist. She saw so little of them.

The crowd milled about to visit and to sample the delights of the carnival. Children and young people congregated around the carrousel, a circle of spokes powered by a pony at the center. At the outside edge of each spoke, an attached booth held two riders.

Vicky joined Diane. "I'm so glad you could come. I have exciting news. My mother is getting married. To Cal Jones. I'm going to be her bridesmaid."

Diane clapped her hands. "Where? When?"

"Out on the farm. We get new dresses. It will be soon."

"You'll have a papa again."

"Yes, but no one will ever take my real papa's place."

"Of course not. Let's go see the moving pictures."

Vicky and Diane flew to the tent where the moving pictures were shown. Inside, people sat on benches facing a white screen. When they were ready to start, the tent flap was lowered and it was almost totally dark.

Then, shadows danced upon the screen until the picture was focused.

The story was about a young Russian woman who was accused of some crime. At the end, she was tied to a horse, and the horse dragged her to death. The whole picture lasted about ten minutes.

Horrified, the girls paid to watch the picture three times, but every time it ended the same way. With tears in their eyes, they stumbled out of the tent.

Matthew and Scott were ambling by. Matthew noticed their tears right away. "What's wrong?"

"A woman was dragged to death in the moving pictures," Diane said, between sobs.

He touched her shoulder. "Not really, Diane. It's just a story. They're actors, just pretending."

The girls looked into Matthew's kind face. "Are you sure?"

"It's true. It's like a dramatic play. Say, why don't you come with us and ride the carrousel." He propelled them all forward and seated himself beside Diane in the booth, leaving Vicky and Scott to sit together.

The girls recovered from their sadness and enjoyed gliding around in a great arc. Diane felt free and breezy, such as a soaring bird must feel. The air cooled her face, heated by the Nebraska sun.

Scott seemed only to endure the ride, not enjoying the company of the girls as Matthew did.

When the ride ended, Matthew asked if they could join the girls for the fireworks display.

Diane smiled. "Yes, of course. We'll all sit on the grass." It seemed to Diane that Matthew filled the void left by her brothers.

Matthew bought ice cream for all of them, a welcome treat after the heat of the day.

In the darkness, the crowd watched the night sky blaze and sparkle to celebrate the birthday of the nation. Diane stole glances Scott's way, admiring his shock of sandy hair. He seemed cold and arrogant toward her, but he and Vicky seemed to be getting on.

At the conclusion of the fireworks, Diane could hear Uncle Robert above the voices of the crowd, sounding like a great bull.

"Catherine, gather up the children. Let's get home. Where have they all run off to, anyway?"

Diane's day of freedom and joy was over. Now it was back to proud Uncle Robert and his timid family. She waved good-bye to her friends, and slipped off to join her aunt and uncle before Robert became more impatient.

Chapter Nine

In late summer, Elizabeth invited Frances and Drew Robinson for dinner. She seated her guests at the table and leaned forward eagerly. "What's the latest news from the *Gazette*?"

Drew, his dark eyes smiling, sniffed the fried chicken eagerly. "My favorite meal. I believe I told you about the surrender of the Russian garrison to the Japanese at Port Arthur in January. The Russo-Japanese War is over."

"That has to be good news." Elizabeth served green beans and fresh beets from her garden.

"Then there was a demonstration in Russia in front of the Winter Palace at St. Petersburg a few weeks later. Several people were shot."

"Why were they demonstrating?"

Drew threw up his hands. "They were strikers and their families, appealing for better working conditions."

"Shot for demonstrating?"

"Yes, and in June there was a mutiny aboard a Russian ship, anchored in Odessa, when a sailor was shot complaining about poor food. The crew responded by tossing their officers into the sea. Now they face death for mutiny. Things must be awful in Russia." He sighed.

Elizabeth shook her head. "Half the U. S. population would be dead if you could be shot for complaining."

"Especially you and my wife." He held up his hands in defense as both of them threw disparaging looks his way. "Just kidding, my dears."

"The biggest news we have," he continued, "is Frances's trip to San Francisco in April to visit her aunt, Mrs.Gwen DeVault. I believe you've met her."

"Indeed I have. She visited you some time ago right here in Plainville. I remember she is a great believer in votes for women."

"Oh, yes." Frances took a dainty bite of chicken. "She can't understand why women can vote in Wyoming and Colorado, and even in municipal elections in Kansas, but not in Nebraska."

"I can't understand that myself."

"She's involved in the Women's Movement. She's also done some work for the Red Cross in San Francisco. You'll have to write to her."

I'd certainly like to write to her. I very much admire Elizabeth Stanton and Susan B. Anthony for all their efforts to get votes for women."

Drew put down his coffee cup. "How are your nieces and nephews getting along?"

"They're fairly well. We don't hear much from Tom out there at the Gephart farm, but Julia's happy at the hotel, Amy enjoys the Schafer children she cares for, and Alex loves training at his Uncle John's blacksmith shop.

"How about the youngest, Diane, isn't it?"

Elizabeth hesitated. "I just don't know. I'm not sure Robert Hoffman is treating her as well as he treats his own children. It must be difficult for her. She's very sensitive. I've thought about seeing Mr. McCall about it."

"You think there's something you can do legally?"

"I don't know. I--"

"Think carefully, Elizabeth." Frances said. "Even if you did have Diane at your house, what would you do about her when you're off nursing with the Red Cross or helping in a home delivery?"

Drew helped himself to potatoes and another piece of chicken. "Robert would probably take any effort to interfere as an insult."

"At Robert's house she does have Rachel for a companion. I'm sure her Aunt Catherine is good to her," Frances said.

"You're probably right. I'm being overly protective, I suppose." Elizabeth shrugged off her concerns. "Tell me about your trip."

"Well, now that Drew has his linotype, he can spare me time for the train trip. No more setting type by hand. San Francisco is a very exciting city, wild and all. Still, Aunt Gwen thinks Caruso may be performing in *Carmen*, the opera. So there's some culture there. I wish Drew could come with me, but he insists he has to stay and get the *Gazette* out."

Elizabeth served peach delight for dessert. "You really ought to be training an apprentice, Drew."

"Yes, I'll have to think about it. The fellow who works here now isn't interested in making a career of newspaper work. I'd like to find somebody with enthusiasm."

When Frances and Drew left, Elizabeth sighed. Her friends thought it unnecessary to worry about Diane. Quite likely the whole town agreed with them. She must accept the unpalatable fact that Diane would stay in her Uncle Robert's house.

◆ ◆ ◆

At their monthly Sunday dinner, Uncle John, after slicing the pork roast, announced that he'd been approached by several men who wanted him to run for county commissioner.

Delighted, Leah said, "Papa, that's wonderful."

"What are your chances, Papa?" Friendly Frank wanted to know.

"I think they are quite good. People are dissatisfied with one of the commissioners"

Uncle Robert appeared miffed that nobody had asked him to stand for the office. "What about your blacksmith business?"

"With more help, I could manage. I'll have to start paying Frank to get him to do more."

Frank perked up and grinned all around. "Wow, imagine that. Pay for work. It's a marvelous concept." The others laughed.

Uncle Robert helped himself to more potatoes. "Wouldn't you need to spend a lot of time in the county seat?"

"For the meetings, yes. I'd be reimbursed for any expenses."

"Papa, what is your platform?" Thelma asked, picking up the potato dish to refill.

"People are complaining about the county roads. We can't improve all of them, of course, but there are some that definitely need repair. At the moment they're practically impassable."

Uncle Robert put a large smile on his face. "Now that you mention it, the road behind our house needs work. Maybe you could do something about that."

Uncle John laughed. "It's a little early to be making those decisions. Besides, I would have only one vote on the commission. And we'd definitely have to work from a list of priorities. I doubt your road would be on it."

Uncle Robert lost his smile at that, but Aunt Catherine said, "John, I hope you win. You'd make a fine commissioner."

"Thank you, Catherine. There's to be a public meeting next week right here in town at the school where the candidates will speak. I hope you come."

Soon Pamela and Diane began to worry. During the week before the meeting, Sonia Jones told everybody she knew that John Hoffman could not run for county commissioner because he was not a citizen. John claimed loud and clear to everyone he met that he had filed the papers to become a naturalized citizen and had every right to run for office.

Meanwhile, John reported to his relatives that several men had stopped by the blacksmith shop to say John had their votes. They were rooting for him to win.

At home, Aunt Catherine told Rachel and Diane that the Hoffman grandparents had arrived from Germany with John when he was a baby. Two sisters living in Omaha as well as Thomas and Robert were all born in the United States, but John had needed to apply for citizenship because he had been born in Germany.

The evening of the public meeting, the school was packed for the speeches by the candidates. Almost every man for miles around, and some women, wanted to hear the discussion. Elizabeth was in the audience.

When the mayor called on John Hoffman to speak, Sonia jumped up.

"John Hoffman is not a citizen of this country. He's ineligible to run for office. He never should have filed. It's illegal. He's lied to everybody."

A murmur arose among the spectators. Rex Jenkins, the moderator, looked at John. "What have you to say about it, John?"

John stood up, a perplexed look on his face. "I filed the papers to become a citizen years ago."

"It's not true," Sonya said in an accusing voice. "I have a county official with me who will say so."

A small man wearing glasses walked to the front of the room and faced the crowd. "Mrs. Jones is correct. John Hoffman filed the Intention to Become a Naturalized Citizen form, but he never completed the process. He is not a naturalized citizen of this country."

Amazed, John sank back down on his chair. "I thought I was a citizen," he said.

Rex Jenkins thanked the county clerk for his information. He hesitated. Finally, he spoke.

"I've known John Hoffman for over twenty years. I know he believed he became a citizen when he filed the intention paper. But, with regret, I must declare that he is ineligible to run for the office of county commissioner."

John Hoffman left the meeting with his head down. For days, he went about his work with a grim face. He told his family he'd been humiliated before the entire community.

Disappointed that John was ineligible, Elizabeth told Diane that he would have made an excellent commissioner. "He's such a good man."

"I feel sorry for dear Uncle John's distress," Diane said.

In time, Elizabeth was pleased to see that John's family and friends convinced him of their high regard and urged him to complete the citizenship process. Time healed his wounds and he eventually became a naturalized citizen. But he never ran for public office again.

◆ ◆ ◆

One crisp autumn morning, Rachel woke Diane early. "Mama is not feeling well, Diane. I've fixed breakfast, but I have to leave early for a project at school. Could you tidy up the kitchen before you leave so Mama can rest?"

As Diane finished washing the dishes, Uncle Robert handed her some money. "Diane, Bob's already gone to school. Go to the train depot with the wheelbarrow to get a box of desert apples. The first train's due this morning with a carload."

"But I'll be late for school."

"Oh, that won't hurt anything." He checked his pocket watch. "Hurry. They might run out of Delicious Apples."

As soon as Uncle Robert left for the bank, Diane removed her apron, hustled out the door and grabbed the wheelbarrow from the shed. At the depot a line formed for the popular sweet apples. People hastened from all over town. Some men loaded two or three boxes into their wheelbarrows. Other families hired the dray to deliver boxes of apples to their houses.

Diane finally bought her box of apples and started home with it.

Sonya Kirkendall loaded her boxes into the farm wagon. *There's that Hoffman brat who stole the hotel business from me. I'd like to pay her back. I'll give her a scare.* She urged her horse forward at a gallop and swerved toward the girl.

Diane, startled, stepped out of the way, and in doing so upset the wheelbarrow. As she attempted to right it, she lost her balance and lay sprawled on the ground. The box broke apart and apples scattered over the walk and the road. Sonya, heading out of town, smiled in satisfaction.

Horrified, Diane had no opportunity to see who drove the wagon. She feared what Uncle Robert would say. Wooden apple boxes were prized for various uses around the house. With tears in her eyes, she ran desperately from place to place, picking up dozens of apples, and placing them in the wheelbarrow. She'd never make it to school on time.

Suddenly, she heard Matthew's voice. "Diane, what are you doing?"

"Oh, Matthew, I broke the apple box. Uncle Robert will be furious. Why aren't you in school?"

"I just took our apples home." He examined the box. "I can fix this. Stay here. I'll get a hammer." He bolted across the street to his house. Within minutes he reappeared and hammered the nails back into place.

"You have a long way to go. Let me push," Matthew said as he helped pick up the apples and load them back into the box.

"No, no. I can do it." Diane lifted the handles. "Thanks so much. Go to school or you'll be late."

"It doesn't matter. The teacher likes me." He grinned. "I insist. You push half a block and I'll push half a block." He decided this was the only way to get her to agree to his help.

"Oh, all right. Then we'll have to run to get to school."

"Okay. We'll race. See who gets there first." He threw the hammer on the walk in front of his house.

Diane won the race. She smiled and waved to Matthew as he set off for his class, and thanked her lucky stars that he had come along. She could always depend on Matthew.

◆ ◆ ◆

A few days later, as Diane was about to go into the root cellar for potatoes and cabbage, she heard a sound in the bushes nearby. Turning, she saw her brother, a small bag beside him, sitting behind a lilac bush, hiding from view of the house.

"Diane," he spoke in a low voice. "I've run away. I walked all the way from the farm and I need to rest. Would you hide me in the cellar?"

"Oh, Tom. You must be exhausted. What are you going to do?"

"If I can get some rest, I can walk into Omaha and find out where to sign up for the navy. I came here because Aunt Elizabeth is away on a nursing case."

"You're not old enough to sign up for the navy."

"I'll soon be sixteen. Anyway, I can lie about it. How will they know? If they won't let me join, I'll go to work at one of the meat packing plants in Omaha until I'm old enough to join up."

Diane knew how hard Tom worked for Mr. Gephart. Perhaps he would have a better life somewhere else. He wasn't even getting proper schooling where he was. Surely helping him was the right thing to do. "I'll leave the cellar door open. You can sneak in to sleep when it's dark."

"I can use my bag for a pillow. Can you get me some food?"

Diane feared Uncle Robert would be angry if he found out that she had taken food and helped her runaway brother. She had to be careful.

"You'll find apples in the cellar. I'll try to bring something from the house after dinner."

"Thanks, Diane. I'll send you a letter to Aunt Elizabeth's house so that Uncle Robert or old Gephart won't know where I am and try to get me out of the service."

At the evening meal, Uncle Robert said, "Herb Gephart was in town today."

Everyone waited. Diane continued eating while Robert watched her. "Seems young Tom ran off. He wanted to know if Elizabeth or anyone else had seen him. Diane, have you seen him?"

Diane avoided Uncle Robert's gaze.

She looked up and shook her head. She had no idea what he would do if he found out she was lying. She had never seen him physically discipline her or his own children, but perhaps that was because they were all afraid to cross him.

He often thundered at them, and warned of dire consequences if they misbehaved, moral consequences as well as physical consequences from him. He used fear of the almighty when it suited his purposes.

Robert finished his meal and left to get ready for his meeting with the Oddfellows. As he went out the front door in the early dark, Diane slipped out the back with dinner leftovers hidden under her apron for Tom. She grabbed an old quilt on the back porch as she went.

To her surprise, Robert went off in the opposite direction from the Oddfellows Hall. Where was he going? Was he lying to the family about his meetings? She was reminded of the time she bumped into him downtown on Saturday night when she visited her sisters and Alex. Eager to take warm food to Tom, she had no time then to think about where Uncle Robert was headed.

Chapter Ten

"I've got food and a quilt to keep you warm." Diane handed Tom a sack filled with bread and butter, warm chicken, sliced carrots, and cookies-- enough for a few meals, along with a jar of water. She doubted that Catherine, scatterbrained as she was, would notice the missing food. "I'd better close the cellar door, but I'll leave it unlocked. You'll be able to push it open and leave early in the morning."

Tom snatched the food and began to chomp on a chicken drumstick. "I haven't eaten all day. I'm hungry and tired. I'll go right to sleep."

"You'll come back if you have trouble, won't you?"

Tom was confident. "What kind of trouble would I have? They need sailors. And I want to see the world. I'll be fine, Diane. Thanks for helping me."

"I have to get back. Aunt Catherine might wonder." Diane kissed him on the cheek and wiped away tears as she headed back for the house. What would happen to him? When would she see him again? Did she and her brother have to grow up before they could see each other?

◆ ◆ ◆

Cousin Bob was an enigma to Diane. He seldom spoke to her, except to grunt or nod or shake his head. But one day he approached her as soon as school was dismissed.

"Do you want to visit Amy out in the country? I'll get our buggy from the livery and drive you out there."

Diane was cautious. "What would Uncle Robert say?"

"We could be back by the time he gets home. Come on, let's get the horse and buggy." He grabbed her hand and pulled her along. Diane followed, thrilled at the idea of an unexpected visit with her sister.

The livery stable stood across the street from the blacksmith shop. Diane, off on a lark, waved to John Hoffman who stood in the doorway as she and Bob spanked down the road in the buggy.

Diane noticed that Bob turned off toward Pioneer Road. "The Schafer Farm is on Homestead Road," she said.

Bob looked away. "This is a shortcut."

The way was rough, not nearly as good as the regular route. In a happy mood, however, she said, "I didn't know there was a shortcut. Shall we sing?"

"I'm not much of a singer. You sing."

Diane started with some carols as it would soon be Christmas. But suddenly Bob stopped the buggy. "What's wrong? Why are you stopping?"

"I thought we'd kiss first." Bob reached over and pulled her toward him.

"What? Don't be ridiculous. We're cousins. I don't want to kiss you."

"Sure you do. You just don't know it." Bob groped for her breast and put his face against hers for a kiss.

She pushed him away. "Stop it. I'm not going to kiss you. Get your hands off me."

Bob's face turned sour. "Okay, brat. If you won't kiss me, I won't take you to your sister."

"Then take me home. I think it's getting late. We won't have time to get there before dark anyway. This is no shortcut."

"You can damn well walk home."

He gave her a vicious shove that knocked her to the ground, and sent the horse off at a speed his father would have deplored.

She picked herself up, groaning. As she brushed herself off, she realized she would have some bruises, but, otherwise, she was all right. She knew she had a long walk, probably a few miles. That did not faze her. An excellent walker, she could cover the ground in no time. But she would arrive home late. What would Uncle Robert say?

The gentle wind did not bother her at first. But, to her chagrin, it began to snow, light flakes at first, then more and more. It grew colder. She increased her pace, fearing the storm more than the dark. If it continued to snow, she wouldn't be able to find her way home.

Though she remembered the way they had come, she did not recall seeing any farm houses along the way. No fences marked the edge of the road. Fear gripped her stomach. She would find no shelter on Pioneer Road.

♦ ♦ ♦

John Hoffman, still in his leather apron, put away his bellows, irons, tongs, and his hammer for the day as the coals in the forge died down. Outside the shop, he found Matthew McCall, waiting patiently for him to finish at the blacksmith shop.

"Why hello, son," he said. "What are you doing here?"

"I'm worried about Diane. I thought she might be here. I couldn't find her after school, and her Aunt Catherine says she hasn't come home.

John remembered seeing Diane with Bob. "I'll go ask Catherine about her again. Meanwhile, you'd better go see her Aunt Elizabeth. She could be over there."

John walked through the falling snow in the dark. It was turning into a norther. He confronted his brother Robert and his family in their living room.

Robert, indignant, said. "I have no idea where she could be. She's supposed to come home after school and help Catherine. She's due for a tongue-lashing when she gets here."

John turned to Bob and Rachel. Rachel knew nothing. Bob turned away.

"Tell us what you know, Bob," John said, in a quiet but firm voice.

Bob hesitated. Finally he said, "I gave her a ride in the buggy. She wanted to walk home."

Elizabeth, along with Frances and Drew who had been visiting her, burst into the room, with Matthew following closely behind. They stood quietly as the questioning continued.

"Where did you leave her?" John asked.

Bob was reluctant, but they all waited for him to speak. "On Pioneer Road," he mumbled.

Elizabeth looked at Drew in horror. "There are no farmsteads on that old road. She's stranded in the storm."

Drew turned to Bob. "How long ago did you leave her?"

"An hour ago."

"She's still a long way off. I'll saddle my horse and go after--"

"I'm coming with you," Matthew said to the group. "Tell my folks where I am."

Elizabeth said, "I'll come too. She's my niece."

Drew took her shoulders. "No, Elizabeth. Stay here. The two of us will find her."

He and Matthew bolted out the door. Elizabeth turned to the Thomas Hoffman family. "What were you thinking, Bob? To leave her stranded in the country in a storm?"

"It wasn't snowing when I left her."

"Even so--"

Robert spoke harshly. "Bob, you had no permission to take the horse and buggy."

"She begged me to take her out to the Schafers to visit her sister. I was just being helpful."

"Don't ever take the horse and buggy again without my permission."

Elizabeth groaned inwardly. All Robert cared about was his precious horse and buggy. Meanwhile, a niece, sheltered in his household, faced danger in the storm.

Chapter Eleven

At the livery stable, Drew and Matthew saddled their horses as the wind howled. Though visibility was limited, they managed to stay on the road. Matthew called out Diane's name as the horses galloped, but he doubted his voice could be heard very far over the norther wind.

His heart sank as he and Drew rode further and further with no sign of her. Along the Pioneer Road cutoff, there was not a house light to be seen.

At last Matthew saw a flash of something that broke up the darkness. Perhaps it was Diane's cream-colored bandana.

She heard the horses' hooves and called out, "hello, I'm here! Here!"

They stopped. When Matthew dismounted she collapsed in his arms. She was exhausted from fighting the wind and cold.

"It's okay, Diane. We'll have you home in no time."

In a weak voice, she said, "I'm so cold."

With Drew's help, he got her onto his horse in front of him. She wore heavy shoes and stockings, but he worried about frostbite as he removed his gloves and slipped them on her hands. Snow continued to fall as he and Drew urged the horses forward.

She leaned against him. *She could always depend on Matthew.*

It seemed forever before they finally arrived at the Robert Hoffman house.

John Hoffman had gone to tell the McCalls that their son had ridden off to rescue Diane. Elizabeth and Frances hustled Diane and the men inside. Hearty beef and vegetable soup stood warming on the kitchen stove. Elizabeth examined the girl's hands and feet as Catherine and Rachel served her.

She had not been so coddled since her mother's death.

"I was so frightened," Diane confided to the women in the kitchen. "How did they know where to find me?"

"Bob told them," Elizabeth said. "Matthew was concerned about you. He couldn't find you after school."

"Bob said he'd take me to see Amy."

"You poor dear," Catherine said. "What a trial for you. We're so happy you're all right."

They finally settled Diane in her bed, warmed by hot bricks wrapped in soft towels. Elizabeth was the last to leave Diane's attic room. "Why did you decide to walk home?" she said.

"I didn't," Diane said. "Bob shoved me from the wagon and left me."

"Why?"

"He was angry because I wouldn't kiss him."

"That horrid boy," Elizabeth snapped. "You must stay away from him in the future. I had no idea he was so nasty. If he gives you any more trouble, let me know immediately."

"Maybe he didn't like my singing," Diane said with a playful look.

"It's good you can laugh at this incident," Elizabeth said, "but please take Bob seriously."

Diane never told Aunt Catherine that her son had pushed her from the buggy and left her on a deserted road. She knew Catherine would be horrified by the information. Uncle Robert said no more about the incident.

For months, Diane dreamed about being stranded all alone, blinded by swirling snow.

She now considered Bob a thoughtless and dangerous boy, and she kept as far away from him as possible. In her bedroom she always remembered to lock the door.

When she told Vicky about the incident, her friend became indignant and always called Bob Bad Bob after that.

He lived up to the name. If he wandered into the kitchen and found her alone, he called her a tattle-tale. Sometimes he made fun of the pink birthmark on her temple. Other times he called her names and made fun of her singing voice, claiming it was terrible. Diane tried to ignore him, but it was hard to ignore a constant bully.

Chapter Twelve

One day Mrs. Muller came to see Elizabeth.

"Could I talk to you for a few minutes?" She stood on the stoop, holding a baby.

"Of course." Elizabeth opened the door wide. "Please come in, Louise. Let's go into the kitchen. I'll make some coffee."

"No, no, I have no time to spare. I must meet my son downtown in a few minutes."

"Please sit down then."

Louise sat. The baby began to fuss so she rocked it in her arms. Elizabeth waited. Finally, Louise said, "I'm expecting again."

Elizabeth knew she had a large family. This was probably not happy news for the woman.

"I want you to help me. I have ten children already. I can't have another baby."

Startled, Elizabeth said, "Louise, there's nothing I can do."

"Your papa was a doctor. I know you assisted Dr. Spencer, and other doctors too. You're a nurse. You could do it."

Elizabeth felt the woman's desperation. Ten children already. Louise must be exhausted. She was tempted for a moment by the woman's plight. Yes, she could do it. A fairly simple procedure. She had helped her father with home deliveries and knew more medicine than most nurses. How she wished she could help Mrs. Muller. Nevertheless, she shook her head. "I'm not trained to treat patients. Besides, it would be against the law."

Mrs. Muller began to sob. "How will I care for another baby? I'm worn out all the time as it is. I have no energy. It's work all the time, from dawn to dusk."

Elizabeth thought about the methods she knew to prevent pregnancy. Her mind wandered back to those golden days with Warren after she had finished nursing training. He had used a sheath, but, being a doctor, he was more knowledgeable than most.

Thoughts of Warren reminded her of the pain she had experienced at his death. A bright future had beckoned for them. Warren had secured a coveted appointment at the hospital, and she had been promised a good position there too. Then hopes and dreams had died along with his death.

"What can I do?" Mrs. Muller's words brought Elizabeth back to the present.

Elizabeth thought she might help in a small way. She had heard of other methods to prevent pregnancy. "Look, it's too late. Have the baby. Then come see me. Perhaps I can help you keep this from happening again."

When the distressed woman left, Elizabeth thought about who might help her with Mrs. Muller's problem. Nobody wrote about ways to prevent pregnancy.

Doctors did not discuss it with their patients. She had heard male doctors tell female patients that they'd had their fun, now they must pay. Never mind that their husbands instigated the fun, and that young girls were often victims of rape and incest.

Still, she knew women had success with various methods. While she had trained as a nurse, she had talked to other nurses and midwives who told her that European women had devices to prevent pregnancy. She would write to those midwives.

She had about six months to find out exactly what they knew, and how to get what she wanted for Mrs. Muller.

Elizabeth spoke to Frances alone as the woman set type in the newspaper office. Frances had avoided pregnancy. What was her secret? How could pregnancy be prevented?

"We've only been married a few years." Frances's pretty face was apologetic. "I consulted a midwife in Lincoln who told me about ways to avoid pregnancy. Drew agreed with me that it would be better to wait to have a family. Starting a newspaper takes the work of both of us and a lot of time. Are you holding out on us? Are you planning to marry?"

"No, no, it's for someone else. She came to me because my papa was a doctor and I'm a nurse. I'd like to help her. She already has a large family. She's worn out, beaten down."

"Women should be told how to limit their families," Frances said, as she worked with the type. "Aside from the dangers of childbirth, their health suffers when they have many children close together, and the children suffer too."

"You're preaching to the converted."

When Elizabeth left the newspaper office she had information from Frances that would help Louise Muller.

She had gathered an assortment of papers about devices to prevent pregnancy when she heard of Mrs. Muller's death, along with the child she carried. Complications of pregnancy. What a waste. She grieved for the woman. She heard that the older children, almost grown, were burdened with raising the younger ones.

Would the woman be alive if she had helped her abort the pregnancy? She would never know. But it seemed ridiculous that women could not get information from their doctors about limiting their families?

Chapter Thirteen

Winter lingered for weeks. Finally, when the March winds blew, the snow began to melt. Elizabeth could smell spring in the air. She collected seed packets and planned a vegetable garden. If she had to leave, Alex would weed and water it for her.

A few blocks away she found Catherine, Rachel, and Diane planning their garden as Bob tilled the plot. The smell of plowed earth and cut weeds and grass filled the air.

She waved as John Hoffman checked his small unusual windmill, so it would be ready to bring up water during the summer. He had also prepared a concrete reservoir to hold water, and made small irrigation ditches for the water to run to the plants. The windmill powered his system, so he had water from the reservoir even if the wind was not blowing.

At the back of the lot, Pamela Hoffman left the chicken pen with a huge basket. Her chickens were laying eggs again.

Elizabeth had been invited to eat with the Robinsons in their rooms. In the *Gazette* office, Elizabeth listened as Sonia Kirkendall complained to Frances and Drew about an editorial with which she disagreed. Drew, along with a new breed of correspondents, tried to report news impartially as they and eye witnesses saw it. In the past, many newspapers had simply reported what their biggest contributors wanted. They also used lurid headlines and half-truths to sell more papers.

Drew reminded Sonia about the need for opposing ideas in the editorial section, thanked her for her opinion, and promised to consider it. His accommodating manner disarmed her, and she left smiling.

When Sonia had gone, Elizabeth said, "Poor woman. Her husband was too young to die."

Frances agreed. "But his death hasn't slowed her down. She's always been a bit scrappy and odd. She likes her own way."

"I visited the patient." Elizabeth frowned as she removed her hat. "There he was, with a simple cough and slight fever and...."

"You don't believe that she--" Frances's eyes widened.

"No, of course not, but it's strange he died like that." Elizabeth shook her head.

Frances gave her a quizzical look. "It's convenient that she married Cal Jones to continue the heavy work he's done for years on her farm."

"Very convenient."

"It hasn't even been a year. They say she was eyeing the field before she settled on Cal. She certainly had other opportunities," Frances said as she set the table. "Sonia never did like me. I don't know why."

"Could be jealousy," Elizabeth said, removing her hat. "You two must be the most attractive women in Plainville."

"Nonsense. Have you heard from those Spencer boys, Elizabeth? Your distance cousins?" Frances took a paper that Drew handed her from the wire.

"I have. Hiram and Phil ended up in San Francisco, working in a warehouse. I rather miss them. It was nice to have the company, and I thought Hiram had developed an interest in Julia while they were at the hotel."

"Wouldn't Hiram and Julia be related?"

"We decided the boys are third cousins to Blanche and me. That's much too distant to present any problems. You'll be going to San Francisco soon to visit your aunt, won't you?"

"Yes, I'm looking forward to it. Aunt Gwen DeVault is expecting me."

Frances scanned the dispatch that Drew had handed her. "I see that some women in England were imprisoned for supposedly obstructing justice. They were attempting to talk to liberal leaders about votes for women."

"Imprisoned for trying to talk about the vote," Elizabeth said, indignant. "Isn't England supposed to be a democracy?"

As Frances spread out a meal of pork chops, buttered peas, and fresh biscuits, Drew poured coffee. "I wonder if the vote is worth all the trouble it will cause," he said. "Many people oppose it. Governments too."

Frances smiled sweetly at him. "That's easy for you to say. You have the vote."

He grinned wryly. "You're right, of course, but I hope you two don't start a campaign in Plainville."

Elizabeth laughed. "I'm afraid two women do not make a campaign. This is the Midwest, after all."

Chapter Fourteen

The city of San Francisco is a peninsula bounded by the Pacific Ocean on the west and by oval-shaped San Francisco Bay on the east and north. Wharves, warehouses, Chinatown, and the downtown are located on the east. Here, at the end of Market Street, an unusually wide thoroughfare, is located the Ferry Building. The ferry runs on a regular schedule across the bay to Oakland.

Away from the waterfront downtown, the city fans out into residential areas.

In downtown San Francisco, Hiram and Phil Spencer rose early Wednesday morning April 18, 1906. They ate breakfast at their downtown boarding house, and headed for the warehouse where they worked, passing through the produce market on their way. By 5:00 o'clock, peddlers were haggling with customers, and noise filled the air.

All was lively. Even the horses pranced more than usual. In the distance, dozens of dogs barked. "Noisy this morning," Phil commented.

They noticed a man waiting for a cable car. Huge drays pulled by horses lumbered by. Motorcars were already out. A woman pushing a baby carriage hurried along the walk.

Phil picked up a handbill from the street announcing the presentation by The Metropolitan Opera of *Carmen*, featuring the famous singer, Enrico Caruso, who traveled to San Francisco to sing.

"Guess we missed the opera last night," Phil said with a grin.

"What a pity," Hiram said, grinning back. "That sure ruins my day. Just as well. What would people have made of our grubby old work clothes?"

As the boys joked, the ground began to shift. The youths had already experienced a minor earthquake in California. Intrigued, they tried to stand straight as the ground rolled and rumbled beneath them. They heard a grumbling and crashing as buildings nearby shifted and cracked.

Then there was quiet for a few seconds. The rumbling started again and buildings shifted back.

When the rolling ended after a few seconds, the crashing noise grew louder. Nearby, wooden buildings collapsed. Brick buildings crumbled and fell to the ground. Broken glass fell into the street. It felt as if the whole world was tumbling down.

All around them was chaos. Trolley tracks buckled. Water and gas from burst pipes flew into the air. Debris rained from the shattered buildings on each side of the street.

Frantic people crowded into the streets and stared at their surroundings.

Some cried in hysterics. Others stared in shock. Hiram pulled Phil to the middle of the street, away from the falling buildings where it was safer. "It was an earthquake. Let's go home and see how our things are."

They raced home and found their three-story boarding house totally crushed, the third story squashed on top of the other two. Where they had eaten breakfast a short time ago, all was rubble.

Phil moaned. "We've lost everything."

"We didn't have much. But I left most of my money at home. I have barely enough to carry me until Friday payday. Do you have cash?"

"Very little." Phil pulled out the meager contents of his pockets. He shrugged his shoulders. "Maybe someone is alive under the rubble."

Along with some other men, they began to tear at the wreckage in an attempt to save the residents. A Mr. Harper, who lived in the house, pulled them off.

"It's useless. They're all dead. They couldn't possibly survive. All that concrete from nearby buildings toppled on top of the house. I had just left on my way to work."

"He's right." Phil pointed across the way where cries for help carried into the street. "Let's help over there." With the assistance of others, they were able to help people out of the building to safety.

For hours, Hiram and Phil helped trapped people out of the wreckage. Wood, cement, shattered furnishings were still falling into the streets. Dust filled the air. They pulled out dead bodies and were forced to leave them at the side of the street.

A few fires started as people in houses still standing tried to use their stoves and found the flues blocked. Firemen raced from one fire to another in their horse-drawn fire wagons. The fires were too fast for them. They set nearby houses on fire and leapt on to even more.

The firemen discovered that the water mains were shattered. They had no water to fight the fires, and communication with the fire station was impossible.

Some people were trapped under rubble as fire headed their way. Passersby saved many of them. But a few could not be helped. One man whose legs were trapped under cement begged to be shot. A civilian took pity on him and shot him in the head.

Refugees whose homes were burned and destroyed began to converge on Market Street, heading for the Ferry Building at the waterfront. Others headed for Golden Gate Park and various parks in the city. Still others raced for the high ground of the Twin Peaks or the San Bruno Hills. One woman ran back to her burning house. She wished to die with her husband, trapped inside.

Finally, Hiram and Phil trudged to the warehouse where they worked. It had completely collapsed. A fleeing straggler told them nobody was inside at the time of the earthquake. The youths were homeless, and now out of a job.

Around them, only soldiers patrolled the streets. Dust and ashes sifted down on the silent streets.

The youths were left exhausted and hungry in the early evening. A soldier told them that food was available at Union Square, a two-acre park of greenery away from the fire. They made their way there and stood in line for canned meat, rice, and bread from a bakery far from the fire.

Tents, sent over from the federal Presidio, were being set up. Phil suffered from a swollen ankle where he'd been hit by a piece of concrete as they worked in the rubble. Since his brother was in pain, Hiram helped set up tents, assisting nearby, unwilling to leave Phil in the park. Besides, they had nowhere else to go.

They heard that the Mayor had fled City Hall in the one automobile owned by the city police. The building, serving as an emergency hospital for a short time, had been destroyed. As the fire approached the hall, the patients had been evacuated to the Mechanics Pavilion. Prisoners were moved to Fort Mason or shipped to the federal prison on Alcatraz Island.

A proclamation by Mayor Schmitz hung on a post in the Square. Citizens were requested to remain at home from darkness until daylight. The Gas and Electric Lighting Company was directed not to turn on gas or electricity. The city could expect to remain in darkness for an indefinite time. Soldiers from the Presidio, the regular police, and special police officers were authorized to shoot looters and persons found engaged in the commission of any other crime on sight. Anyone could be killed on the least suspicion.

Hiram read the proclamation and wondered what had happened to the Constitution. Didn't the President have to declare martial law?

And the ridiculous request to remain at home was laughable. What about the hundreds of people who no longer had a home?

That night, Hiram and Phil, along with thousands of other refugees finally went to sleep on the grass. They did not sleep long.

Word came that the fires had spread and merged into one towering inferno, swallowing the waterfront. Since the water mains were all broken, firemen were trying to dynamite buildings along a fire line to stop the fire.

The downtown was gone. The blaze was headed their way.

♦ ♦ ♦

In Plainville, excitement kept Diane from falling asleep. She looked forward to staying with Aunt Elizabeth for several weeks, while Uncle Robert and Catherine and their two children traveled to Iowa to visit Catherine's parents.

Diane relished escaping from Uncle Robert's perpetual frown and Bob's insults. Several times she got up to slip things into her small traveling case to take to Aunt Elizabeth's house.

The next day, Aunt Elizabeth paid them an early visit. Robert, having just finished breakfast, invited her in. "Elizabeth, what a pleasant surprise." His hands lingered a second longer than necessary on her shoulders as he started to help her out of her coat.

"Good morning, Catherine, Robert. I can't stay." Looking flushed, she shrugged off his efforts. "There's terrible news. There's been a huge earthquake in San Francisco."

Catherine put her hand to her mouth. "Isn't Frances Robinson in San Francisco now?"

"Yes." Elizabeth frowned. "Drew has had no word from her. He's very distraught. My cousins are in San Francisco too."

"Good God." Robert sat down.

"The Red Cross is calling for nurses. I want to leave as soon as possible."

"But you'll have Diane."

Elizabeth's eyes begged them to understand. "The earthquake started fires. The city is burning. People will have injuries. They'll need nurses."

"We've got our train tickets."

"I'm sorry. Any other time."

Robert's eyes narrowed. "So a bunch of strangers in San Francisco are more important than our plans."

"I'm very sorry."

Robert flushed with anger. "Why don't you take her with you? She looks older than fourteen. No one will guess how young she is. Surely they need all kinds of volunteers."

Catherine piped up. "She's a very good worker. Knows a lot about cooking and serving. You'd be able to keep an eye on her. Besides, look at all those ten-year-olds and even younger who work in factories and mills."

"There's school--"

"We'll have Bob and Rachel read to keep up. But you hardly need worry about Diane. She makes excellent grades."

In the corner, Diane held her breath. She hoped to be with Aunt Elizabeth. Traveling with Uncle Robert and Bob to visit strangers held no interest at all.

"I'll have to think about it. What if she's in danger?" Elizabeth turned to Robert. "Does Thomas Hoffman know that Blanche is dead? Where his children are?"

"John wrote to him. He didn't answer. So I guess he doesn't care."

His words hurt Diane. She remembered little about her father, but it stung to hear that he didn't care for his children.

Elizabeth tapped her foot and considered Diane. "What do you say, Diane?"

"Let me come. I can help. I won't be any trouble."

"We'll have to work all day. There won't be any time for fun. We may have to sleep on the ground in tents."

"Yes, I don't mind."

Elizabeth studied her only a moment longer. "You can serve people food, peel potatoes, that kind of thing."

"I don't mind."

"Get your bag then. We can lengthen your skirts on the way and put your hair in a bun. You can use your mother's combs to hold your hair back. Maybe we can make you look sixteen. I have to go home and pack a few things to catch the afternoon train leaving for San Francisco." She sailed out the door.

Within minutes, Diane had grabbed her small case and raced to follow Elizabeth, waving good-bye to Catherine and Rachel as she sped by.

At her house, Elizabeth threw basic medical supplies and personal items into her traveling bag as Diane watched, ready to run errands if asked.

At a knock on the door, Diane found Julia on the doorstep, crying in distress. "Diane, I've got to talk to Elizabeth." She brushed past Diane, and found Elizabeth in the bedroom.

"Aunt Elizabeth, have you heard anything about Hiram and Phil?"

"No, I'm sorry. I haven't. Drew doesn't even know if his wife is alive."

"I've been writing to Hiram. If you find out anything about them, will you let me know?"

"Of course. I'll wire Drew and he can get in touch with you. Try not to worry. I'm sure most of the people will survive. They usually do."

Diane walked with Julia back to the hotel. "I'm sorry about our cousins," she said. "I'm going to work for the Red Cross with Aunt Elizabeth. If I see Hiram and Phil I'll tell them you're worried about them."

Julia hesitated. "They're just friends of mine, of course, and shirttail relatives," she explained. "You'll be a comfort to Aunt Elizabeth. Take care, little sister."

Diane pranced back to Elizabeth. She didn't want to be left behind in Plainville.

Chapter Fifteen

In San Francisco, all the sleepers in Union Square woke up to hollering and crying in frantic voices. "The fire is coming this way! Wake up!! Hurry! Run toward Van Ness Avenue. Run to the Ferry Building. Go to Market Street."

Hiram yanked Phil to his feet and the two fled with their blankets. Despite his wounded ankle, Phil managed to keep up with Hiram. The brothers stopped to rest in front of a small undamaged house. It was surrounded by daisies and rose bushes. A wrinkled, but spry old woman rushed out with cups of water.

"You poor boys. Sleep here in the yard with your blankets. The fire won't get this far." She peered at Phil's ankle. "It's swollen. We should keep it cold. I have water in the barrels. We'll wrap it in wet rags."

She hurried back inside and reappeared with dampened cloths, some cold cooked chicken, bread and water. "Here, eat this," she offered. "Get as much sleep as you can. Who knows what tomorrow will bring. My man is bedridden. Everybody calls me Granny Moreno."

Thanking the kindly old woman, the brothers settled down with their blankets for a second time to catch some sleep.

♦ ♦ ♦

The train carrying Elizabeth and Diane chugged down the track, heading west, spewing smoke outside. Inside, it was crowded, noisy, and dirty. Elizabeth, filled with anxiety about her cousins and Frances Robinson, sat straight, horror filling her thoughts. Diane watched from the window and failed to notice the dirt.

Around them, people talked of Roosevelt's trust-busting, of suffragettes being arrested for picketing the dwelling of the Prime Minister, (10 Downing Street in London), but mostly about the earthquake and the fires in San Francisco that had resulted from the earthquake. The city was in flames.

People were horrified. "Our family lives near Market Street. They must be burned out. Where could they go?"

"They can't all live out in the hills."

"Golden Gate Park, maybe?"

Worried passengers stewed about their friends and relatives and the terrible tragedy taking place in their nation.

Through the rolling plains, the high mountains, and the fruitful valleys of California the train sped. Once, as the train neared the city, they were stopped beside a string of freight cars filled with refugees from San Francisco. Their clothes were soot-covered and they looked tired and hungry.

♦ ♦ ♦

In San Francisco, Phil's ankle seemed better in the morning. So he and Hiram ate cold biscuits with milk provided by Granny Moreno, and set off to see where they could help.

People wandered about the streets, seemingly dazed. The youths passed soldiers digging latrines. Meanwhile, in the hills close to downtown, mansions burned.

They heard from one man that houses were to be evacuated and dynamited in order to provide a firebreak and protect residential districts. They hoped to make Powell Street the fire line.

The fire raged as the mayor and his advisory committee, forced to flee their headquarters for the second time, left the endangered North End Police Station and moved into Franklin Hall on Fillmore Street, a mile from the nearest fire line.

From there, they made the final decision to make Van Ness Avenue the firebreak. Expensive residential districts between Powell and Van Ness would have to be destroyed. The fire had become a roaring furnace.

Word spread that refuge centers were set up in Golden Gate Park and in the Presidio, both far from the fire area. Some people snatched up what they could and headed for the camps. Others begged wagon drivers to haul their possessions, often offering exorbitant sums of money.

As the fire raged on either side of Market Street, people fled to the Ferry Building at the end of the street in order to cross the bay to Oakland. With so many people aboard, the passengers were allowed to take only what they could hold onto the ferry.

Around Van Ness Avenue, people were ordered to evacuate their houses scheduled for destruction. Since they were in the area, Hiram and Phil helped them remove their possessions to the far side of Van Ness. The refugees, many still in shock, sat on pianos, tables, chests, sewing machines. Flames shooting up a few blocks away filled them with terror. The fire sounded like cracking wood, crushing buildings and crackling flames.

Phil heard a woman ask others, "Has anyone seen Granny Moreno?"

Phil turned toward her. "Do you know her?"

"Yes. She's a neighbor. We thought she left, but no one has seen her."

"Granny Moreno?" Phil said to his brother. "They've moved the fire wall and she's behind it."

Hiram groaned. "And her husband is bedridden."

"We'll have to go for them. Maybe we can carry them on our backs. She couldn't weigh more than eighty pounds."

"But how do we get through the soldiers?"

"Let's run over to Market Street. It's so crowded nobody will notice what we're doing. Then we can double back to her house."

They sped toward Market Street. The thought of the danger to the old couple spurred them on. Smoke drifted everywhere in the air and choked their lungs.

When they burst into Granny Moreno's house, they found her kneeling beside her husband's bed, praying.

"We've come to take you to the other side of the firebreak," Hiram said.

"Oh, you dear boys." She breathed a sigh of relief. "There's a wheelbarrow for him in the back." Granny Moreno grabbed a half-filled sack and stuffed more garments and food inside.

Hiram and Phil lifted the old man onto pillows and blankets in the wheelbarrow, and piled on extra blankets. "I'll carry you on my back," Phil said to Granny.

"Carry me! I should say not. I've got two good legs. Lead the way."

As Hiram pushed the wheelbarrow, Phil carried one of Granny's gunnysacks. To their surprise, she had no trouble keeping up with them, even carrying a large parcel slung on her back. They could see the flames licking through buildings a few blocks behind them.

This time they headed straight for Van Ness Avenue. When the soldiers saw Hiram and Phil pushing the old man in the wheelbarrow, they motioned them through the blockade. Immediately, they were surrounded by friends and neighbors who had worried about the couple, and now took them under their protection.

"I didn't see how I could get my man out," Granny told them. "I couldn't lift him into the wheelbarrow. By the time I realized I needed help, everyone had gone. These boys saved our lives."

They had rescued the old couple just in time. The soldiers fired cannon at houses, and the boom of dynamite deafened ears. All night the racket continued.

While they battled the fire, the first train load of food and medical supplies from Los Angeles arrived in Oakland, across the bay.

The exhausted firemen worked hours trying to contain the fire at Van Ness. By midnight the fire leaped across in one place.

Chapter Sixteen

All Thursday night the firemen fought the blaze, encouraged by the chief. In some cases they attacked the flames with horse blankets, sacks, and rugs. Volunteers used brooms and potato sacks, whatever was handy.

Late Friday morning things looked better. Hiram noticed that the wind had changed and was blowing the inferno back over ground that was already scorched.

The navy brought thousands of feet of hose pipe. As Hiram and Phil held up wet blankets to protect the firemen who held the hoses to the fire, they were joined by a couple of reporters who had run out of film for their cameras.

In the early morning hours on Saturday, the fourth day of the tragedy, the firemen declared the fire on Van Ness Avenue was finally out.

Another volunteer who had worked beside the Spencer boys and the reporters said, "Do you fellows have a place to sleep?"

All four admitted they did not.

"Come with me. You can sleep on my porch in the Western Division. We still have some food left too."

The four exhausted men followed him, leaving the fire to the firemen.

The reporters introduced themselves. "I'm Vince Morris from Omaha and this is my brother Scott, learning the business. I publish a small newspaper there."

"We've been to Nebraska. We spent a few months harvesting ice in the winter. I'm Hiram, and this ugly fellow with the limp is Phil, my brother."

Phil, not at all ugly, grinned.

"You should get off that foot." Hiram gave him a hand. "Tomorrow we'll go to Golden Gate Park so you can give it some rest. Maybe see a doctor. On the way, I'll be able to give some help while you rest for spells."

"We have to get to Oakland to send telegrams," Vince said. "My wife will be worrying if we don't. We heard about the run you made to save Granny Moreno and her husband. She's been telling everybody about it. If I ever have a fire, I'd like to have you two to fight it. When did you last sleep?"

"Wednesday night, before the fire got so big."

The four, covered with black dust and grimy clothes, flopped onto the floor of the porch, while their host sought food and a basin of wash water.

"They're still working to save the Bay Shore and put out a fire in the Mission District." Vince spread out on the floor. "I just haven't the energy to follow up on those."

Scott yawned. "With the wind turned, they'll probably be stopped soon too."

"Now if someone could stop the soldiers from looting the evacuated buildings," Hiram said, stretching.

Vince grimaced. "I've heard some horrible stories: They've shot people coming out of houses with their own possessions, threatened people to get them to evacuate, shot a deaf man who didn't hear their orders."

Their host brought out blankets, mats, bread, and canned meat. "We can't start a fire for coffee," he apologized. "Besides, we're short of water. You'll have to drink wine."

"I'm willing to do my share for the cause. I don't mind wine." Vince grinned. "We wouldn't want you starting a fire and causing more trouble."

"Hell, let's all sacrifice," Scott said, pouring glasses from the bottle.

After they ate, the four of them fell asleep immediately.

Chapter Seventeen

The next day, on their way to Golden Gate Park, Hiram and Phil were stopped by gun-carrying soldiers. Pointing at a number of dead bodies stacked in an open area, the soldiers ordered Hiram and Phil to help bury them.

"Not the kind of help I had in mind, but I don't feel like arguing with a damn gun," Hiram told Phil. He picked up a shovel, and the two got to work. Phil limped and slowly helped with the digging. By this time the stench was nauseating and the flies swarmed around them. Now and then rats appeared from the open sewers. The soldiers raised their guns and shot many of them.

They had dug graves and buried several bodies when Phil called to Hiram. "I know this woman. It's Mrs. Robinson from Plainville."

Hiram looked at the small body and agreed. "See this bruise on her head. She was probably hit by flying debris from a building. What a tragedy. She was beautiful. Look at her long black hair."

They wanted to take something from the body to show her people if they ever saw them, but they worried that the soldiers would shoot them for stealing from the dead.

Hiram asked one of the soldiers if he could take the woman's scarf to return to her husband. He would need to know what had happened to her. The soldier shrugged. "Be sure you take only the scarf."

Hiram stuffed the scarf in his pocket. Perhaps he could mail it, but in the back of his mind, he could not shake the belief that they would be back in Plainville someday. He often thought of pert and pretty Julia Hoffman at the Plainville Hotel.

When they finished that job, the soldiers allowed them to leave. As they headed off, Hiram looked back over his shoulder and saw soldiers removing and pocketing jewelry from new bodies that were laid out on the ground.

♦ ♦ ♦

On the other side of San Francisco Bay, the train pulled into the Oakland Station and unloaded. Diane and Elizabeth hurried to catch the ferry. Refugees from San Francisco poured into the street. Even though the fire was contained by now, they looked dirty and desperate. A Red Cross station in Oakland was there to help them.

Elizabeth and Diane identified themselves as a Red Cross nurse and a worker. They were allowed to cross San Francisco Bay on the ferry. Otherwise, sightseers from outside San Francisco were not allowed.

Elizabeth held a small map of the city in her hands. With the help of ferry workers and harried residents, she located Mrs. DeVault's house in the Western Addition on the street map.

Residents told her the house was probably still standing as the fire had not reached that location. It would be a long walk, but Golden Gate Park, the site of Red Cross operations, lay in the same direction.

They were about to set off on foot when they noticed a Red Cross wagon being loaded with supplies from the ferry.

Elizabeth spoke to the driver. "We're here to work with the Red Cross at the Golden Gate Park. Could we get a ride as far as the Western Addition?"

"Sure, lady." The driver, busy with his loading, didn't even stop to look at her. "We'll take you as far as we can."

It didn't take them long to reach their destination, but they stared in dismay at the charred ruins of the downtown as the wagon passed through.

True to his word, the driver dropped the two women off a few blocks from the DeVault house.

Mrs. DeVault was overjoyed to see them. She hugged Elizabeth and could barely refrain from sobbing.

"What a horrible time we've had. We still have no word about Frances. She left after the earthquake to help out at Union Square and never returned. Mr. DeVault took the carriage to look for her, but she wasn't there. The army confiscated our automobile. Then Union Square was hit by fire. Oh…." She wrung her hands, unable to continue.

Elizabeth burst into tears. As her sobs subsided, she said, "Frances is my best friend. I don't know what I'd do without her. Have you wired Drew again?"

"Yes, I sent a wire off to her husband as soon as I could with a friend who left for Oakland. See here, Elizabeth, the whole town is mourning. My house has escaped the fire. Our area is safe. Many of the Red Cross people are staying in tents, but you must stay with me. I need your presence."

"Are you sure we won't be a burden. I've brought my niece, Diane, to work with me. She's energetic and smart."

"Hello, Diane. You're both very welcome. As it happens, my house is full of refuges. You'll have to share a room."

"That's very good of you. We want to get to work as soon as possible."

"It's too late today. I insist you get a good night's rest. In fact, some of the people at my house could use your nursing skills. It's practically impossible to get a doctor right now."

That evening Diane and the maid boiled water and carried kettles of it to the sick room as Elizabeth tended small burns and changed dressings at the DeVault house. Sleeping mats covered the drawing room and parts of the hallways.

In the distance, they could hear explosions as the fire department blew up damaged buildings, many in danger of toppling over on people.

"Most of these visitors will be going to the Red Cross tents as soon as enough have been set up for them. Some are still looking for friends and relatives. Others are volunteers too."

Mrs. DeVault poured coffee for Elizabeth as she and Diane ate supper. "In the morning, my driver will take you to Golden Gate Park in the carriage."

Elizabeth shook her head. "I've no intention of showing up at the aid station in an expensive carriage. I'm sure you have better uses for it at this time. Write down the directions and we'll walk. I understand it's not far."

"No, it isn't far. I suppose you could walk." Mrs. DeVault sighed. "It's hard to help someone as independent as you are, but I do see your point."

♦ ♦ ♦

The next day, Elizabeth and Diane left early for Golden Gate Park. They found army tents stretched out in rows as far as the eye could see. Other volunteers, desperately trying to feed and care for hundreds of homeless residents, welcomed them and put them to work. Elizabeth nursed in the Red Cross first aid tent while Diane, with two other women in another tent, ladled coffee from buckets set on planks between sawhorses. They also served soup, canned beans, fresh beef, and biscuits to refugees and workers who ate at long tables.

Shocked, worried, exhausted, people filed through the line, and accepted the food as they sat on makeshift benches and examined the faces of others, looking for relatives and friends.

Diane heard residents talking. "Do you suppose it's true that Congress has voted to send two and a half million dollars for relief?"

"That's what I read."

"You have a newspaper?"

"They printed the newspapers in Oakland and brought a bunch around this morning. Old Teddy is going to help us. President Roosevelt is sending a Dr. Devine to handle relief operations. Sure hope his help is divine." The man chuckled at his joke.

A knowledgeable woman said, "Roosevelt doesn't trust our esteemed mayor to distribute the money." Diane had heard that the mayor was suspected of graft and corruption.

"Chicago has pledged additional money and is sending a Mr. Bicknell to handle it. Guess they don't trust the mayor either. People in Chicago can understand what a fire can do. They were burned out in a massive fire years ago."

"As a matter of fact, I've heard people from all over the world have offered to help."

"And people right here," Granny Moreno said. "Jess and I were saved by two young fellows who risked their lives to come back for us."

Her remark led to further tales of bravery during the earthquake and fire.

Diane fed firewood to the stove standing in the Red Cross tent. It was laden with several pots of food. A six-foot-tall woman with long, wavy, brown hair asked to take her picture standing in front of the tent. She carried photographic equipment and wore a wide smile.

Diane hesitated. "I think you should ask Elizabeth Spencer. She's my aunt and she's nursing in the first aid station."

The woman studied her. "How old are you, anyway?"

Diane lowered her voice. "I might be too young to be working here. Please don't tell anyone. I can work as well as the others."

The woman gave her a benign smile. "I see. Well, I can't tell what I don't know."

From the first aid tent, Elizabeth, carrying a tray filled with soup, bread, and milk, strode toward the two of them. "Diane, we should eat something now. They have canned milk available. Have some with your meal."

Elizabeth looked with curiosity at the woman and her camera. "Hello. I'm Elizabeth Spencer and this is my niece, Diane Hoffman."

"I'm Molly Potter. I'm a photographer. I'd like to take a picture of your niece."

"Why?"

"That's how I make my living. I'll be selling the pictures to a magazine."

"How interesting. Well, I suppose it will be all right."

"I'll wait until she's eaten. I need a rest anyway." She plopped down beside Elizabeth and Diane on an old bench someone had provided for the aid workers to sit on, and pulled out a sandwich from her bag. "Did you just arrive today?"

"Last night. We're staying with Gwen DeVault."

"I see. I've heard of her. Quite active in social causes, isn't she?"

"Yes, I believe she is. She has dozens of refuges in her home right now. She's taken us in because I'm a friend of her niece...." Elizabeth faltered. She didn't want to believe that her friend was dead.

Molly touched her hand. "I'm sorry."

"I can't dwell on it right now." Elizabeth raised her head and shook it. She had to concentrate on her work here.

Intrigued by Molly, she questioned the woman. "Where are you staying?"

"With my brother and his wife. They live in Sam Mateo, a few miles down from the Peninsula, to the south. I caught a ride with a neighboring banker this morning in his buggy. The day of the earthquake Peter Giannini and his employees removed all the fixtures and the bank's money from the vault and hauled it all away in a produce wagon. They wisely took it to his home because later his bank burned down. He's now set up a stand in the city to start loaning money to people so they can rebuild."

"That's amazing." Elizabeth sipped coffee. "Do you travel often?"

"Yes, I do. It's an interesting life. You may have seen some of my pictures." Molly mentioned several magazines and their dates of issue.

"Have you taken many pictures of this catastrophe?"

"I have. Some devastating pictures. The fire has consumed property worth millions, plus hundreds, maybe thousands, of lives. It's been difficult to fight because the earthquake broke the water mains."

"I understand it also broke the sewer lines, and that rats are running in and out of them. That could cause trouble later on. Rats carry disease."

"They sure don't need that here." Molly drank water from a jar she'd brought.

Elizabeth didn't want to cause a panic about the possibility of plague. "Maybe it won't happen," she said.

When Diane was ready, Molly took a picture of her at the entrance to the tent. Then she gathered up her camera and tripod.

"I'll send you a copy of the magazine when I get it. Now I must get going and earn my daily bread. Maybe I'll see you again, little Miss Red Cross and Elizabeth." After securing Elizabeth's address, she tramped off, politely greeting some armed soldiers on her way.

One of them made a suggestive comment. Elizabeth stopped and stared at him, hands on hips. "What did you say, soldier? Speak up so everybody can hear you."

Shamefaced, the soldier walked away as bystanders stared. Mollie, taller than he, made a formidable figure. She winked at Diane and continued on her way.

The soldiers then strolled around the camp, eyeing everything somewhat suspiciously. Finding nothing out of order, they marched off.

"I've heard they're shooting looters on sight," one man told the others. "Be careful not to get in their way or give them the wrong impression."

Concerned, Elizabeth said, "Hear that, Diane? Please don't wander off."

Elizabeth had also heard some frightful stories about soldier abuses.

"They shoot suspected looters on sight, but they broke into rail cars filled with liquor and helped themselves to the drink," she told Diane.

Elizabeth stood. "I must get back to work too." *Would it be safe to walk to the De Vault house late in the day?*

Chapter Eighteen

When it started to get dark, Mr. and Mrs. DeVault arrived with a wagon full of patients who needed to see doctors.

"You must accept a ride back to our house," Gwen said. "We've been cooped up all day, caring for refugees. Automobiles and carriages have been commandeered by the army, and we've had a devil of a time getting a wagon to carry off the wounded. We're getting short of food so we needed to bring the refugees here."

"We may be able to buy food before long." Mr. DeVault said. "I've been told that some businesses near the burned areas downtown are opening up already."

"What resilience. But not everybody wants to stay," Elizabeth said, relieved to see the wagon. "I've heard many have moved out. The Southern Pacific has given free one-way passage to earthquake refugees fleeing San Francisco."

♦ ♦ ♦

The next afternoon, between the dinner and supper meals, Diane sat down to rest on a bench outside. A man and a youth, both clean-shaven, carrying small notebooks and pencils, began to interview the few people still lingering after a meal.

"We're from the press in Omaha," the man said.

The youth walked over to interview Diane and two other workers.

"Diane Hoffman," he said, surprised. "You look much older. What are you doing here?"

It was Scott Morris, the boy Diane had met at the Plainville Independence Day celebration the previous summer when he had been visiting Matthew McCall.

She smiled. "Hello, Scott. I'm here to work for the Red Cross with my aunt."

Scott sneered. "I suppose your family can come down here without worrying about making a living. Must be nice to be part of the elite."

"Why, I...." Diane was at a loss. His words stung. What was he talking about? What family did he mean? Aunt Elizabeth worked for a living. Diane didn't feel a part of Uncle Robert's family. Besides, were they elite?

"What are you doing while people are starving and dying?" He gave her a hostile stare.

"Why, I'm brewing coffee."

"Oh, that's very helpful." His voice sounded like a sneer.

"Yes, well, I notice you're not busy saving lives," she said in a sarcastic voice.

Scott turned away from her and addressed one of the women named Ida. "I'm Scott Morris, working for my brother, Vince Morris. He publishes a newspaper in Omaha. Did your homes survive the fire?"

"We both live south of San Francisco. Our houses weren't badly hit by the earthquake. We've come over to help."

"That's very commendable of you. Did you feel the earthquake where you live?"

"Did we feel it?" Nina said. "Of course we felt it. But our homes are fine."

"Now that makes sense. Living close by, coming to help." He turned to Diane. "Was it really necessary to come all the way from Nebraska?"

Taken aback, Diane stared. "Well, my aunt's a nurse. She's also been trained in Red Cross procedures and she's taught them to me."

"Are you sure all these extra people aren't just in the way?"

Diane had no reply to that. She walked off to pour coffee to a man who was waiting.

Ida eyed him curiously. "You're being a bit hard on her, aren't you?"

"I don't think so. Why are all these Red Cross workers from so far away necessary?"

"They are necessary. The residents of San Francisco are still in shock, looking for relatives, burying their dead. They're cleaning up the rubble and planning how to rebuild. We make it easier by providing for their basic needs until they have shelter and food of their own. For that, we need willing workers like young Diane. She's been a godsend. Where she comes from is unimportant."

Chastised, Scott wandered off to look for news elsewhere, muttering. "Rich ladies, nothing better to do." Every time he thought about Diane's wealthy father and how he swindled his own papa out of land, he boiled with rage.

For the next few days, Scott and Vince checked with the police, the army, the fire chief and Mayor Schmitz's headquarters for news to telegraph home for their Omaha newspaper.

At the end of each day, they visited the Presidio and the Golden Gate camp to find items of interest. Afterward, the reporters ferried across the bay to send their wires and to stay at their hotel.

They accepted coffee from the Red Cross, but no food, believing it should be reserved for the refugees. Molly brought her own bread and cheese and drank only water.

One day Scott walked up to Diane's work table as she talked to Molly, Ida and Nina. "Some of Mrs. DeVault's neighbors aren't very charitable. I've heard them make ridiculous remarks about the people from Chinatown and the area south of Mission. Their wealth has made them blind to tragedy."

"People who live in glass houses shouldn't throw stones," Scott said.

She stared at him for a minute with those remarkable eyes, and then walked away and busied herself with serving utensils.

Ida and Nina looked at him and said nothing. He found the atmosphere unpleasant and sauntered off. "Let me know if you have anything newsworthy," he said over his shoulder.

♦ ♦ ♦

As time passed, Diane became acquainted with people at the camp. The refugees wandered from tent to tent, looking for a lost child or missing family member. They put up signs describing the missing. More than once, Diane entertained a child while people sought relatives. She told the children folk tales and taught them games she knew.

The refugees nursed their wounds and sought news. Her heart went out to them. She wished she could do more.

A man who called himself Todd came to the camp one day. He hung around the service tents. Diane wondered why. Most of the refugees looked for relatives or talked with friends and acquaintances, exchanging information, making plans.

Something about Todd was not right. He didn't act like the other refugees. Could he be dangerous? She watched him furtively as he nursed a cup of coffee in the early evening when it was almost dark.

After the driver walked off, Todd suddenly jumped up onto the seat of a wagon filled with as yet unloaded Red Cross supplies.

Diane, standing near the wagon, feared what he had in mind. He had been watching the wagon. A second after he jumped onto the seat, the athletic girl grabbed the edge of the wagon and vaulted into the back, her full skirt making it possible.

Unwilling to lose the badly needed supplies, Diane began to shout, "He's taking the food. "Help! Help!"

"Get off!" screamed Todd, turning his head to yell at her as he urged the horse forward.

Diane was thrown off her feet into the bed of the wagon, toppling boxes and crates, but she had no intention of abandoning the supplies. She plunged forward and attacked the man from behind, pulling him into the wagon bed. He struggled with her and swung a fist to hit her in the head.

Chapter Nineteen

When Todd jerked and then dropped the reins, the horse slowed. People came running to catch up with the horse and wagon. Vince and Scott yanked Todd from the wagon and wrestled him to the ground.

One man said, "We should turn him over to the soldiers." The crowd murmured assent.

"That's no good," Vince said. "They'd just kill him for stealing. Hardly a capital offense." He turned to Todd. "Where were you going with all the food, Mister?"

"We're running out of food on our street. There's no place to buy anything." Todd stared at them, defiant. "And no money even if there was food."

"Tell the people to come here." Elizabeth told him. "We can't allow anyone to take this much food. People might try to sell it and that would be wrong."

"You're going to let him go?" a man said, frowning at Vince.

"Do you really want to see him shot for stealing food?"

The crowd became quiet. In a low voice, Scott said to Todd, "Get out of here while you can."

Todd, knowing when to become scarce, took off in a dead run. When Diane leaped down from the wagon, Molly clapped her hands. "Well, little Miss Red Cross. You saved the food."

The crowd agreed, and Diane blushed at their praise. "I didn't figure he had a right to that much." She rubbed her head where Todd had hit her.

You could have been hurt," Elizabeth said with concern. "Let me look at your head."

"I'm sorry, Aunt Elizabeth. I didn't think about that."

"Looks like you'll have a bump, but there's no blood," Elizabeth announced.

Scott watched Diane. *Quite a little jumper for an heiress.*

◆ ◆ ◆

As the days went by, some refugees left the park to rebuild their lives in their old homes. Since the landscape was totally changed, they often had trouble finding the lots where their homes had stood. It presented a problem for decades.

Though millions of dollars had been lost in the disaster, people were willing to start over.

One evening, Elizabeth and Diane headed for the DeVault home very late. She and Diane were both exhausted from long days of work.

Vince saw them start off. "Scott and I can see you home. We're headed that way," he called, running to catch up.

Elizabeth turned. It would be dark before they arrived at the DeVault home. She hated being alone in the devastated city. "Why, thank you, Mr. Morris. How thoughtful of you."

Scott gulped and trailed behind his brother who walked beside Elizabeth. To Scott's surprise, Diane shuffled over to Elizabeth's other side, as if seeking protection. Her action galled him. He hadn't exactly hurt her. Why should she avoid him?

Vince talked about fire insurance as the group strolled down the residential streets, untouched by the fire. The two reporters had been interviewing people about it all day.

"It appears the majority of the insurance will be paid, even from companies that will be put out of business. Some of it will not, of course, and much of the city was uninsured."

"It's surprising that so many are planning to stay here," Elizabeth said, enjoying the night air.

"We met a couple of young fellows who are undecided about whether to stay or to go. They helped dig people out and fight the fire for days. Phil hurt his ankle and it's still not quite well."

Elizabeth stopped and looked up into his face. "Did you say Phil? Who was the other one?"

"Hiram."

Elizabeth beamed. "They're all right? Do you know where they are?"

"Of course," Vince said. "We visit them."

"They're our cousins."

"What a coincidence. They're in the park. They must have been in a different food line. I'll show you where they are tomorrow."

The next day, Elizabeth and Diane found Hiram and Phil at their tent. "We've been worried sick about you. I'm so glad to see that you're all right."

Elizabeth hugged and kissed them both. Diane held back. She had only seen them a few times in Plainville.

"We're fine. Phil got a bruised ankle, but it's almost well now."

Hiram wore a broad smile. "We sure didn't expect to see anyone else from Plainville. We actually buried a lady from there. It's a small world."

Elizabeth turned cold. "You buried someone from Plainville?"

"Yes, we were ordered by the soldiers to bury the bodies. We recognized Mrs. Robinson, the newspaper publisher's wife."

Elizabeth's legs could not hold her. She sank down onto a cot in the tent and covered her face with her hands.

"Oh, we're sorry," Phil said. "We should have realized that you knew her."

Diane kneeled down to be close. She put her arms about Elizabeth.

Then she turned toward the brothers. "Are you sure? How did you know it was Mrs. Robinson? Maybe it was someone who looked like her."

"The soldiers let us take her blue scarf. Maybe you recognize it." Phil rummaged in a bag and pulled out the scarf.

Elizabeth reached for it and touched the soft silk. Her worse fears had come true. "It's hers. Drew gave it to her for Christmas. I'll miss her very much. She was my best friend."

"Take the scarf," Hiram said, "and give it to her husband."

Diane spoke up. "Julia is my sister. She's worried about you two. She asked me to let her know right away if we find out anything about you."

Hiram, blushing slightly, looked sheepishly at Phil. "I'll write to her today. They say the post office is sending all mail out of San Francisco free these days."

Elizabeth dabbed at her eyes with a handkerchief. "What are you going to do now?"

"We've been waiting for Phil's ankle to heal. Our boarding house and our work place were both toppled in the earthquake. We'll have to earn some money soon. I hear construction has started already."

♦ ♦ ♦

After the women left, the young men considered the visit. Finally, Hiram spoke. "Phil, I say, we haven't lost anything much here. What say we catch free Southern Pacific railroad rides as far as possible and make our way back to Nebraska?" He remembered a brown-haired hotel maid with sparkling eyes in Plainville.

Phil laughed. "It wouldn't be because you want to see Julia again, would it?"

Hiram reddened. "Watch your mouth, little brother. Maybe we could board with Elizabeth again. We've seen California. Now let's go back to Nebraska."

"When shall we leave?"

"Very soon. We now have friends in Omaha too. Vince and Scott Morris want us to write to them and keep in touch."

Elizabeth asked Vince to send a telegram from Oakland to Drew Robinson informing him of his wife's death. He was to mention the blue scarf and the fact that she had been recognized by Hiram and Phil Spencer. Drew was also to let Julia Hoffman know that Hiram and Phil were safe.

"Of course. I'm wiring my wife today too," Vince said.

Elizabeth's most difficult task was informing Mrs. DeVault of her niece's death. "She died trying to help out. Try to remember her spirit," Elizabeth said.

The number of medical and Red Cross volunteers in San Francisco soon exceeded the need as Scott had somewhat predicted. Elizabeth and Diane had filled an immediate emergency, but now they were free to go.

The train home cut through fruitful valleys in California, snow covered mountains and plateaus in the Sierra Nevadas and the Rockies, and then the rolling plains of Nebraska. As the train neared Plainville, corn shoots were thrusting up from the earth.

"What a lot of corn," Diane marveled.

"Nebraska grows oodles of corn. Some people say there are thirty-three ways to cook corn," Elizabeth told her.

"Really? Name some."

"Well, corn on the cob and cornbread come to mind. Can't you think of any?"

"Cornmeal muffins and cornmeal mush. Some people would say corny speeches, but you can't cook them."

Elizabeth chuckled. "Keep thinking and you'll come up with more."

Chapter Twenty

In their farm house outside of Plainville, Sonia Kirkendall waited for Cal to come in from the field for his midday meal. When he entered their small frame house, she kissed him on the cheek and gave him a sultry look. She was pleased he seemed to be in a good mood.

She had a serious matter to discuss with him and needed him to agree. Usually, he did as she wished, but this was different. He might let his exaggerated sense of morality get in the way.

She had set the table with particular care: Fork on the left, knife and spoon on the right, cup to the right of the plate, the water glass on the top right, above the knife. She'd baked apple pie for dessert with cinnamon sprinkled on top--his favorite.

While he washed up, she put the fried chicken and potatoes on the table. As she poured the coffee, she said, "I was terribly disappointed when the doctor said I can't conceive any more children." She wiped her eyes with a handkerchief. "You so wanted a child. It's almost too much to bear."

I don't actually believe that old fool. I'm sure I could get pregnant. It must be my two husbands who are the problem. Two of a kind. What rotten luck. I'm tired of waiting. Maybe Cal could get another female pregnant.

Cal took a large bite of a drumstick. "I'm sorry. I know you want another baby. But it's not so important to me."

"It's not fair. Every man should have a son." Sonia sat across from him. Cal was a strong, ruggedly handsome man. She very much wanted his child. She imagined a number of sons who would all look like him, but have her brains. She could sit in church surrounded by her strong boys, the envy of the community.

"We'll just have to make the best of it." Cal calmly ate his dinner.

Sonia took a deep breath. "Vicky is old enough to have a baby."

Cal stopped eating. "So? Is she getting married or something?"

Sonia spoke quickly. "She could have your baby. It wouldn't have to affect her at all. We could raise it as her little brother or sister."

Cal stared at her. After a long time, he said, "impossible." He took up his fork again.

"When she starts to show, I can take her to my friend's home in Omaha. Nobody would know. I'd come back with a baby and she could come back to school."

"That's ridiculous." Cal stared in disbelief.

"She adores you, and she owes you a lot. It would be a way of paying you back. She'd be giving me a gift too--my life's desire."

"She likes me all right, but--"

"I could go downtown to visit some evening for a few hours."

"I don't think--"

"I know you want a child as much as I do. This is a way to have one. I long for a baby of yours."

"Sonia--"

"Imagine us raising a child together, your son, and a part of it would be mine too."

Cal pushed his plate away. He'd lost his appetite. He'd never been able to refuse Sonia anything.

Sonia relaxed, and began to eat. Cal would do it. She'd soon have a baby of theirs, Cal's child, and her grandchild. She might have to push him, tell him how much she wanted a baby of his, make all the arrangements, but in the end, he'd do it.

◆ ◆ ◆

At the Plainville train station, Drew Robinson and Matthew McCall greeted Diane and Elizabeth.

Elizabeth threw her arms around Drew and sobbed. "I'm so sorry, Drew."

"She's at peace, Elizabeth. We have to get used to it. I know she lost her life trying to help." Then he indicated Matthew. "We both came to carry your bags home. Robert and Catherine are not back yet, so Diane will be staying with you."

The two started out, with Elizabeth holding Drew's free arm. Diane followed, with Matthew, carrying her bag, trailing along behind.

"Did you know her well, Diane?" Matthew asked, moving up beside her.

"No, I didn't. But Aunt Elizabeth said Frances Robinson was her best friend."

"I'm sorry. I thought about you. Now that you're back, I wonder if you'd go to the church social with me next month. I'll come by for you. I'd like to hear about your travel."

Surprised, she said, "I don't think Uncle Robert would allow it."

"Your uncle isn't back yet."

She brightened. "Then I'll ask Aunt Elizabeth. She'll probably let me. I'll see you then."

"I'm sure it will be all right," Elizabeth told Diane when she asked. "But you must remember that you're not to date anyone steady until you're eighteen. That's what your mother wanted and that's four years away."

"I don't think this is really a date, Aunt Elizabeth. After all, Matthew is an old friend."

"He's certainly attentive," Elizabeth said. "On another matter, I have a letter from Hiram and Phil. They're coming back, and they want to board with me."

"That's wonderful. I'm going to go tell Julia right away." Diane dashed out and marched to the hotel. Julia was serving coffee in the dining room. When she had a moment she joined Diane near the door.

Diane burst out, "Hiram and Phil are coming back to Plainville."

"Oh, Diane, how sweet of you to come tell me. I got a letter from Hiram. Mr. Baker has offered jobs to him and Phil here at the hotel. He needs help with many of the chores."

"That's good." Diane was somewhat disappointed not to be the bearer of the news first. But Julia looked overjoyed, and Diane was happy for her sister.

◆ ◆ ◆

Vicky Kirkendall pounded on Elizabeth's door.

Elizabeth yanked the door open. "What is it? What's wrong?"

"It's my stepfather." The distraught girl's hair was in disarray. Her eyes were wide with fear.

Diane rushed to her. "What's wrong, Vicky?"

Elizabeth guided her to a chair. "Sit down and tell us."

"He tried to..., he wanted me to.... When I wouldn't, Cal attacked me. I barely managed to get away. I ran most of the way here."

Elizabeth and Diane were speechless.

Finally, between sobs, Vicky said, "I can't go back there. I can't fight him off. I've run away."

Elizabeth spoke up. "Of course you can't go back there. Do you want to talk to the sheriff about this?"

"Oh, no, I'll get my mama in trouble. He said they wanted me to have a baby for them. I don't want a baby. I just want to get away from Cal."

"Dear God." Horrified, Elizabeth nevertheless thought quickly. "You can stay here for the time being. Diane and I have clothes you can wear."

"Oh, could I? They don't want me anyway. They just want a baby." She continued to cry. It was hours before Vicky quieted down enough to sleep.

The next morning, Elizabeth heard at the store that Cal and Sonia were asking people around town about Vicky. Seems she had run away.

Elizabeth knew they would show up at her door sooner or later. She had no legal right to shelter Vicky. But she would not send the girl back into the house where Cal Jones lived. She went to see Drew Robinson.

She explained everything. "What can we do?"

Drew pushed his typewriter away. "The law might not help. The sheriff could decide she'd made up the whole thing, and even if not....Why don't we try the Reverend. Appealing to their morality might be more useful."

Reverend Rice invited them into the parsonage. Somewhat timid, he was a good man, nevertheless.

"We need help." Elizabeth sat down. "A young friend of my niece has been attacked by her stepfather. For her safety, I'd like her to come live with me, but she's only fourteen. We thought, with your support, we could convince her mother and stepfather that she can't go back home."

"You say he attacked her? He has the right to discipline her."

Elizabeth shook her head. "I mean he sexually attacked her. Apparently he and her mother think she should bear a child for them."

"Surely you're mistaken," the minister said, aghast.

"No. If you'd seen how upset she was when she came to my door last night, you'd believe her."

"Bring her over here to my wife and me for the time being. I'll talk to Cal and Sonia if they come by. Go see Mr. McCall about legal issues."

Elizabeth hurried home and told Vicky and Diane to go to Reverend Rice's home. Then she and Drew rushed to Mr. McCall's law office on Main Street.

Mr. McCall was not optimistic about Elizabeth's plan to have Vicky stay with her. He thought Vicky was unlikely to want to cause trouble for her mother. If she was not willing to make an accusation, there was little that could be done. Her mother could insist that she come home.

Discouraged, they headed back to Reverend Rice's house. "What can we do?" Elizabeth said.

"We can threaten to expose them," Drew said. "As a last resort, we can threaten to use the *Gazette.*"

They reached the house just as Sonia and Cal marched up, their faces set.

"Where's Reverend Rice?" Sonia demanded. Her stare was stone cold as the door opened to reveal him. "The neighbors tell us that Vicky and Diane just arrived here. Vicky is to come home with us."

Chapter Twenty-One

Elizabeth stepped forward to confront Sonia. "I can't allow that. She's afraid to return home for fear her stepfather will molest her."

"Ridiculous," Sonia said, as she pushed Elizabeth to get inside. "You're making things up. You think you can do anything you want in this town, you old meddler."

Drew spoke up. "We'll tell the sheriff and everyone in town about your plot to impregnate her with Cal's child."

Sonia stopped. "How dare you? Where did you hear such a fantasy?"

"It's true," Vicky screamed from inside the house. "He told me so."

Reverend Rice stepped forward. "It would be better for all concerned if you would allow her to stay with Miss Spencer."

"Leave Vicky with Elizabeth and get out of town," Drew said. "If you do that, we'll keep this unfortunate incident to ourselves. She'll soon be old enough to leave home anyway."

Pulling Sonia with him, Cal backed up. Sonia hollered, "She's my daughter. She has to come home with me. You witch," she said to Elizabeth. "I'll sue."

Cal hushed her. "Leave it be, Sonia. It's better this way."

"How dare they interfere?" Sonia fought Cal's efforts to subdue her. At last Cal quieted her and the two disappeared down the street.

Diane put her arms around Vicky. "You'll be safe with Aunt Elizabeth."

Elizabeth took the two girls home, and plied them with hot chocolate to help Vicky forget the outrageous attack. She pampered the distraught girl, bringing out clothes for her to try on so she'd be suitably dressed.

The next week, it was all over town that Sonia and Cal had moved away from their rented farm during the night, leaving Vicky behind.

Catherine said to her friends, "It's just like Elizabeth to take in a waif, like she took in those two cousins of hers. Sonia told a friend of mine that she and Cal planned to move further west. Her mother thought Vicky would be better off here."

For a time, Vicky seemed unhappy about losing her mother, but as Sonia had often ignored the girl, the two had never been close. Vicky eventually regained her high spirits. She felt safe and comforted with Miss Spencer.

♦ ♦ ♦

At Drew's insistence, Elizabeth wrote several articles about the San Francisco earthquake and fire for the *Gazette*. She worried that the articles would be constant reminders of the beautiful, loving wife that Drew had lost.

Though his face wore a haunted expression for months, he edited and published all the articles. The whole countryside was interested in the biggest catastrophe of the century so far.

One late afternoon after the paper was put to bed, Elizabeth and Drew walked through town out to the verge and beyond for fresh air. The day was calm and peaceful. Fluffy clouds hung in the vast blue sky. A bird twittered on a roadside ash tree. Insects buzzed around them as the two talked newspaper business and world events.

They wandered onto a small bluff where they could watch the sun sink over the plowed fields, turning green.

"Frances was almost certain she was going to have a baby," he said suddenly. "We'd finally decided to have a child."

"Oh, Drew. I'm so sorry. You lost two of them."

He gave her a pained look. "I'm afraid I think only of Frances."

How wounded he looked. How would he ever find anyone to replace beautiful Frances? They were the perfect intelligent couple: He, sturdy and striking. She, petite and fine-boned.

"I miss her too. I've never met a lovelier person in my life."

"I know you're hurt too, Elizabeth. Your friendship has meant a lot to me."

"And yours to me," Elizabeth said. She and Drew turned back toward town.

"We'll get over our grief in time, but now it hurts."

She took his arm to let him know she felt the same way.

Occasionally, she invited him to dinner, along with Vicky, Diane, Alex, and the Spencer boys. She invited Julia at the same time and watched romance deepen between Hiram and her oldest niece.

Phil and Hiram told them all about a Halloween prank pulled off by town boys the previous year. They had herded a cow to the top floor of the school house. When it was discovered who had done it, the boys were ordered to remove the cow. They tried to lead it down the stairs, but it balked. No amount of persuasion and pushing could get Bessie to go down the steps.

"They finally had to get a farmer to help them," Phil said, laughing.

"How did the farmer manage it?" Julia's eyes were wide.

"By backing the cow down the steps, of course," Hiram said. "Any farm boy could tell you that."

As time went on, Phil took a keen interest in the newspaper business. He asked Drew endless questions and visited the *Gazette* office. Drew considered offering him a job there.

♦ ♦ ♦

Uncle Robert and his family returned from their trip full of stories. Robert seemed less brusque with Diane, perhaps because he had finally noticed that she caused little disruption in the house, and was enormous help to Catherine, who wasn't feeling well since their trip.

Now and then he surprised Diane by asking how school was going. Apparently, she was now worth speaking to.

But when Aunt Catherine told him that Diane was planning to attend the church social with Matthew, he angrily refused permission.

"You and Rachel are much too young to be running around with boys," he announced at the dinner table. "I'll have no one who lives in this house going on dates until they're sixteen."

Diane and Rachel sadly left the room. Two years to wait, and no certainty that they could date even then.

At school, Diane told Matthew that she could not go to the social with him.

"Ah, well," he said, with resignation. "We'll see each other there anyway." He would have liked to walk her to and from the social, but he had to wait for that.

Chapter Twenty-Two

That spring, Rachel, Diane, Vicky, and Eric the Red were ready for graduation from the eighth grade. In preparation for the required test, they and other eighth graders quizzed each other at odd moments.

"Recite the names of the presidents," Diane said.

Vicky gave her a mischievous look. "President number one, president number two, president number three."

"Be serious."

"Okay. Washington, Adams, Jefferson...."

"That's fine." Diane said, when Vicky had named all twenty-six, concluding with Theodore Roosevelt. "How many states are there?"

"Forty-six states."

"Name them."

"All of them?"

"I guess not. They probably won't expect us to know them all."

The examiner, a short, thin man with a thin mustache, came to their school and passed out the tests. He told them not to talk while they worked on the questions. The examination lasted all day.

Rachel and Diane walked home for lunch and found Catherine had made vegetable soup with ham bones. Diane did not care for it, and she ate very little. By the end of the day she felt faint.

But when the results were announced, it developed that all fifteen of the eighth graders in Plainville had passed the test.

Miss Blue, their teacher for the last two years, gave the students a short speech about the opportunities for those who would continue school, and for those who would now begin their working lives. She asked them to conduct themselves well at the diploma ceremony, and said she had enjoyed having all of them in her class.

Diane would miss their excellent teacher, who greeted the students each morning in her white waists and long, dark rustling skirts with a pleasant smile. With her red hair and her immaculate dress, she was a handsome woman.

Some people thought it strange that she had never married. She was surely over twenty-five, they whispered, and she wasn't even walking out with anyone.

For the graduation ceremony at the county seat, Elma Black, a classmate, invited Diane, Vicky, and Rachel to ride with her in her father's automobile. Elma's father insisted on picking up each girl at her home, creating chatter and gasps from all the curious neighbors when he tooted the horn in front of Robert Hoffman's house.

Uncle Robert opened the door and asked about all the commotion. "Oh, sorry, Mr. Hoffman. I didn't want to disturb you by knocking on the door," said Mr. Black.

Robert withdrew, mumbling. "A honking horn is not disturbing?"

Rachel and Elma wore new dresses that reached their ankles, making them feel grown-up. Vicky wore her bridesmaid's dress from her mother's wedding. Drew and Elizabeth found it, along with the rest of her garments, at the house that Cal and Sonia had vacated.

Elizabeth had spruced up one of Blanche's dresses for Diane, a princess gown in green chiffon velvet, and had added a lace collar. The longer skirts made the girls feel grown up. The sashes on the girls' wide-brimmed hats were tied around their necks to keep the hats on and to keep their hair from blowing in the wind. Mr. Black drove slowly to avoid disturbing the girls' outfits.

Graduates from all over the county had come to receive their diplomas. Many of their parents from nearby communities sat in the audience. A county official spoke to the audience and pointed out how favored the participants were to have advanced so far in the educational system.

By contrast, he mentioned, nearly two million children throughout the country between the ages of ten and fifteen who were employed in factories, farms, and cotton mills.

Never had the future of the country seemed so promising for young graduates. The twentieth century offered tremendous opportunities for young people, with new occupations from which to choose. It was a glorious time.

Inventions such as the telephone, telegraph, typewriter, sewing machine, steam engine, self-binding harvester, motorcar, and electric lights would simplify life. Greater advances were undoubtedly ahead. A new age was dawning, and these youth would be a part of it. Progress, prosperity, and peace were their future.

As they left the courthouse, the girls breathed sighs of relief, while the boys threw their caps in the air and caught them again. For some, their school days were now over, and they went whooping from the building.

On the way home, the girls examined their diplomas carefully. "Will our futures be so different?" Elma asked her father.

He became philosophical. "I think so. Life will be better for young people, especially for you girls. You may even get to vote someday."

As the girls thought that over, he said gloomily, "everything's changing."

His melancholy mood was not shared by the young ladies. On the way home they gaily sang "Meet Me in St. Louis," a song made popular at the time of the 1904 St. Louis Exposition and Fair in the Missouri city.

But the economy was due for a fall.

Despite the lavish predictions, the country experienced a panic in 1907. The decline began earlier in the year, but by the autumn there were runs on several banks before J. Pierpont Morgan in New York managed to stem the alarm with large temporary infusions of money that he and other financiers provided.

Near Plainville, Mrs. Schafer finally succumbed to tuberculosis and died at the farm, leaving Amy Hoffman in full charge of the Schafer household and children.

Still, for women there was encouraging news in 1907. Elizabeth and Pamela could barely contain their enthusiasm when they learned that Finland became the third country, after New Zealand and Australia, to give women the vote. In their March election several women even won seats in the Finnish Parliament. Surely women would be granted the vote in the United States soon, and become full citizens. Their votes could change the country for the better.

In Plainville, the best news of 1907 came late. Julia Hoffman and Hiram Spencer were to be married early in 1908.

Chapter Twenty-Three

Hiram met the two Omaha newspapermen, Scott and Vince Morris, along with Vince's wife, Maggie, at the train station. He ushered them into two of the finest rooms in the hotel. Hiram and Phil had seen Scott now and then when he visited Matthew McCall during the summers. Since their meeting at the time of the San Francisco Earthquake and Fire, they had remained friends.

"I'm sorry your sister couldn't come with you. What's her name?"

"Ann," Maggie said. "She's visiting friends. What a pleasant hotel."

"The hotel dining room will be closed tomorrow for the wedding," Hiram said. "We're to be married there."

"I congratulate you," Scott told the older man. "I see your bride is named Hoffman. Is she any relation to the wealthy Omaha Hoffmans?"

"Her father, Thomas Hoffman, lives in Omaha. But he deserted the family. I heard he married again. His five children have all been raised here. Julia is the oldest at twenty-two."

"What about the mother?" Vince said, setting their bags down. "I see by the invitation that the Bakers are hosting the wedding."

"Their mother died a few years back. The Bakers have given Julia a home and work since then. Phil and I work for them too."

Scott frowned in puzzlement. "Who are the other children?"

Hiram counted on his fingers. "Let's see. There's Amy, who keeps house out on the Schafer farm and looks out for two small children for a widower. Tom ran off and joined the navy. Alex lives with the preacher and works with his Uncle John Hoffman in the blacksmith shop. The youngest, Diane, lives with another uncle, Robert Hoffman.

"What? I thought Diane lived in Omaha. I supposed she was a daughter of the wealthy Omaha Hoffmans."

"No, no. She might be Thomas's daughter, but she has a more difficult time than any of the others. Her Uncle Robert is a proud, stern man. He owns the bank."

"Good lord. I completely misunderstood. I thought she was rich."

Hiram laughed. "Robert Hoffman is fairly prosperous. But he's not about to share any of his wealth with a niece. Julia says she and Elizabeth Spencer have to make sure the girl has proper clothes to wear."

"How is Elizabeth?" Vince said.

"She's well. Phil and I boarded with her for a time, but now we have rooms in the back of the hotel."

"Together?"

"Of course not. I'll be with Julia, and Phil has his own small room."

Vince, laughing, slapped him on the back. "I'm glad to hear it. We can hardly wait to see you stand in front of the preacher."

Phil laughed. "Get settled and come down for coffee."

♦ ♦ ♦

Hannah Baker had put a great deal of thought into Julia's wedding, the biggest one that Plainville had ever seen. With no daughter of her own, this was her opportunity to act as mother of the bride. Elizabeth had worked with her on the white satin wedding dress. George Baker gave the bride away.

Hans Schafer brought Amy Hoffman, wearing a fluffy pink dress, to town in the wagon to serve as bridesmaid. Phil Spencer acted as best man for his brother. With extra help from people in the community, a full meal would be served in the dining room.

When Scott saw Diane he noticed she had matured considerably and seemed even prettier than he remembered. Her sturdy young body had grown a little taller, her skin glowed, her dark hair waved into soft curls, and her alert blue eyes danced with excitement.

He had determined to apologize to her for acting so rude in San Francisco. After the ceremony, as the guests milled about, he looked for an opportunity to talk to her alone, but she was always surrounded by people.

At one point, as the guests stood waiting for the meal to be served, he joined her in a small group that included his brother, Vince, and Maggie Morris, Drew Robinson, Elizabeth, and Robert Hoffman. To his disappointment, Diane moved to the opposite side of the circle when he came up beside her. Well, what could he expect? He'd been intolerable. Still, it galled him.

Vince was talking shop. "From what I gather over the wires, a crisis was barely averted this fall. They're calling it a panic. Fear of banks failing. What do you know about that, Mr. Hoffman?"

"There was a money shortage." Robert seemed pleased to explain. "The shortage affected building projects, construction, and financing for bonds most of the year. According to the experts, several large demands on money were responsible: the costly Russian-Japanese War, the job of rebuilding San Francisco, railroad expansion programs, and a late crop season tying up the farmers' cash. Along with other calls for money, these big programs limited the supply of capital."

"For the worker, the result was fewer jobs," Drew said. "Record immigration for the year created even more competition for work, I understand."

"My cousin in Indianapolis writes of much unemployment there," Elizabeth said.

Maggie grinned at the group. "President Roosevelt even had J. P. Morgan for tea at the White House after the panic was resolved, presumably in gratitude."

They all chuckled or smiled. By enforcing anti-trust laws, President Roosevelt had angered big money interests. The antagonism seemed to be mutual. Eventually, Roosevelt understood the danger the economy had faced, and the contribution J.P. Morgan made by resolving the money crises.

Robert frowned. "I gather some financiers are urging Congress to create a Federal Reserve of some kind that could lend emergency money to stop runs on healthy banks. A central bank, more or less. I'm not sure I approve."

"Perhaps the economy will pick up after this debacle," Elizabeth said.

"We're glad to be in a position to make more loans. Like most bankers, I feared a financial collapse."

"Our circulation has picked up some," Vince said. "Everyone wants to learn about it."

Drew looked at Elizabeth." You should be heartened, Elizabeth, to hear that Florence Nightingale, that famous British nurse, was awarded the Order of Merit for her success at saving lives during the Crimean War."

Elizabeth laughed. "And about time too. After fifty years. They're lucky she was alive to receive it. She's eighty-seven years old."

"Better late than never," Maggie said. "She was the first woman to get it. Do you nurse much, Elizabeth?"

"Now and then in a private home or with the Red Cross. Dr. Williams sometimes asks me to assist in difficult cases. But there is a local midwife."

"Elizabeth also writes articles for my paper," Drew said.

Vince turned to Elizabeth. "Drew showed me a couple of your articles. Well-written. Perhaps you'd like to submit some of your work to us if you feel you'd like a larger audience."

"How kind of you." Elizabeth blushed. "I'll do that."

"Are you those muckrakers that President Roosevelt talks about?" Robert said.

Vince laughed. "I suppose we are. We like to expose evils when we find them."

"And sell more papers?" Robert nodded knowingly.

Scott felt he had something to say. "The public needs to learn about the abuses of the railroad, and all the things that Lincoln Steffens, Ida Tarbell and Thomas Lawson wrote about."

"Yes, well, you're young."

"And Frank Norris in his fiction too," Diane said.

Scott felt pleased. At least, Diane didn't mind supporting his position.

At dinner, the guests found platters piled high with roast beef, potatoes, and carrots. The aroma of baking rolls and rich coffee filled the air. Later, the young couple cut the wedding cake, served with vanilla ice cream, a rare treat.

Scott had no chance to talk to Diane alone. He exchanged a few words with his old friend, Matthew McCall, as the diners found their places. Envious, he noted that Matthew was seated by Diane.

It suddenly seemed important that he talk to Diane and let her know how foolish he felt about his comments to her in San Francisco. What a jerk he'd been. Only his resentment at Thomas Hoffman for the way he had treated his own papa had prompted such rude behavior.

But he never got a chance to talk to her. All during the reception he attempted to find her alone, but she was always surrounded by people. Once she sailed past him, giving him a nod and an indifferent gaze from those striking blue eyes. Before he could turn around and approach her, she was talking with Leah Hoffman, a cousin he gathered, from the snatches of conversation that he caught.

Aunt Catherine was absent from the wedding, as she did not feel well. Diane watched Uncle Robert chatting with Mrs. Smith. *What could they find to talk about?*

Diane and Vicky learned from Amy that another marriage would take place soon. Amy planned to marry Mr. Schafer, her employer on the farm.

"He's ten years older than I am, but he's a wonderful man. I love his children and the farm." Amy brimmed with happiness.

"Oh, Amy, I'm so thrilled for you. Will it be a large wedding?" Diane hugged her sister.

"No, no, nothing like this. We may just drive to the county seat, get married, and drive right back. We can't leave the farm chores for long. The children will come with us."

Pleased to find Drew laughing and enjoying the wedding reception, Elizabeth glowed when he led her to the floor for a dance. He commented that the guests seemed to be enjoying themselves.

"Are you enjoying yourself, Drew?"

He studied her. She'd chosen a peach satin gown, setting off her wavy chestnut hair, swept up with combs. "When you're with me, Lizzie, I always enjoy myself."

She swallowed. *Was he teasing her, feeling the effects of the wine they had shared before the ceremony?*

"I never really got a chance to thank you properly for the help you gave us when Vicky ran away. I didn't know who to turn to."

He shrugged slightly. "I was happy to help. I hope you feel you can always call on me. How is she getting along?"

"Vicky is thriving. She's very resilient and grateful for everything. I don't think her mother gave her much attention."

"So you have a young person in your house again after all," he said, watching her with a glint in his eye.

Was he teasing again, because he knew how badly she'd wanted to raise her nieces and nephews?

"You look lovely in that dress," he said. *Well, that was straightforward enough.*

The next morning, Vicky told Elizabeth that after the reception, a group of gleeful young people had gathered at the window of the newly married couple's first floor room. They came to shivaree them. They banged spoons against pans and made a huge noise, the idea being to keep the newly married couple from their business as long as possible.

But Hiram and Julia had exchanged their room for the night with Phil, and none of the guests had discovered it. When Phil stuck his head out of the window to complain about the racket, they sheepishly withdrew.

Chapter Twenty-Four

In the spring, Diane and her classmates finished the tenth grade at the Plainville School, the highest grade offered. Diane, Vicky, Eric the Red, and a few others were excited about attending the local two-year normal school which trained teachers and offered classes in other vocations. Diane knew Uncle Robert expected her to earn her tuition by helping Catherine with the housework in all her free time.

Robert's children left his home as soon as they were able. Rachel, to everyone's surprise, married a local boy right after school let out. She told Diane about their plans to go to Oregon.

"We'll be staying with Conrad and Ann Bauer. They're Germans who lived in Plainville and became friends with Uncle John and Pamela. Aunt Pamela arranged it because she knew we wanted to leave and start our own farm."

"How long will you be staying with them?"

"Only until we can get our own place with a little money that Ralph's parents left him."

Robert Hoffman was furious. He vowed he would disown his daughter, disinherit her, and never see her again. Diane tried to stay out of his way while he vented his anger. He berated John Hoffman and Pamela for giving Rachel information about the Oregon couple.

He had suffered a serious blow when Bob left home for Omaha. Now, both of his children were gone. He began to pay some attention to Diane, especially since his wife was ill.

As Catherine's health got progressively worse, Diane, at sixteen, struggled with the chores in Robert's house.

"Well, it's nothing new," Diane told Vicky on an autumn visit. I've handled much of the housework for a long time."

"Poor Diane." Vicky commiserated with her. "Ironic, isn't it. I get to live with your generous Aunt Elizabeth, and you have to live with that cranky old uncle. Why don't you run away too?"

Diane finished drying dishes and sat down across from Vicky. "Who would I run away with? Uncle Robert barely lets me out of the house."

"If your Uncle Robert comes home unexpectedly, I'm leaving. I'd like to do something nasty to his things while I'm here, but he'd probably blame you if I did."

Diane laughed. "Vicky, you're impossible. He wouldn't say anything impolite to you if he did come home."

"It's his look of distain, as if he's the lord of all he surveys. And he treats you like a slave. He's a heartless dictator. Before long, you'll be old enough to do what you want."

"I don't think I could leave Aunt Catherine while she's sick. She's been good to me. Besides, I feel sorry for her. I think Robert's seeing another woman."

"You don't say?" Vicky leaned close.

"Oh, I shouldn't have said anything. The only proof I have is that he sometimes claims to go to lodge meetings, and then I've learned that none of the lodges meet. And I've seen him go to Mrs. Smith's store when he said he was going to a lodge meeting. One time I heard them in the back of the store when they didn't hear me come in. He called her 'darling.' I left before they saw me. But I certainly never heard him call anyone else 'darling,' not even Catherine."

"Why, that old rascal."

"Promise you'll say nothing to anyone."

"All right, I promise. So he's seeing the widow Smith. That witch. I still don't think it's fair to you."

◆ ◆ ◆

Every evening after classes, Diane hurried home to tend to Catherine. The rest of the family used the outhouse, but Catherine could not walk far, so Diane emptied her chamber pot, saw to Catherine's needs, and prepared the evening meal. After dinner she tidied the kitchen and hauled wood and water into the house.

On weekends she scoured upstairs and down and scrubbed the linen and the clothes. She ironed Robert's numerous starched shirts and vests. Sometimes Vicky came over to help hang clothes on the line or to dust the furniture.

One morning Diane said, "Don't you and Aunt Elizabeth have laundry to do today?"

"We finish before you do, slow poke. We work faster." Vicky said, fishing for clothespins in the bag. "Just kidding. With two of us, it naturally goes faster."

Later, the two strolled to the butcher shop for meat, and to the general store for supplies, where they observed Mrs. Smith. An attractive woman, she seemed to enjoy visiting and laughing with all the patrons. They could not help but admire her.

On the way home, Vicky said, "tell me again the names of your cousins that are in your Uncle John Hoffman's family."

Diane thought. "Jack's the oldest. He's off in the army. Thelma is next. She's married. Then comes Frank. He's called friendly because he gets along with everybody and is always smiling. He works with Uncle John at the blacksmith shop. Leah works at the post office. The others call her prissy, but I think she's just talented and capable. You know Eric the Red, who is our age. And the two youngest are Barbara and Samuel. Samuel is interested in airplanes. Barbara is always interested in the latest fashion. She's the redheaded beauty with the creamy complexion. Everyone makes a fuss over her."

"Are you and the others jealous?"

"A little, I suppose, but she's such a sweet thing. She's also confident and cheeky."

The girls stopped at Uncle John's house, where Aunt Pamela was feeding the chickens in the back yard. Diane always bought fresh eggs and fresh fruit in season. John's family tended a small orchard of mulberry, cherry, and pear trees.

Eric the Red and Frank were off working, but Leah had slipped home for the midday meal. Aunt Pamela and the girls stopped their work for a few minutes to visit over coffee and fresh cinnamon rolls, shelling peas as they talked.

"Give us some to shell," Vicky insisted. "We don't dare sit here and do nothing."

Aunt Pamela handed them each a bowl of pea pods fresh from the garden. "Did you hear about the automobile that Hans Schafer bought?"

Vicky's eyes widened with excitement. "An automobile?"

"Yes. They must be doing well."

"Phil has read a lot about automobiles," Leah said.

"I've heard Drew Robinson claim that we'll all be riding in automobiles before long," Diane said. "Henry Ford has lowered the price."

Vicky clapped her hands. "I can hardly wait."

"Phil is writing about automobiles in his newspaper articles," Leah said. "He's a great writer."

Thelma, a married woman at twenty-two, was visiting her family. "Did you girls hear that in London a huge crowd of people demonstrated in Hyde Park for votes for women? Mrs. Pankhurst was one of the speakers. She was in jail, you know, for asking for the vote.

"In jail?" Diane became indignant, echoing her Aunt Elizabeth. Surely jailing women for seeking the vote was not right.

"Yes, she's been involved in the movement for some time. Even after being jailed, she still demonstrates."

"Phil has written articles about the suffrage movement," Leah said.

"I hope they get the vote," Vicky said. "Then maybe we'll get to vote in Nebraska."

"Phil is building his own house, you know. It's out on Pioneer Road." Leah stood to go, picking up her wide-brimmed straw hat.

The others saw Leah to the door as she headed for the post office. Leah said, "Oh, look, the sun's out."

"Did Phil do that?" Vicky said with a bland look.

Leah gave her a sour glance and stomped off, as the others, grinning, stared at Vicky.

"How long has Phil been working on that house?" Vicky said.

"Forever, it seems," Thelma said. "Hiram claims he's never been in a hurry about anything."

"How about proposing to Leah?"

"I haven't heard that he's done that either. Did you hear what happened the other night when Phil brought her home in the horse and buggy? He lingered so long talking to Papa and Leah in the house that the horse got impatient and went back to the livery stable without him."

Diane bent over with laughter. "Smart horse."

"There are other men in town who dawdle at courting," Thelma said. "Drew Robinson for instance."

"Oh?" Diane raised her eyebrows. "Is he courting someone?"

"It's been two years since his wife died in the San Francisco earthquake. Surely he'll marry again. I know a couple of women who wouldn't mind being pursued by him." Thelma had a knowing look.

Diane missed the point, if there was one. "Aunt Pamela, may I borrow last month's *Good Housekeeping* magazine?"

"Of course, Diane. Take the latest one too. We've all read it by now."

◆ ◆ ◆

One late afternoon, Drew drove up to Elizabeth's house in a Haynes Touring Car, a convertible. At the toot of his horn, she opened the door. "We've put the *Gazette* to bed, Lizzy," he hollered. "How about coming for a spin?" Nobody else was allowed to call her anything but her full name. Drew was special. She took the nickname as an affectionate gesture.

"Drew, come on in," she said from the doorway. "I'd love to. I didn't know you'd bought an automobile. I'll just be a minute."

Before she settled herself in the car seat, Elizabeth tied a veil over her hat. They both had to wear goggles and dusters. Then Drew cranked the car, jumped in, and they were off in billows of dust across the prairie. At twenty-five miles an hour, they bounced along on the dirt road for some time before Drew stopped the car in front of the Schafer farm.

The frame house stood back from the road. Behind the house a crumbling soddy provided a playhouse for the children.

Amy Schafer and the children ran out to greet them. "Where did you get it?" Amy said, admiring the vehicle.

"In North Platte. Thought we'd visit some."

"Do come in. Hans is still working, and Hansy is with him. I'll put the coffee pot on. Can you stay for dinner?"

"Oh...I don't know--" Elizabeth said.

"If it's no trouble," Drew said, smiling. "The car needs to cool off, and I'd like to talk to Hans. I must get the farmer's view now and then." Elizabeth suspected he wanted to show off his automobile and compare notes with Hans about their vehicles.

Amy added kindling to the kitchen stove and filled the coffee pot with water from the hand water pump over the sink. "No trouble at all," she said, as she got out her good coffee cups. "I've just killed a chicken for dinner."

Her stepdaughter churned butter in a jar by shaking it back and forth. "Yes, and it flopped all over the yard," she said, her eyes shining with excitement.

Before they sat down, Amy got out her Brownie Kodak Camera and took a picture of Elizabeth and Drew standing in front of the convertible, with the children standing beside them. "I'll give you a copy when I get them developed," she said.

Elizabeth studied her niece. "How are you feeling? Is Hans happy to become a father again?"

"I'm fine, and he's elated." She laughed. "You know how farmers welcome children, especially boys, to help with their work. Can you come when it's my time?"

"You're not having a midwife?"

"I'd rather have you and the doctor if you can get here."

"It would be my pleasure." Perhaps it would be best for Amy to have a doctor. Of her three nieces, Amy was the smallest and most delicate.

♦ ♦ ♦

That autumn, Elizabeth attended at the birth of Amy's baby boy. It was a difficult birth. Dr. Williams told Elizabeth that it would be dangerous for Amy to have more children.

Elizabeth was saddened to hear the news because she suspected that Amy wanted more. "Have you told her?"

"I was hoping that you would tell her," Dr. Williams said. "You being her aunt and all."

When Elizabeth talked to Amy, the girl said, "Hans has a boy and girl already, so he shouldn't be too disappointed. But how can we prevent it?"

Pleased that Amy had accepted the news so easily, Elizabeth said, "There are ways."

"How do we find out about them?"

"I happen to have some information. I'll bring you some papers I've received from midwives. Then you and Hans can decide what you want to use."

"Oh, thank goodness. I'd hate to have to tell him that we'd need separate beds."

"I'm happy to say that won't be necessary." Elizabeth already had the information that Amy needed to preserve her health. She had gathered all of it for Mrs. Muller. At the time she'd had no idea that it might save her niece's life.

♦ ♦ ♦

At the Robert Hoffman house, Aunt Catherine sometimes tried to get up and help Diane with the work, but she soon sought her bed again. Dr. Williams could do little for her.

"I'm such a burden, Diane. How I wish I could help you."

"Shush. You've got to rest and get well. I really don't mind."

"If only Rachel were here to help. But I hope she's happy off there in Oregon. Why did she have to go so far away? I do miss her. What would I do without you and Elizabeth? You're like a daughter to me. Elizabeth is so attractive. Her shorter hair is very flattering. How is Drew Robinson getting on since his wife died? I know Elizabeth is his friend."

Diane listened to her chatter. Sometimes, Catherine dozed off in the middle of a sentence.

Elizabeth stopped in now and then at Robert's house to check on Catherine and to see Diane.

Robert hired Eric to plow up the spring garden plot and left Diane to plant and care for it. He hired Alex to chop wood. Since Catherine had become ill, Diane usually missed the Independence Day celebration. When she did go, she left early.

"I'll miss you at the park. You'll not be able to hear your Uncle Robert's talk," Vicky said with a touch of sarcasm.

"Oh, wouldn't that be a shame," Diane said, rolling her eyes. "As if I don't hear him talk all the time."

"You won't get to see Matthew."

"True. I miss seeing him now that he's off studying law."

On autumn days, Vicky helped Diane can tomatoes and green beans, and put up jams and jellies.

"What do you hear from Bad Bob?" Vicky said, as the two picked wild plums for jam out in the country.

"He seldom writes. Uncle Robert wrote to him about Aunt Catherine being sick. You'd think he would write to his mother. It would please her."

"He's a queer one. Look, I've got a full bucket of plums. Let's see if we can find some wild chokeberry and buffalo berry for jelly."

One day the two ambled to the limestone post office, the only such building in the town. They needed to purchase stamps and wanted to see Leah at work.

Vicky said, "Diane, now that you're sixteen, is your Uncle Robert going to let you go out with boys?"

Diane gave her a grim look. "And when would I have the time to go out anywhere? It's work, work, work with Uncle Robert."

"You're far too meek, Diane. Everyone needs some social life."

"Tell that to Uncle Robert."

"Oh, fiddle, faddle. Your uncle should move with the times. Matthew will be home over Christmas. I suspect he'll invite you out. I'm going to the church social next week with Eric the Red."

"Is that so? I had no idea. When did this interest start?"

"I was surprised myself when he asked me, but I've always liked him. I thought he'd want to be a blacksmith like his papa, but he's so much fun in our education classes."

"Well, my brother Alex is prepared to teach too, even though he's learned a lot of horseshoeing. But with everybody buying cars and trucks, Aunt Elizabeth wonders if we're going to need horses in the future. Blacksmiths will have no customers."

That very evening, Amy called Diane on the telephone. She and Hans Schafer would be coming to town on Saturday, and they'd be riding in their new automobile. They invited Diane for a ride. Excited, Diane discussed it with Uncle Robert in the kitchen.

"Who will look after Catherine?" Robert said, removing his vest.

"Well, who looks after her all week? She'll be fine for a little while."

"You really shouldn't be gadding about when she needs your care. Besides, I'm buying an automobile myself. When I get it, you can take a ride with me."

Diane's voice was cold. "So generous of you. If you think Catherine needs someone here on Saturday, you can close the bank early and stay with her yourself. I'm going for a ride." She stalked off.

Robert's surprised voice followed her. "Well, if it's that important to you...."

Diane felt a small sense of power. She had, for the first time, defied her overbearing uncle.

Chapter Twenty-Five

In the spring, Elizabeth, dressed in a blue broadcloth suit trimmed with white lace, prepared to leave Diane and Catherine after only a short visit.

"You look very smart today," Diane said. "That suit gives you a stately look. Doing something special?"

"Yes. Drew is taking me for a drive. Then we're having supper in the hotel. Drew says he wants to repay me for all those home cooked meals and for my help editing copy while Phil's been sick these last few days."

"Does Phil have anything serious?"

"No, no. Just a touch of something. He'll be back, thank goodness. He's a wonderful assistant for Drew, though it took him long enough to ask for the job." Elizabeth hurried off.

That evening, Drew sat across from Elizabeth at a table in the quiet hotel dining room.

"Now that Diane and Vicky are enrolled in the new normal school, will they teach?"

"That's what they're training for."

"So your days as substitute mother are nearly over. What will you do now?"

"Well, I...." She noticed his amused expression. "You're making fun of me. Truth is, I usually manage to keep busy. Somebody always seems to need a nurse."

"And you must be a good one. Elizabeth, have you ever thought of marrying?"

Surprised to hear the question from him, she hesitated before answering. She hadn't thought of Warren in a long time. She had mentioned him to no one except Blanche. Even Frances knew nothing about him. But time had passed and her heart had healed. "In nursing school, I loved a doctor. We were to be married, but he died in a terrible carriage accident. Afterward, I decided to come back to Plainville."

Drew took her hand. "That explains a lot."

"I was very depressed, unable to do much for days. My sister and my nieces and nephews brought me through that time, though the children didn't know about it, of course." She looked up. "So I have some idea how you felt about losing Frances."

His eyes were filled with compassion. "There comes a time when we have to put it all behind us and get on with life."

"Of course, and I admire how you've been able to do that, even though Frances must have been the most perfect wife in the world. She was so beautiful."

"Yes, she was, but so are you."

She gave him a doubtful look.

"It's true. You move like a ballerina. Your hair is a glossy, rich brown, your complexion is unblemished, your eyes are friendly and intelligent, and your lips...."

He stared at her lips, while Elizabeth felt her face turning red.

Finally he said, "Elizabeth, several men in town show by the way they look at you that they would be interested if you gave them any encouragement."

She laughed. "I'm sure you're mistaken."

"Take the butcher, for one."

She looked up, startled. "What? Why, we have nothing in common."

"Sometimes that doesn't matter. Marriage is an economic arrangement."

"It matters to me." She looked at him closely. "Are you trying to marry me off or something?"

"I'm just sounding you out. Do you and I have things in common?"

She was speechless for a moment. She had admired him for years. Finally, she said, "yes, we do. We're both readers, writers, Progressives.

We're interested in events beyond Plainville, but still enjoy living here." She glanced at their empty plates. "And we both love fish."

He burst out laughing. "Come on. Let's walk down by the river. It's a lovely evening."

They strolled beside the water, silver in the soft moonlight. Frogs croaked in the spring evening. The warm silken air caressed Elizabeth's skin.

He stopped and put his arms about her waist. "Could you love me, Elizabeth?"

"Oh, Drew, of course I could. I do." He'd never touched her in that way before. She held her breath.

"You must know I love you. Would you marry me?"

She smiled with radiant pleasure. But still she hesitated. "You've paid me a great honor, Drew. But I must tell you I have responsibilities. I own a house that must remain in my name so the children inherit it."

"You don't give up everything when you marry."

"Married women often do. Their husbands own their paychecks, their property, their children, in fact, their bodies."

"Where did you get this idea?"

"It's in the suffrage literature. It's true in many states. I'm not sure about Nebraska."

"Then we'll talk to McCall and make sure the house remains in your name, and that the rights of the children are secured. Is that your only concern?"

"Will you resent my being involved with Blanche's children? Or my rushing off to help the Red Cross?"

"I'm not asking you to be my slave. I want a woman with a life of her own, interests of her own. If you weren't happy, I wouldn't be happy."

She gave him a bright smile. "I believe you mean it. One more thing, I don't want a dozen children."

"Of course not. Nine should be plenty."

She looked at him with horror, until he said, "I'm teasing, Elizabeth. Since you'd be the one to have them, it should be your decision."

She breathed a sigh of relief. "All right, then. I'd be proud to marry you."

Beaming, he kissed her for the first time, a long sensuous kiss that left her breathless. Kissing her nape, he stroked her back and her shoulders, and caressed her full breasts.

Finally, he stood back. "How soon?"

Overwhelmed, she said, "as soon as you like." Her body responded to his urgency, even as her mind was having trouble keeping up.

"Tomorrow? We'll talk to McCall in the morning."

"It might take longer than that for the license and all."

"So we'll start tomorrow. Thank God Phil will be back to work. I'll think of you all evening, my dear."

♦ ♦ ♦

Early the next afternoon, Elizabeth dropped in to see Catherine. She had exciting news for Diane.

"I can only stay a minute. Drew and I are getting married."

Startled by the news, Diane recovered quickly. "But that's wonderful. The whole town's been wondering about you two."

"I phoned Julia to ask her and Hiram to drive to the county seat with us and serve as witnesses. You know how everyone listens in. And those that don't hear it on the party line quickly hear it from those who do. It was an easy way to get the word out." Elizabeth chuckled.

Then she reflected. "I never expected to marry. I thought I'd spend my life looking forward to visits from my nieces and nephews. But you're all grown now. And Drew and I have much in common."

Diane said, "You don't have to apologize for getting married."

"Frances was so beautiful. I didn't dream Drew would ever want me."

"Why, Aunt Elizabeth, you're beautiful too."

Elizabeth smiled and blushed. "How sweet of you. But no one will ever be as beautiful as Frances was."

Diane shook her head. A woman didn't have to be petite with long, black hair to be beautiful.

♦ ♦ ♦

When he visited Plainville, Bob was allowed to drive Uncle Robert's new motorcar. He dashed about the streets, frightening horses and pedestrians alike.

There was talk of regulating the new vehicles, but nothing had been done so far.

Soon after they were married, Drew and Elizabeth invited Diane to drive out to see Amy in their automobile. Aunt Pamela offered to sit with Catherine for a few hours.

The three barreled along the road, stirring up dust. On the road in front of them, the dust stirred up by another automobile obscured their vision.

As they drew near the Schafer house, Drew stopped the car. "I can't see a thing. We'd better wait until the dust has settled."

Diane could barely see the car ahead of them. But as the dust settled down, she peered into the distance. "That looks like Uncle Robert's car," she said.

"What would he be doing out here? Doesn't he stay close to the bank?"

"Maybe it's Bob." Diane said. "Leah told me he's taken a fancy to one of the Muller girls." Diane hadn't welcomed his visit home. He still managed to insult her every time he saw her.

Drew cranked the automobile again, jumped in, and took off. Suddenly, he slammed on the brakes, bringing the vehicle to an abrupt halt. Ten-year-old Hansy Schafer lay stretched out on the side of the road, bleeding profusely. All three of them raced to the boy, Elizabeth removing her duster to put over him in case of shock.

"Are you all right?" Elizabeth said, feeling for his pulse.

"I don't know. I hurt all over." Blood poured from his torn shirt.

"What happened?" Elizabeth ripped off the lower part of her underskirt and handed it to Drew to apply to the wound at Hansy's side.

"A car hit me. I came over to wave to them."

"Who was it?" Elizabeth said, checking the boy's legs for further injuries.

"I don't know."

"What kind of car was it?" Drew said.

"I don't know."

"He might have a broken leg," Elizabeth told Drew. "I think you should go phone Dr. Williams from the Schafer farm. Tell him to bring splints so we can move him. Diane, go along. Get cloths and water to wash his face and to drink. It's hot. He's probably thirsty. I'll stay with Hansy."

Drew and Diane rushed off to do as Elizabeth said. At the Schafer farm, they found Hans at home for the midday meal. While Drew phoned Dr. Williams, Amy and Polly gathered jars of water and cloths to clean Hansy.

"Aunt Elizabeth thinks he has a broken leg. Dr. Williams will bring splints, but we need a large board to move him here," Diane told Hans. "His leg should be kept straight, and he might get sunstroke if he stays out in the sun."

"I'll bring a board in the wagon." Hans raced for the barn.

Diane did not wait for Drew to finish on the telephone or for Hans to hitch up the horse. She hurried down the road where Elizabeth watched Hansy. With the water, Elizabeth washed his wounds and his face and got him to drink.

Drew charged up with a sawhorse and set it on the road to stop any automobiles as they tended to the boy.

"We'll soon have you home, Hansy," Diane said. "Your papa is bringing the wagon to take you there as soon as Dr. Williams says so."

Elizabeth and Diane spoke with Hansy, to keep him company and to gauge his condition by his remarks.

When Dr. Williams drove up, he put Hansy's leg in a splint with Elizabeth's assistance. Finally, they gently lifted him onto the large board and hauled him off in the wagon to the farm house.

Amy settled her stepson in bed. Dr. Williams set the boy's broken leg and stitched up his side. Hansy whimpered in pain, but did not cry out.

"How did you know to move him on a board?" Dr. Williams asked Diane.

"I heard Aunt Elizabeth talking about it once."

"It's good you listened," he said as he finished with the boy. "It saved some time and protected the leg from further damage."

On the way home Drew said to Diane, "are you sure it was Robert Hoffman's car ahead of us? If it was the car that hit Hansy, we should report it to the sheriff. The driver should have stopped and offered aid."

"I'm sorry. I only got a glimpse of it. It wouldn't be fair for me to say so if I'm not sure."

"Of course not," Elizabeth said, "but it would be just like Bob to drive off without stopping."

"We need some rules of the road for automobiles," Drew said. "I'll write an editorial about it this week."

At the Robert Hoffman house, Catherine told Diane that Bob had rushed around the house and then left early to catch a train to Omaha. At dinner, Uncle Robert said nothing about driving out in the country during the day.

Later, Diane slipped out to look at the motorcar. It had been cleaned all over. She found a small wave on the right front fender (not an actual dent), a slight scratch in the paint, but nothing else. It seemed suspicious, but not suspicious enough to make an accusation.

◆ ◆ ◆

During the Christmas holidays, Diane talked to Matthew after church. He asked her to attend the church social with him that evening. She decided that she was now old enough to do as she pleased. So she agreed.

Vicky, Eric the Red, and the other young people sang songs, and nibbled on sandwiches and cookies at the church. As they balanced their coffee cups on their knees, Matthew told Diane about his law studies. Diane listened, pleased to have her old friend home again. The four left together and tramped through the hard snow to their homes.

Uncle Robert had said nothing when Matthew stopped by for her. But when she entered the house after the social, he exploded. "Why do you want to spend time with that boy? He's poor as a church mouse. Catherine was asking for you. You should have been here."

Diane knew Uncle Robert had never liked Matthew after he had shown up his son by rescuing her in the blizzard. It was probably embarrassing for Robert that Bob had left her stranded.

"You're her husband. You should be able to care for her. What's the matter? Did you have a lodge meeting tonight?" She meant to sound sarcastic.

His brows lifted. "I--"

"You've had so many lodge meetings lately that I'm surprised to hear there are that many lodges in Plainville."

"How dare you." His face turned red.

"Some of them must be hidden in the country *or in stores*."

She gave him no chance to respond, or to determine her meaning. If he gave it some thought, he would realize she knew about his visits with Mrs. Smith. She checked on Catherine in her bedroom, and then clambered up the stairs to her attic room.

When Robert brought his horse to his brother's blacksmith shop to be reshod, John Hoffman said in a friendly way. "I hear that Diane is spending time with Matthew McCall."

Robert frowned. "Young vagabond."

"Oh, I wouldn't call him that by any means." John patted the horse on the flank and began to heat his anvil and shoe. "He's studying to be an attorney, like his father. People say he's bound to make a name for himself, being so clever and popular with everybody. He'll make a good living too."

"Oh?" Robert stroked his chin. "I hadn't heard."

"Couldn't hurt to have a lawyer in the family, you being almost a father to Diane. Never know when you might need legal advice."

"Well--"

"You can thank your lucky stars that Diane came to you. I imagine she's been a great help with Catherine."

"Well, yes--"

"Your generosity is being returned many times over," John said, with the straightest face he could manage.

"Well, I guess you're right."

From then on, Uncle Robert said not a word about Diane's meetings with Matthew on the holidays.

The next time someone mentioned Matthew's name during Sunday dinner at the John Hoffman house, Robert said, "It's good to have a lawyer for a friend. Never know when you might need legal advice."

Diane's jaw dropped. *What had happened to Uncle Robert?*

Chapter Twenty-Six

After two years Diane, Eric the Red, and Vicky were ready to graduate from normal school with twelve years of education. Diane was now prepared to make a living for herself, something she had wanted forever it seemed. She was free of Uncle Robert. Catherine's health was no better, but Robert could hire someone to care for her.

Aunt Elizabeth and Drew proudly watched the graduation ceremony, but Uncle Robert did not bother to attend Diane's graduation. In view of Uncle Robert's absence, Matthew's presence, away from his law training, pleased her. He gave Diane a book of poems for a graduation present.

The juniors treated the graduates and their friends to a sunrise breakfast. Rising before dawn, the young people gathered in a grove near the river. As they fried bacon and eggs over a makeshift fire, they chattered about everything, from their recent sighting of Halley's Comet and the death of Mark Twain, to their plans and dreams for the future.

A few would go on to higher education. Eric the Red was headed to college with the help of money sent from Jack, his older brother. Vicky landed a teaching position in a country school and arranged to board with Hans and Amy Schafer, who lived in the area. Elma Black got work with the telephone company.

One classmate, Lila, would marry one of Diane's cousins, Friendly Frank Hoffman, now twenty-three. A large gregarious man, he worked with his father in the blacksmith shop and tinkered with engines whenever he had time.

The young graduates were entering adulthood at a grand and glorious time for the nation. Everyone knew the twentieth century would exceed in grandeur all previous centuries in history with peace and prosperity for humankind.

The future beckoned with exciting innovations. Airplanes flew, automobiles raced about the country.

They were part of tremendous changes sweeping over the nation. They could help correct the ills of society by voting and becoming involved in movements to abolish child labor, gain votes for women, and protections for workers. Their dreams were filled with optimism.

One evening after graduation, Uncle Robert came to talk to Diane in the kitchen just as she entered the back door with an armful of wood for the next day.

"I hope you won't go away to teach, Diane. Catherine's getting worse and she needs you here."

Diane dumped the load into the wood box. "Why, Uncle Robert, I have to teach. What's the sense of training if you can't make use of the knowledge? You can hire a housekeeper and a nurse."

"It wouldn't work. Catherine depends on you. She wouldn't want anybody else. I've heard that Miss Blue is finally getting married. I'll talk to the school board members and see that they give you the job."

Diane burned with anger. "How dare you! I don't want any special favors from you, certainly not a job that was given to me through your influence."

"Please, Diane." He began to wring his hands. "How can I look after Catherine in the evenings and on the weekends and keep this house up by myself. I don't know what I'd do if we didn't have you." His proud face pleaded.

Diane glared at him. She felt that she owed him nothing. But Catherine was another matter.

"Oh, all right. I'll try to get a position on my own in town. But you have to stop seeing Mrs. Smith."

Robert gasped. "What? Why--"

"I know you're seeing her. And it's only a matter of time before everyone in town knows it too, if they don't already. It must stop. It's not right, and it's an embarrassment to Aunt Catherine."

"Why, you--"

"You know I'm right. If you want me to stay here and be your housekeeper, you must stop seeing her."

Robert fell silent. After a time, he said, "we can work out a schedule and alternate evenings."

She held her ground. "Perhaps you didn't understand me. You *will* stop seeing Mrs. Smith."

His tone was resigned. "You win. Stay with us and I'll do as you say."

"Now you've got it. Why, you're a mind reader, Uncle Robert. I'll see about teaching in town. Don't talk to anybody about me. I can get a job on my own." When she left him, he was still shaking his head in disbelief over the knowledge of his shy little niece.

Though she'd won his concession, Diane dreaded the thought of staying in Uncle Robert's house.

◆ ◆ ◆

The next morning Diane went to see about the teaching job in Plainville. It was evident to her that the principal had not been influenced by Robert. She mentioned that Diane's papers and references looked exceptional. She had two other applicants, but within a few days, she offered Diane the position.

Diane was conflicted. She wanted the job, but it meant another year of servitude in Robert's house. Elizabeth, on one of her visits, tried to console her.

"At least you'll be getting valuable teaching experience and a salary. This will give you some independence."

Diane now had Miss Blue's teaching position. She hoped she could live up to her high standards. When she had plans in the evening, she expected Uncle Robert to be with his wife. After all, she caught up on nursing tasks after school--fixing a tray for Catherine and seeing to her needs. At least Uncle Robert could keep her company.

One evening, Diane and Vicky joined Matthew in his father's yellow Rambler to see a famous film in McCook, *Birth of a Nation*, reputed to be technologically advanced. It turned out to be about the Klu Klux Klan.

As they exited the theater, Matthew, astonished, said, "It's a racist film and employs stereotypes."

"I read that the film has drawn complaints from colored people in Portland, up in Oregon," Diane said. "They don't want it to be shown there."

"Golly," Vicky said, "haven't the producers read about talented black leaders like Booker T. Washington, and W.E.B. DuBois?"

As they entered a dark street, a young woman ran up behind them. "Matthew, girls, could I get a ride home with you?" She looked frightened.

Through the darkness, Diane saw Lillian Muller. "Why, of course, Lillian," Diane said, "How did you get here?"

"I came with Bob Hoffman. I didn't realize when we started that he'd been drinking. He's driving recklessly and seems belligerent this evening. I'm afraid to go home with him."

"Come with us." Matthew led her toward his car, with Vicky holding an arm around her." They were parked on a side street, some distance from the theater.

Diane followed them. Bob came up behind her and grabbed her arm. "What's going on?"

"Lillian is riding home with us, Bob. You shouldn't be driving while you're drinking. It's not safe."

"Who the hell are you to tell me what to do, you little pauper?

"I bet it was you that hit Hansy Schafer and broke his leg. You shouldn't be allowed on the road."

Bob's fist shot out and caught her on the side of the head so hard that she staggered backward, stumbled on a large rock and crumbled to the ground. Stunned, she saw and heard everything as from a great distance. As she listened, Bob's running footsteps grew faint.

"Diane, come on." It was Matthew and Vicky calling her. She could only moan.

She heard people run up to her. All three of her friends stood over her. "Good God, what happened?" Matthew said, kneeling down.

"Bob hit me."

"Why, that brute. I'll go after him," Matthew said.

"No, no, it's too late," Diane said. "Please, don't. Besides, what can you do?" Vicky and Lillian helped her up. "I'm all right. Just dizzy. He's angry. We had words. I need some meat for my face. It's probably going to swell and bruise.

"You're right. I'll stop at that restaurant on the way out of town and get a steak. We're going to report this to the police tomorrow," Matthew said.

♦ ♦ ♦

Diane heard Bob come home late that night. She was relieved to hear him leave early in the morning.

When she and Matthew talked to Police Chief Collins, he asked about witnesses.

"No, it was dark," Diane said. "We were arguing...."

"Your face doesn't look bad."

"I put a steak on it."

"Aren't you related to Bob Hoffman, Miss Hoffman?"

"Yes--"

"This looks like a domestic dispute to me. I don't get involved in such matters."

As Diane and Matthew walked to Uncle Robert's house, Diane said, "I remember now that Chief Collins has some dealings with Uncle Robert's bank. He probably didn't want to get involved."

Bob stayed away from Plainville after the incident with Lillian and Diane.

♦ ♦ ♦

On one of her visits to the Robert Hoffman house, Vicky said to Diane, "Are you getting serious about Matthew?"

"Not really," Diane said, removing clothes from the washing machine drum to send through the wringer. "He's like a brother to me."

Vicky gave her a doubtful look.

"It's true," Diane said. "We've known each other for years, since we've both lived here all our lives. He's new to you because you moved here later."

"I wonder if he sees it that way. He probably wants a wife. It looks to me as though he's eager to join his father's law practice and become a solid citizen of Plainville. They say he's planning to build a house.

"I suppose so." Diane gathered clothespins. "He has prepared to join his father's practice."

♦ ♦ ♦

Robert kept his promise not to see Mrs. Smith. When Diane had plans after school, Robert stayed with Catherine himself. Over time, he became a more loving husband than he had ever been before.

During Diane's second year of teaching and caring for Catherine, it became evident that the woman needed full-time nursing. Every morning as Diane set off for school, she worried about leaving her aunt alone.

During the summer vacation, Robert coaxed and pleaded with Diane to quit her job, and look after his wife.

"Tell him he has to pay you the wages of a nurse," Elizabeth said, over coffee in the kitchen on one of her frequent visits. "It's only fair. You're certainly doing the work of a nurse and that of a housekeeper too."

"That would be so mercenary," Diane protested.

"Well, look who's the mercenary one? Robert can well afford to pay you. After all, you'll be giving up your teaching salary to look after Catherine."

By the time Diane had decided to give up her job, Elizabeth had convinced Robert that he should pay Diane a nurse's wages.

♦ ♦ ♦

April 15, 1912, the sinking of the magnificent luxury liner, the *Titanic*, shocked the nation. Elizabeth wished she were with the Red Cross workers who aided the distressed survivors, but it was too far away for her to go.

People were outraged to learn that there were not enough lifeboats on board to save all the passengers. Those in first class were loaded into the boats, while most of those in steerage were left to drown.

Drew, in his editorial, wrote that it was a disturbing comment on our society. The tragedy led to calls for legislation that would require more lifeboats on ships.

According to the newspapers, the disaster came at a bad time for feminists. They planned their third spring parade up New York's Fifth Avenue on May 4th. The story of chivalrous men surrendering their seats on the boats to save women (at least first class women), led some feminists to withdraw. Others thought it disrespectful to hold such a militant march so soon after the tragedy.

Nevertheless, Mrs. Blatch, daughter of the famous Elizabeth Cady Stanton, went ahead with preparations. The time turned out to be ripe. Shop girls, factory workers, nurses, typists, teachers, clerks, artists, housewives, society ladies, and celebrities walked in solidarity. It seemed the crowd supported them, a change over the previous two years. In 1911 a mere 3,000 marched; in 1912, over 15,000.

The Men's League for Woman Suffrage, 619 men--artists, poets, editors, philosophers--marched along with the women, heads erect, eyes forward. There were fewer hecklers asking:

"Who does the cooking at your house, mister?"

"When are you washing the dirty dishes?"

Newspapers commented on the size of the crowd, but the *New York Times* editor warned, "The situation is dangerous." And went on to describe the havoc that would result when women got the vote.

Nevertheless, Elizabeth, Diane, and their friends cheered when they heard about the increased numbers in the parade. Public opinion must be leaning toward votes for women.

♦ ♦ ♦

When the women in Plainville got together over Christmas, they talked about their gender gaining the ballot in several states: Washington in 1910, California in 1911, and in 1912, the new state of Arizona, along with Kansas and Oregon.

"Do we need the vote?" Thelma said, her baby boy in her arms as she visited in her mother's kitchen. "What if a husband and wife voted for opposite candidates? They'd just cancel each other out."

"Not all women are married," Leah said. "Anyway, that isn't the point. Everyone should have full rights of citizenship--married or not."

Aunt Pamela removed fresh apple strudel from the oven. "I read about a big parade in New York for women voting."

Leah poured coffee for the women seated around the table. "Phil says the men won't go for votes for women because they believe that the women will vote for prohibition."

"They don't want their fun to end," Aunt Pamela said. "Some of them go to the polls and then go drink at the taverns. Or, in the cities, the candidates buy them drinks and the men go vote for them in return."

"Drew says the brewers oppose women's suffrage for that reason. They've persuaded legislators in many states not to vote for it," Diane said, "but according to Aunt Elizabeth, plenty of women in the suffrage movement would prefer not to be associated with the drys. It dilutes their fight for women's rights. Furthermore, they don't all support prohibition."

"Do you realize there are women who do not even want to vote?" Vicky said in disbelief. "The Omaha papers interviewed one woman about suffrage, and she said she was suffering enough, and was too busy to be bothered with the suffrage movement."

There were smirks from the women.

"I don't think anything will change much if we do get the vote," Thelma said. "Most women will vote with their husbands."

"Oh, for goodness sake, Thelma," Barbara sputtered as she poured more coffee. "That attitude has kept women down for centuries."

Diane, pleased to visit her cousins while Elizabeth stayed with Catherine, said "I would have voted for Theodore Roosevelt and the Progressives if I'd had the vote. I've always admired Roosevelt for defying the trusts and creating national parks."

"Roosevelt was a good president," Aunt Pamela said, "but he had his two terms as president. Eight years is enough. If it was good enough for George Washington, why not Teddy Roosevelt?"

"Roosevelt took votes from President Taft when he broke off from the Republicans," Leah said. "If he hadn't, Woodrow Wilson would not have won. But I'm glad he did. It's time a Democrat became president."

Diane, bouncing Thelma's two-year-old boy on her lap, looked at Leah. "How is everything at the post office?"

Leah, perfectly groomed in a simple lawn shirtwaist and a health skirt, said, "I like my job, Diane. Now I must be getting back. My dinner break is over. Phil and I are getting married, in case you haven't heard"

"Does he know that?" Vicky said, wearing a bland look.

"Ha, ha. You're so funny, Vicky."

After Leah had gone, Vicky said, "How does she stay so fresh? Not a hair out of place. Wouldn't you just love to splash a juicy tomato on her?"

They all laughed at the scandalous remark. "That's an awful thing to say, Vicky," Diane said, still chuckling.

"Aw, I'm just kidding. I love her shorter skirt. I'm going to shorten some of mine."

"Those walking skirts must be healthier since they don't brush the floor and pick up dirt," Aunt Pamela said. "Less cloth to clean too."

"But they expose the ankles," Thelma said.

"If that bothers you, you can always wear short boots," Barbara said, raising her foot to show them her own dainty laced boots. "They're very fashionable. All the pictures in *Vogue Magazine* show them. I find the shorter skirts convenient." She stood up. "I have to get back to work too. I have gobs of typing to do this afternoon at the office. Mr. McCall has been busy."

"Are you still seeing Keith McCall?" Vicky said.

"I am. Like Frank, he's clever with motors. The two of them are always fooling around with some motorcar. Keith wants to get an automobile of his own."

"Doesn't everybody?" Aunt Pamela said as she took her younger grandson in her plump arms.

Chapter Twenty-Seven

Bob Hoffman, still living in Omaha, visited his mother in Plainville when he learned she was failing day by day. Though she did not enjoy his visits, Diane saw how it pleased Aunt Catherine to have him home. She patted his head and told him she was not really very sick.

He smiled and told her he missed her. She would soon be whisking about the house, he said. She gave him a wan look, too tired to argue about it.

"Will she recover?" Bob said to Uncle Robert in the kitchen.

Distressed, Robert said, "the doctor doesn't think so. There's nothing any of us can do. I'm glad she got to see you. You should come home more often."

"Yes, well.... I got a letter from Rachel," Bob said, looking unhappy to be back in Plainville and finding Catherine so ill. Diane knew his mother had always been his particular supporter. "Rachel's saddened, but writes they have no money to come back."

Bad Bob had not given up his hateful ways. When he found Diane in the kitchen alone, he said, "Papa says he's paying you to look after Mama. After all my papa and mama have done for you, I think that is very greedy."

"I'm sorry you feel that way, Bob, but I did have to give up my teaching salary to stay home with her."

"My folks took you in when no one else would. I think you owe them care when they're sick."

"You chose to leave home. It's obvious Aunt Catherine's care is not a big concern of *yours*."

He raised his fist as though to strike her. Just then his mother called from the other room.

Bob lowered his arm and gave Diane a look of distain. "That ugly birthmark on your face is getting bigger. I don't see how anyone can stand to look at you." He left the room.

Diane held back the quick tears that came to her eyes. But as she thought about it, she realized that she could expect little else from Bob. He'd always been ill-mannered and thoughtless. It was foolish to let his cruel remarks hurt her.

She knew she was not pretty like Aunt Elizabeth, or Mrs. Robinson had been, or as Vicky was with her beautiful long blond hair. But, despite the red birthmark on her face, she knew she was not ugly. She'd try to ignore his remarks as she'd done in the past. She hurried to Catherine.

For several months, Catherine fought death. But in April, she died during the night. Despite his often cavalier attitude toward his wife, Uncle Robert seemed stricken. She had always looked up to him. Diane knew he depended upon Aunt Catherine as a source of admiration and love, even during her illness.

♦ ♦ ♦

When Scott Morris entered the Red Cross First Aid Building in Dayton, Ohio, after the flood, he found Elizabeth Spencer working there. He smoothed back his sandy wind-blown hair and sat down beside her as she finished her lunch at a large table. The room was full of chattering people, but she recognized him at once.

"Why, Scott Morris, how nice to see you. Is your brother with you?"

"No, Miss Spencer. Vince had to stay home. Maggie is facing confinement in the next few days. He finally trusts me enough to handle a news story on my own."

Elizabeth laughed. "Please call me Elizabeth. Actually, I'm Mrs. Robinson, although I don't mind my maiden name."

"I heard about your marriage. Drew Robinson is a lucky man."

"How sweet of you. How are Maggie and Vince and your young sister?"

"They're all fine. Maggie did all right during the first birth, so they expect no trouble with this one."

"I'm glad to hear it. Have you seen Molly? She's here taking pictures."

"Still? By golly, she's a trooper, isn't she? I'll look forward to talking to her."

"She may not recognize you. You've changed a lot since the San Francisco earthquake."

Scott grinned. "I suppose I have. Is Diane here?" He had been searching for her face among the Red Cross workers who poured coffee, and handed out scoops of food. All the way to Ohio on the train, he had looked forward to talking to her, apologizing for his words in San Francisco.

"No. Her Aunt Catherine just died. She had to stay for the arrangements and the funeral."

He was quiet for a time. Then he spoke. "Has Diane ever said anything to you about me?"

Elizabeth raised an eyebrow. "No-o-o, I don't believe she has. Should she have?"

"I'm afraid I insulted her badly when I spoke to her in San Francisco. And she was so young; fourteen, I believe."

"Have you talked to her about it?"

"I haven't had an opportunity. You see, her papa cheated my papa out of some land in Omaha, and I blamed her at the time. It was stupid of me."

"Well, I wouldn't worry about it. It hasn't marked her for life or anything like that. Although he lives in Omaha, I haven't heard about Thomas Hoffman for years. He married my sister."

Scott nodded. "I see. He's become very wealthy working for the railroad, doing their dirty work. He's probably responsible for the high freight rates, land swindles and who knows what all."

"I'm not very fond of him myself, to put it mildly," Elizabeth said dryly. "He left my sister Blanche and five children for another woman. How is that marriage working out?"

Scott said, "I couldn't tell you about his marriage. We're not in their social set. But I haven't heard of them having children."

"Well then, I should pity him. Later, when he becomes more interested in his offspring as men do, his five in Plainville might not want anything to do with him."

"Say, there's Molly. I'd recognize those beautiful six feet anywhere. Molly, come on over." He stood up to beckon the photographer over.

"Well, look who's here." She stretched out her arms to embrace each of them. "Good grief. Is this the brash boy who knew all about reporting in San Francisco?"

Scott burst out laughing. "Since then I've learned that I know practically nothing. College taught me that. You look wonderful, Molly."

"Aw, go on." Molly blushed. "Let me take a picture of the two of you together. You've grown and you're very well-proportioned. Someday you might be as tall as I am."

"Ha, ha. I imagine I will, Molly."

They obligingly posed, and she snapped the picture. "I'll send you a print," she said, and began packing her camera, tripod, and supplies. "I've got to get to work."

"I've admired your photographs, Mollie," Elizabeth said. "I'm especially intrigued by those of working people in the mines and textile mills."

"Thank you. Laborers often work under terrible conditions. I hope to call attention to their plight," Molly said.

♦ ♦ ♦

Before she returned to Plainville, Elizabeth visited her first cousin, Lucille Gilbert, in Indianapolis. The Gilberts lived in a large, Tudor brick house in a fashionable neighborhood.

"You must stay over with me. I'll take you to see all your relatives and the sights," the vivacious Mrs. Gilbert said. "I have my own motorcar and we'll be able to get around. You know, my father was a doctor too.

Grandpa Spencer was prosperous enough to send both of his sons to medical school. You must tell me all about your father."

"Of course. And I'd like to hear about Grandpa Spencer and my uncle."

Lucille nodded. "You will. Now, Indianapolis boasts some sights. The poet, James Whitcomb Riley, was an Indiana man. We'll drive by President Benjamin Harrison's house. He's the only ex-president we can claim in Indiana. The house is beautiful."

"Let's see, he was in office before Cleveland, wasn't he?"

"Yes, he was the twenty-third. After him were Cleveland and Mckinley. When McKinley was assassinated, Vice-President Theodore Roosevelt completed his term.

"I wish Mary Beard was in town. She's a friend of mine from this state. You'd be interested in her, I know. She's worked for women's rights and she edited *The Woman Voter* the last two years. It's a publication of New York's Woman Suffrage Party."

Elizabeth removed her hat. "She sounds interesting."

"Oh, she is. She and Charles Beard lived in London when he went to Oxford. She got involved with the suffrage movement and working-class organizations over there."

"Tell me more."

"Well, lately, she's been showing some reluctance to support the Equal Rights Amendment. She believes it would be detrimental to working women."

"Would it? I know Alice Paul, as leader of the Woman's Party, is working to get it accepted," Elizabeth said.

"Mary's interested in protective legislation in the workplace and feels it would be lost if the Equal Rights Amendment passed."

"A difficult question, I can see."

Lucille jumped up. "Get some rest and we'll go for a spin before supper."

True to her word, in the next few days, Lucille led Elizabeth on visits to distant relatives, early Quaker meeting houses, and numerous museums. At last, weary but exhilarated, Elizabeth boarded a train for home.

Carol Albrecht Dare

◆ ◆ ◆

Back in Plainville, Elizabeth sat in a chair as Diane went through Catherine's things. "What will you do now, Diane? Robert can no longer plead Catherine's illness to keep you."

Diane shrugged. "I haven't had time to think about it. Maybe I can fill in for the other teachers when they get sick. Teaching positions won't open until next fall. Meanwhile, I can apply at the telephone company."

"Come stay with Drew and me in your mother's old home."

"Who would iron Robert's many shirts and cook his meals." Diane's voice dripped with sarcasm.

"Those chores are no longer your responsibility."

Diane sighed. "I know, but I'll stay for a time, until he recovers from his grief."

Elizabeth studied her niece. "Sooner or later you're going to want to leave him. Have you thought about becoming a nurse?"

"I've hardly thought about anything beyond Catherine the last few months."

"Well, give it some thought. You'd make a fine nurse. And the settlement money that your father provided for you will help see you through nursing school."

Diane sat down on the bed. "You've told me how difficult nursing school is. I'm tired from the funeral and the years caring for Catherine."

"Of course you are. It is difficult. The days are long, and there's little time off, but things might get better. I've read about legislation in California to extend the Eight-Hour Law for Women to student nurses. Anyway, once you graduate, you'll have independence. Private nursing is satisfying, and you can refuse a job if you wish.

"Most importantly, you'd be serving your fellow humans when they most need care and comfort."

"I've always admired your work as a nurse and as a volunteer with the Red Cross," Diane said, as she folded the last of Catherine's clothes. "I'll certainly think about it."

Elizabeth had barely unpacked when word came about a tornado in Omaha. It had cut a swath through the city a quarter of a mile wide. One hundred forty people were killed and many more injured. Twenty-five hundred were left homeless.

She wondered about her friends there: Scott, Ann, Vince and Maggie Morris. How tragic if something had happened to them.

The Red Cross was feeding and aiding the wounded and desperate. Elizabeth immediately telephoned Diane. "Come with me, Diane. It will get your mind off Catherine's death."

Diane did not hesitate. "Yes, I will. I'll come by for you in the morning. We can walk to the depot and catch the early train."

♦ ♦ ♦

Uncle Robert was none too happy about Diane leaving. "Why do you want to go running off with Elizabeth on her romps? Who knows what trouble you're likely to get into." He paced the long kitchen as Diane finished tidying up after their meal.

She ignored his words. "I've shopped for supplies. You should find enough food to last several days. The laundry and ironing are all caught up. I've brought in wood and water."

She left him in order to pack her small bag. How pleasant it would be to live with Elizabeth. Robert could hire someone to keep house for him. Her savings would have to last until she decided what she wanted to do.

She had often dreamed of becoming a nurse. Now that she had rested after the long vigils with Catherine and the funeral, the work did not seem quite so forbidding.

Chapter Twenty-Eight

Scott Morris parked his bicycle and strode toward the Red Cross Headquarters for Visiting Nurses in Omaha. It served as a relief station for distressed residents who had lost their homes and all their possessions in the tornado. Maggie and Ann Morris had joined other volunteers to serve hungry people who lined up for food and medical attention.

The minute she saw him, Diane turned away. Disturbed, he decided to confront her despite her efforts to avoid him.

"Miss Hoffman," he said loudly on approach, "may I speak to you for a few minutes?"

Trapped, standing a little apart from the others in the large room, she stopped and waited for him to reach her. People were still lined up to get refills of coffee.

"I've been hoping to ask your forgiveness for my unpardonable behavior in San Francisco when you worked for the Red Cross. I've realized how unkind I was to belittle your work, and it has given me much discomfort. I came to realize how hard you worked and what comfort you gave to patients. I admire your Red Cross work. Could we be friends?"

She seemed speechless. "After seven years!" She said at last. "It's caused me some discomfort too. You attacked me for no reason at all."

"Actually, I thought I did have a reason. Let me explain."

"Mr. Morris, you don't need to explain anything. Your thought processes mean nothing to me."

"You're being unreasonable."

Maybe I am. Just as you were in San Francisco."

"Will you at least listen to me?"

"Mr. Morris, I accept your apology. Now please leave me alone." She marched off, leaving him in distress.

Maggie strolled over to her young brother-in-law. "Something wrong, Scott?"

"She hates me because I was unkind to her in San Francisco."

"She'll probably get over it."

"Doesn't sound like it," he said, staring after Diane. "Well, I must get to work. Your husband expects a story this afternoon." Depressed, he pedaled off on his bicycle.

Meanwhile, Elizabeth talked to Diane. "What happened? You practically ran from Scott."

"He's a very rude fellow. He insulted me and the Red Cross when we saw him in San Francisco."

"That was seven years ago!" Elizabeth said.

"Still--"

"I've always found him to be very polite. It sounds as if he'd like to make it up to you."

"I don't care one way or another." Diane gathered up dirty coffee cups and carried them off to the kitchen.

Maggie insisted that Elizabeth and Diane stay overnight with her, Vince, and Ann while they were in Omaha. Since it meant fewer provisions for their needs from the Red Cross supplies, they agreed.

When the Red Cross was ready to leave Omaha, Maggie Morris told them they had to stay over one more day. The wealthy Daytons were hosting a party in their enormous mansion for all the workers and volunteers who helped after the tornado, including the Red Cross workers.

Elizabeth protested. "We have nothing to wear to a party."

"I'll loan you dresses to wear. They might be a little long for Diane, but should otherwise fit. We can baste up the hem temporarily on her dress."

Elizabeth glanced at her niece. She needed the diversion. The poor girl had been almost housebound for years. "That's very kind of you," she said. "It sounds like fun."

They found a low-cut dress of primrose faille, with white satin collar and cuffs, for Diane. "You look like a pretty spring daffodil," Vince said when he saw her."

He settled the four women in his Maxwell, and drove to the Dayton mansion. When they arrived, they found people in the ballroom waltzing about the floor. Maids wearing black uniforms with white aprons served glasses of punch from trays.

Scott greeted them in the ballroom, but, having been rebuffed earlier, made no attempt to talk to Dianne. He noticed that she had fashioned an attractive lock of hair over her right temple to cover the pink birthmark. Although the soft wave lent a dramatic flair to her face, he considered it totally unnecessary as the mark did not detract from her pretty features in the least.

Suddenly, Maggie said, "Look. There's Thomas Hoffman. I wonder why he's here."

"I understand he contributed a large sum of money to the relief effort," Vince said.

Diane stared at her father. His distinguished face sported a handlebar mustache. Several people stood around him. They sought his attention. Scott moved up behind her. "Don't you recognize your papa?"

She seemed too astonished to snub him. "I haven't seen him since I was five years old."

"That's very sad."

At last Thomas looked in their direction and seemed to recognize Elizabeth as well as Diane, who stood breathlessly beside her aunt. After a few moments he headed in their direction.

"Hello, Elizabeth," he said, smiling.

"Hello, Thomas. How are you and your wife?"

He missed the slight sarcasm in her voice. "She's ill this evening with a slight head cold. This lovely young lady must be Diane. I heard that the two of you were here." He took Diane's hand and examined it carefully.

Showing a broad smile on his face, he looked up. "Are you enjoying Omaha?"

She gave a short laugh. "We've been working hard. We haven't had much time for sightseeing."

"I see." He examined her closely. "In that case, would you take a drive with me tomorrow? We'll see the sights of the city."

She started to decline, but Elizabeth interrupted. "That's a wonderful idea. I'm going to need extra rest. We can delay our return by one day. No harm done." She turned to Thomas. "We're staying with Vince and Maggie Morris."

"Till tomorrow then." Thomas gave them a slight bow and left. As he strode off, a group of people immediately surrounded him.

Diane stood in apparent shock, staring after her father.

Behind her, Scott said, "You're attracting attention. You need to do something. Let's dance." He swept her out onto the floor. She seemed too shaken to resist, saying nothing.

By the end of the dance she had recovered her composure. Though Scott badly wanted to resume his case for her friendship, he decided the time was not right. He left her with Elizabeth.

♦ ♦ ♦

The next day, Diane sat beside her father in a closed carriage. It smelled of leather and fine cigars.

Thomas said, "I understand you've been looking after Robert's wife."

"Yes, but she didn't survive my nursing."

Thomas laughed. "I'm sure your nursing had nothing to do with it. I'm sorry Catherine's gone. Were you very fond of her?"

"Yes, she was good to me. She was hurt when Rachel and Bob moved away."

"John wrote to me about that. What are your plans now?"

"I may finally get training as a nurse. Now that I'm twenty-one, I'm old enough for nursing school."

"Let me help you with expenses."

"That's not necessary. It won't cost a lot. I can use some of the settlement you left me."

"You can keep that for later. I want to help."

Diane turned to look at him. Like all his children, he had blue eyes and rich brown hair, graying at the temples. "Of course, if you wish. Why did you never come to see us?"

Thomas turned his face away. "My wife is extremely jealous. She doesn't want me to have anything to do with my family."

"I see." Courtesy required a comment. Is she seriously ill?"

"No, no, nothing serious. Tell me about your brothers and sisters."

Diane smiled. "In case you haven't heard, you're a grandfather now. Amy has a darling little boy."

"I heard," he said in delight. "John wrote to me."

"Julia will be a mother soon too. Tom's in the navy, and sailed around the world in Roosevelt's great fleet."

"What a remarkable experience." His eyes shone with excitement.

"Alex's been going to college. The settlement you left each of us made it easier for him."

"I'm proud of all of you. Do you suppose, if I were able to get away, the others would welcome me?"

"I can't say for sure. I suppose they would welcome you. But once I start nursing school, I won't get back to Plainville for more than one week each for the next three years."

"Then all I can do is hope the three years pass quickly."

As they walked in the park, she told him about his Hoffman nieces and nephews, about all his former neighbors, about his hometown.

He listened raptly, and she thought she saw a longing for home in his expression.

When he deposited her at the Morris house, she had forgotten any bitterness she held against him.

♦ ♦ ♦

Diane soon made up her mind. Back in Plainville, she told Matthew that she was planning to start nursing school in the summer.

"Do you have to? It sounds like a grueling experience."

"Yes, just as your law training was. If I want to be registered as a nurse, I have to get training. I've always admired Aunt Elizabeth, and she's dedicated to her work."

"Three years is a long time. Are you sure you want to be a nurse?"

"For years my greatest pleasure has been making Aunt Catherine comfortable and looking after her," Diane said. "I believe I have a calling to nurse. I also want the independence that Aunt Elizabeth enjoys. God knows I've had none of that in Uncle Robert's house, and neither did his wife."

Matthew studied her eager face. "I...I'll miss you."

"And I'll miss you too. But we're young. The time will go by quickly."

He gave her a chaste kiss and left her at her doorstep, a disappointed suitor.

Chapter Twenty-Nine

A few weeks later, Diane, along with twenty other young women dressed in gray dresses with starched white aprons, sat in the hospital lecture theatre as the superintendent of nursing welcomed the students. She warned them that they must behave honorably at all times. If they did not, they would be expelled.

The new students would serve as probationers for three months. If they were deemed worthy at the end of that time, they would become student nurses.

At first, the probationers would spend only a few hours in the wards each day, arranging flowers, making up empty beds, and caring for bathrooms, the diet kitchen, linen closets, chart rooms and other duties as assigned.

Most of their time would be spent in classes in anatomy, physiology, bacteriology, urinalysis, medical drugs, and hygiene.

Gradually, they would be spending more time on the hospital floor and less time in the lecture hall.

As they finished their first day of lectures and flower arranging on the ward, a student named Becky winked at Diane and said, "I can hardly wait to spend more time nursing and less time listening. Just think, no walking out with a man for three whole years, except on our vacation time at home--if we're lucky."

Diane loved the uniforms and the starched white aprons. The gleaming waxed floors of the hospital and the stimulating lectures invigorated her. The smell of disinfectant did not offend her senses.

The students were housed in a building next door. Several beds stood in each long room. "Apparently, privacy is a thing of the past for us," Becky said.

The next day, they learned more about the running of the hospital. The superintendent and assistant superintendent taught most of the classes, but surgical supervisors taught surgical techniques. An instructor from the Manual Training School taught cookery and dietetics. Physicians lectured in many of the classes, held in a basement room of the nurses' dormitory, or a lecture room in the hospital.

Third year students served as head nurses and assigned duties to senior and junior nurses. They wore a black band encircling their caps, designating them as head nurses.

Three years seemed far away. Diane, Becky, and the other students buckled down for a rigorous round of study and work. Diane wanted to make her papa proud of her and to show Uncle Robert that she could make it. At the end of three months, only one student failed to pass the probationary period.

As their work on the floor increased and the classes decreased, they fought fatigue at the end of the day. Sometimes Diane could barely get her legs to move. The nurses fell into bed late at night and were awakened early in the morning. Their ten-hour days sometimes stretched even longer when they had not finished their cleaning duties.

Though ward maids scrubbed the hallways, the students did their own share of heavy cleaning. Becky said to the others, "I had no idea that practically all the work in hospitals is done by the student nurses."

"It's cheaper that way," Maxine said. "Even when the students are on private nursing assignments, the hospital collects pay for the work they do."

"No wonder the hospitals in California fought so hard against extending the women's eight-hour day to student nurses," Diane said, scrubbing a counter. "They apparently make most of their money through the labor of young women."

"I guess we won't be getting jobs in hospitals when we graduate," Becky said, "since all the drudgery is performed by student nurses. Only a few nursing supervisors are needed. We'll have to go into private nursing on our own, or get jobs in public health."

Despite their rigorous days, the nurses joked among themselves. When Diane left the dinner table one day to check on a patient with a right arm injury, Becky said with a grin, "Remember not to bandage up the left arm." Diane chuckled, along with the other students, at the medical joke.

Some of the cases they observed on the ward tore at Diane's heart. The orderlies brought in young girls and women who were victims of brutal rapes and botched abortions. Victims of industrial accidents and incurable diseases looked to their care. What could be more important than healing their wounds, and giving them comfort?

Still, when she thought about three years of toil, most of it in housekeeping tasks, she wondered if she had made the wrong decision to train as a nurse. Still, she couldn't bear the thought of telling Elizabeth that she couldn't handle the work.

Despite the drudgery, the classes and the hospital interested her. She saw many nursing routines she had not known when she had looked after Catherine.

On the other hand, she wondered why the food trays were carried one by one to the patients, often some distance away. When she asked the assistant superintendent, Miss Cone, why wheeled trucks carrying several trays were not used, the woman said the food would be cold when it arrived at the patient's bed.

Lids over the plates and thermoses would keep the food warm, but apparently no one thought saving nurses' steps was worth the bother of trying those methods.

Soon after her conversation with Miss Cone, a head nurse named Bonnie Grell, confronted her in the hallway.

"Miss Hoffman, if you have any other criticisms to make, please come to me and do not bother Miss Cone about them."

"I don't understand."

"I'm referring to your ridiculous comment about expensive wheeled trucks for carrying food trays."

"It was just a suggestion."

"I don't think Miss Cone, who has years of nursing experience, needs suggestions from a first-year nursing student."

"I didn't mean to question her experience or her authority."

"Nobody cares about your silly ideas here. You'd best keep them to yourself if you wish to become a registered nurse."

"Yes, Miss Grell."

Miss Grell could keep her from succeeding in nursing school. She felt distressed to find herself in an oppressive situation similar to the one she had escaped at Uncle Robert's house. She had to keep her bright ideas to herself, at least until she finished her training.

In late spring, Diane received a letter from Vicky.

> I have lots of news from Plainville. Leah Hoffman, and Phil Spencer are finally getting married in August. Phil is finishing up the house he built for them.
>
> Leah is thrilled. I hope you can arrange to get home for the wedding, for there's to be a reception in the yard of her father's house.
>
> Elizabeth has taken a job as Town and Country Nurse for the Red Cross. She travels in a Model T and visits patients all over the countryside. She seems pleased with the work.
>
> Barbara Hoffman, and Keith McCall are still walking out together. I sometimes go to the movies or a dance with Matthew McCall. We miss you.
>
> Your friend,
> Vicky

On their half day off during the week, the students usually laundered personal items, washed their hair, wrote letters and took care of other chores. One afternoon, when Becky and Diane were both free, Becky suggested they jump on a streetcar and go shopping since they hadn't been to a store in months. Diane needed a new hair brush and white shoe polish.

Becky chatted about her large family as they poured over the store displays. "They've moved into a larger apartment. They need more room because Mama just had her eighth baby. My older sister is getting married. We're so happy that she had not started working at the Triangle Shirtwaist Factory when fire broke out because it killed one hundred forty women who were working there."

Diane shook her head. "I read about the fire. How awful. The doors were locked on three floors, and only a few women escaped. I've wondered why the doors were locked."

"The owners feared theft of materials." Becky fingered dress material on display.

"Because of that, all those women lost their lives? It's so tragic."

"The tragedy did end in some good results. It prompted the needle workers to go on strike afterward, and has led to some safety legislation in the factories."

Diane paid for her purchases. "I read that the Red Cross collected money for the families of the victims."

"That's only fair. Their families depended upon them for their livelihood."

On their excursion, the energetic Becky occasionally skipped a short distance as they went from one store to another. "My older brother joined the army. I suppose it's a good occupation if you want to travel a little and as long as we are not going to have any more wars."

"Yes, the short Spanish-American War at the end of the century was our last war. But our real conflict was the Civil War over fifty years ago. Cousin Jack has been in the army for years. He gets home so seldom that I hardly know him."

"It seems they are often fighting in the Balkans though," Becky said.

"True, but that's far away." Diane gazed in a store window at some of the newer dresses.

"It's far away, but there's a civil war raging in Mexico which is closer."

"I read a book where the author wrote that war was unprofitable for both victors and vanquished."

"It may be, but I guess they haven't heard about it in Haiti. There's trouble there too."

Diane turned toward Becky. "Are you determined to spoil my good mood?"

Becky grinned. "No. I'm just being realistic. I wonder if the world will ever be completely free of war."

"International arbitration is making progress. Some leaders are trying to make war obsolete."

Becky looked doubtful. "Well, I hope they succeed. We should be getting back. I have letters to write. Miss Cone thinks we should spend our half day off on Sundays attending church and reading the Bible. That doesn't leave much time for writing."

"Yes, and I'm sure Bonnie Grell is keeping track of what we do."

♦ ♦ ♦

When the hospital was crowded, patients slept on the floor. Then the nurses were so busy they were unable to do all the regular work assigned to them. Patients called to Diane for this or that as she went through the ward on errands.

At such times, Miss Cone brought the nurses together and lectured them on the necessity of keeping up the work. The students listened and then rushed around all day trying to do as they were told.

Sometimes, after a lecture, the students laughed when they left Miss Cone. They knew they wouldn't be able to finish everything that day, but all the most vital work for the patients would be finished.

One day Diane received a letter from Amy.

> You'll never believe what happened. Our father visited all of his children in Plainville. He even visited Tom when our brother was here on leave. I know you saw Papa at the Omaha party, but I never expected him to actually look us up.
>
> Papa's wife is quite ill, but since her mother is visiting her, he felt free to come see us in his touring car.
>
> He seems contrite that he hasn't seen us over the years. Julia treated him coldly, but I want my son to know his grandfather.
>
> He stayed for dinner with us and played with little Tommy. He was pleased that I gave my son his name. I always liked it, and Hans already had little Hansy named for him. Papa, Tom, and Alex talked for hours and saw a picture show together in town.
>
> We're all looking forward to your holiday in August when we'll go to Leah's and Phil's wedding.
>
> Your loving sister,
> Amy

Chapter Thirty

At the end of the year, Miss Cone called Diane into her office. "Bonnie Grell has given me reports on all the first year nurses," she said.

Diane waited.

Miss Cone went on. "She tells me that you have trouble taking orders."

Diane didn't know how to respond. "I was not aware of that. Did she mention any specific incidents?"

Miss Cone frowned. "No. It is just a general impression she has."

"It's difficult to answer an accusation like that."

"Yes, and I'm willing to let it go, since she didn't give me any specifics."

Diane breathed a sigh of relief.

"But I must warn you that you'll be under extra scrutiny here next year."

Diane gulped. She had tried hard to be a proper nurse. Becky had suggested that Bonnie Grell resented it when Diane went over Bonnie's head to discuss patient trays. Well, Bonnie Grell would leave this year. The lower level students would no longer have to put up with her.

Diane thanked Miss Cone and left, determined to continue working consciously as she always had, despite Bonnie's erroneous remarks.

♦ ♦ ♦

At the Plainville train depot, Elizabeth and Drew welcomed Diane home for her yearly vacation. Elizabeth examined her closely. "You look pale."

Diane embraced her aunt. "I've spent all my time indoors in a hospital. Not much sun in there."

"We'll take some walks and cure that."

"I began to think that Leah and Phil would never get married."

Carol Albrecht Dare

"Hiram says he was never in much of a hurry to do anything. He figures he has forever on this earth. He certainly kept her dangling," Elizabeth said.

Drew picked up Diane's traveling case and led the way around the ditches the city had dug for the new water system. "All your friends and relatives look forward to seeing you tomorrow," he said, as they walked to the large house where Diane had spent the first thirteen years of her life.

After dinner, Elizabeth asked how she liked working in a hospital.

Diane put her coffee cup down. "It's very hard work, and the hours are long."

"Yes, I know." Elizabeth clucked in sympathy. "There's no shame in giving up the training if you think nursing is not your calling."

"I want to nurse. I enjoy the lectures. I just wonder if all the scrubbing and cleaning I'm doing is preparing me."

Elizabeth was quiet as she served apple cobbler. "Perhaps you should train as a doctor, like your grandfather. It's not unheard of. Several women have become doctors in the United States and in Europe."

"No." Diane sighed. "Nursing has been my dream. I'll stick with it. As a registered nurse, I'll be able to provide comfort like body rubs and reading to patients."

♦ ♦ ♦

Vicky, spending the summer with Elizabeth, burst in from an errand with greetings for Diane. "I have to talk to you about Matthew."

"Of course. Come up to my room." Diane sat on the bed and left the chair for Vicky, whose blond hair swirled around her shoulders. "I suppose you've been seeing lots of picture shows now that they're showing them here in Plainville," Diane said.

"We have. Your redheaded Cousin Barbara does fine on the piano. When the action is heavy, she speeds up the music. When the love scenes come on, she plays slow, romantic tunes." Vicky playfully rolled her eyes around.

"She's lucky that Aunt Pamela taught her to play." Diane waited for Vicky to speak about Matthew.

"Do you remember," Vicky said, "that you told me you thought of Matthew as a brother?"

"Yes, I do. A very dear brother." Diane spoke warmly. "I saw as much of him after my mother died as I did my own brothers."

"We've been seeing a lot of each other."

"Yes, you wrote to me."

"I hope you still think of him as a brother," Vicky wrung her hands, "because Matthew and I are getting married."

Caught off guard, Diane managed to recover quickly. "That's wonderful. I...had no idea."

"It doesn't bother you?"

"No, I told you. We're like brother and sister. But I thought you and Eric--"

"Eric the Red is seeing someone else." Vicky sighed in relief. "I'm glad you're not upset. I wouldn't want to do anything to hurt you."

Diane felt a sense of loss. Matthew would be spending his time with Vicky, and not with her. Her former companion had found a closer companion.

Leah, immaculate as always, wore a cream-colored dress that swirled well above her ankles, along with dainty white boots. She and Phil took their marriage vows in the yard at her home. Uncle John happily gave his second daughter away. As bridesmaid, beautiful Barbara nearly stole the show in an aqua gown which complemented her auburn hair.

The guests feasted on succulent baked chicken, raised by Pamela in the back plot, with corn on the cob, fresh cucumbers and juicy tomatoes, all served on long tables adorned with freshly picked gladiolas, raised especially for the wedding.

From Omaha, Vince, Maggie, Ann and Scott Morris joined the group milling about the lawn. By now, they knew several people in Plainville. They had made it a habit to attend the Independence Day Celebration as well as the occasional circus in order to visit friends at the same time.

After the ceremony, the young people danced in the living room and on the long porch to music drifting out of the house from the phonograph. Scott wanted to talk to Diane and make things right between them. When she arrived, he joined her at the first opportunity.

"Hello, Diane." He wore a dark suit, his curly, sandy hair neatly combed back, a smile on his earnest face. "Do you like nursing school?"

She gave him a wry look. She appeared to be more comfortable with him since they had danced together in Omaha. "That isn't exactly the word I would use."

He laughed. "I suppose not. I've heard nursing school is very difficult."

"How about you?" She slowly smoothed the waist sash on her dress. "Still covering the news for your brother?"

"Yes, since graduation. He's nine years older than I am and I can learn a lot from him." He frowned. "The news from Europe is not good. For weeks now, even the stock market has been closed in order to avoid a fatal collapse of all values."

"It's heart-breaking," she said. "Now that the Germans have invaded Belgium and France, will it be an all-out war, do you think?"

"All the large countries of Europe have declared war." He quietly admired her apricot health dress. The shorter length gave her more freedom of movement. Of average height himself, she seemed small and fragile, but he knew she was not. Any girl who could jump into a wagon bed as she did in San Francisco was not frail, but supple as a willow.

"War seems unthinkable in this day and age." She sipped a fruit punch. "Such progress has been made in international cooperation with organizations such as the International Telegraph Union and the International Postal Union and many others. Why, I read about a conference in 1899 in which the powers of Europe consented to a limitation of armaments and arbitration of disputes with an International Court."

"Yes, but arbitration was voluntary and then ignored during the Balkan Wars of 1912 and 1913, when the nations went back to their old habits of settling things among the most powerful heads of state."

"If only that crazy Serb had not shot the Archduke of Austria."

"Yes, the June assassinations." Scott recognized that she had more interest and knowledge of world affairs than most people. "According to Vince and his friends though, the nations of Europe have been competing in an arms race for some time, and it took only a small incident like the shooting to set off a confrontation."

"Thank God President Wilson declared our neutrality so we can stay out of it," she said. "Did you hear Matthew McCall, and my friend, Vicky Kirkendall, are getting married?"

"He told me a short while ago." Scott's heart had jumped at the news that Matthew was no longer courting Diane. "I was surprised. I got the idea that you two--"

"No, no. We're just friends. Here come my cousins, Eric the Red and Frank, with Frank's wife, Lila. Your sister Ann is with them. I'm sure they'd like to visit with you."

The young people soon began to talk about automobiles. Friendly Frank, who had opened an auto livery near the blacksmith shop, told his favorite joke. "When I suggested to one farmer he should buy more fuel, he told me he didn't want to give his car any more gas. He was weaning it."

As they all laughed, Eric the Red said, "I'm glad you're selling gasoline. People tell me it was downright inconvenient to buy it at the drugstore."

To Scott's dismay, Diane wandered off, smiling at acquaintances, exchanging a few words with old friends.

Uncle Robert joined Diane for a few minutes and told her about bank business. She told him about nursing. He seemed genuinely interested.

About her, the conversation revolved around events heating up in Europe, the price of wheat, and the new water system in Plainville. Nursing school seemed far away.

Farmers talked of plowing up additional prairie land. They figured the demand for grain would increase with a war in Europe.

Elizabeth and Drew exuded happiness. Strange they had no children. Of course, they were both nearing forty. Julia and Amy each had a small boy in tow, along with Amy's stepchildren, Hansy, fifteen years old, and Polly, eleven.

Cousin Barbara and Keith McCall were inseparable. Diane expected an announcement of another marriage soon. Brother Alex was seeing one of the Muller girls whenever he got home from college.

If she had not decided on nursing school, would she be planning a wedding? She shrugged the thought away. By the time she finished her training, she'd be twenty-four, almost past the marrying age. Besides, as a child disgraced by the abandonment of her father and marked with a disfiguring birthmark on her temple, who would want her? Perhaps she'd never marry.

Vicky, Matthew and Scott strolled over to her. "Diane, Matthew and I want to be married at the county seat on Tuesday," Vicky said with a huge smile. Her eyes were aglow. She did not hide her infatuation with Matthew. "Keith McCall and Barbara will be standing up for us, but we'd like you and Scott to come too. You're our best friends."

Surprised to hear their marriage would be so soon, Diane stammered. "I...I..."

"We wanted you to be the first to know," Vicky said, still not sure how Diane felt about the situation.

"I'd be honored," Scott said. "I planned to stay over anyway, even though the rest of my family has to get back." He appreciated the offer, and the opportunity for an outing with Diane was irresistible.

"We'll be living with Matthew's folks until we get our own place. I'll be teaching in town next year. Please say you'll come, Diane."

As close as she and Matthew were, Diane had never thought of him as a date or as a husband. Still, as he and Vicky stood together in front of her, their arms almost touching, it hit her like a brick that he would never be her friend in the same way again. Vicky had taken her place.

"Of course I'll come. Do you have a dress? How can I help?" What else could she say?

Diane left the party with Slim Jenkins who walked with her the short distance to Aunt Elizabeth's house. He seemed slightly in awe of her status as a nurse in training.

♦ ♦ ♦

The next day, the six young people rumbled off to the county seat in two cars for the marriage of Matthew and Vicky. Beautiful Barbara rode with Keith McCall in his own Model T. All the girls wore shorter skirts these days, but Barbara's light green was the most daring, reaching just below mid-calf.

For her wedding day, Vicky wore short white boots and a sky-blue gown, accenting her blond tresses. After the brief ceremony in the courthouse, they stopped for an afternoon meal at the side of the road. The newly married couple would enjoy a family dinner with wedding cake in the evening, hosted by the McCall family.

Scott and Diane spread out a blanket. With the blue sky as a cover over the flat landscape, and the lazy heat, it felt like the greatest place on earth to Diane. They feasted on ham sandwiches, potato salad, and lemonade, kept cool with plenty of ice. Sunflowers nodded beside the road. In the hot sun, insects buzzed around them. But the day was too lovely for the young people to be bothered by them.

Matthew talked about the house he was having built.

"We're to have an indoor outhouse," Vicky said with a proud smile. Vicky looked forward to a home of her own. Diane knew that despite Elizabeth Spencer's welcoming care, Vicky had always felt a little like a needy guest.

As for Matthew, Diane realized that becoming a family man and stable citizen had become important to him. The oldest son in his family, he had always taken on special responsibility.

"Are you a lawyer too?" Scott said to Keith, as he bit into a sandwich.

"I am," Keith said. "Two of us are with Papa in the business now. I'm the baby of the group and get the difficult work."

Smiling, Matthew threw a small pebble at his feet. "Always complaining." Matthew seemed truly happy.

After they had eaten, Keith said, "I see cottonwoods at the edge of this meadow. Let's amble over to the water. We can wade in it and cool off."

Everyone got up except Diane. "Sorry. I walk miles every day in the hospital. I think I'll just enjoy the view here."

Scott sat down. "I'll stay with you."

When they were alone, he said, "I'm still surprised that Matthew and Vicky decided to marry."

Diane gave him a small smile. "I always thought of him as a brother or a cousin. He's had plenty of time to fall in love with Vicky. Since I think she's wonderful, I couldn't be happier for her."

"You and I have known each other a long time."

"Yes, we have."

"How was the visit with your papa?"

"Wonderful." Diane's eyes glowed with pleasure. "He's been to see my sisters and brothers too."

"What?" Scott couldn't hide his surprise. *Over ten years gone and Thomas Hoffman finally makes a trip to visit his children?*

"His wife is jealous of his children, but he managed to visit them in Plainville when Tom was home on leave from the navy. Papa is very thoughtful and generous."

Scott could not let the remark go. "Why, no he's not. He's a grasping, lying swindler."

Diane jumped up. "How can you say such a thing?"

Scott rose too. "He cheated my father out of land for the railroad."

Diane stared at him. "Can you prove that?"

"I don't have to. I know it's true. Papa told me about it before he died."

"And your papa couldn't be mistaken." Her sarcastic voice irritated him.

"He wasn't."

"You arrogant turnip. Go to Helena." She glared at him, anger coloring her face.

"How can you keep defending a man who abandoned his family?"

"What do you know about it? Uncle Robert stayed with his family and made them all miserable. He practically made his wife a slave."

Scott felt contrite. He hadn't realized that she lived with such an uncommonly pathetic family. "I'm sorry. I heard he was selfish."

"I'm going wading." She marched off across the meadow to join the others, startling a sage grouse as she passed.

"Your papa is not what you think," he shouted to her back.

He stood in anguish, watching her lithe figure receding. What had happened? He had meant to become better acquainted. Now things were worse.

On the ride home, Diane and Scott spoke very little. The others could not help noticing. "It's a bit icy in here," Vicky said. The remark dropped like a stone in the brittle silence.

As they left Diane at Elizabeth's house, Vicky said, "Diane, I want to see you before you leave. Maybe you'll feel better."

Diane gave her a wistful look, and headed inside.

♦ ♦ ♦

The words with Scott had depressed Diane. Happy for Vicky, she still felt abandoned by Matthew. Her constant companion was gone. In fact, with Vicky getting married, it seemed she'd lost two best friends. She felt shut out.

For years, she had sought love and acceptance from Uncle Robert. She had hoped for it from her father, but she would not be seeing him often. Aunt Elizabeth, her biggest supporter, had married Drew. Now her best friends, Matthew and Vicky, had found each other. There was no one for her.

Diane was not one to worry others with her concerns. She said nothing to Aunt Elizabeth and Drew about the argument with Scott. At supper that evening, Elizabeth asked for an account of the marriage at the court house. Diane told her about her day, omitting the heated discussion with Scott.

Drew told them more about the crashing European war and about the opening of the Panama Canal. "About time," he commented. "They've been ten years working on it, but it's a marvelous achievement."

"Just think how much time that canal will save when ships don't have to sail around the tip of South America," Elizabeth said, as she served plum cake.

"I just wish we could have acquired the rights to build without being so ruthless," Drew said, finishing his coffee. "I've heard some reports of terrible mistreatment of the natives."

"Well, you know how self-confident President Roosevelt was," Diane said. "When he made up his mind about something, there was no stopping him. We should be thankful that most of his actions in this country were beneficial to ordinary people."

"Men lost their lives building that canal." Drew looked concerned. "Most of them were poor natives of the area."

The following day, when Vicky came to the house to talk, Diane told her about arguing with Scott. "He's always been insulting and I want nothing more to do with him."

Puzzled, Vicky said, "I always thought he was pleasant and polite."

Diane rolled her eyes. "Yes, he puts on a good act."

Vicky looked at her for a time. "You're acting foolish," she finally said. "Several girls at the wedding showed great interest in him."

"I could have told them how boorish he is."

"I wish you'd give this more thought, Diane. I can see you're angry with him, but he's finished journalism school and has a good career at his brother's newspaper."

"Vicky, I'm never going to be interested in Scott. Slim Jenkins walked me home from the wedding the other night. Now he's a fine fellow."

"In my opinion, he doesn't begin to compare with Scott."

"That's your opinion," Diane snapped. "Now that you're a married lady, it doesn't concern you."

"Well, that's a catty remark. Maybe we can talk about it another time."

The next day, Diane regretted her snippy attitude with Vicky. Why had she been so abrupt? Was she jealous that Vicky married Matthew? No, she knew she did not feel the way Vicky did about him.

It was the conversation about Scott. Diane wanted to forget she had ever met Scott Morris. Vicky's pleasure in his brash manner galled her, especially when she found him so annoying.

One morning as the two lingered over morning coffee, Elizabeth told Diane she was going to have a baby in the winter.

Diane tried to hide her amazement. "That's wonderful. I thought maybe you'd never have one."

Elizabeth's hand ran over her stomach in a loving, protective stroke. "We weren't ready. But now I have work here, and I won't be traveling around the country for the Red Cross. So we decided to try for a child. We're also a bit surprised, though we're overjoyed."

"You weren't ready?" Diane said, perplexed. "But how--"

"There are ways to prevent pregnancy, Diane. You'll probably be learning more about it in nursing school. Not from the instructors, but from the students. Sheaths and pessaries can work."

"I wasn't aware--"

"Most women aren't, but they should be. Especially those whose lives are endangered by childbirth. For instance, Dr. Williams advised Amy not to have any more children."

"I...I didn't know."

"Childbirth is often difficult. I see no reason why Amy should endanger her life to have more children. Hans already has two."

"Of course not." Diane knew of several large families that struggled because there were so many babies. She had seen women worn out with the care of them, and their bodies aged with the bearing of them. "I want you to know about such things, Diane. Even if you never need the information for yourself, you might be able to help other women and even save lives."

Diane agreed that such knowledge would be invaluable.

Chapter Thirty-One

When Diane returned to nursing school, she was allowed more time with patients. Despite terrible illnesses and accidents, they were generally friendly and grateful.

Diane combed the beautiful golden hair of one young girl who was almost too sick to sit up. Sometimes the pull on her head caused pain, but when Diane showed her how she looked in the mirror, she smiled with pleasure.

That autumn, many typhoids were brought in, and one attempted suicide. Diane took temperatures and bathed five patients every day, sometimes more, and tended to bedsores.

On meal breaks, the nurses put patient care away and exchanged information about their visits to their homes during the summer.

"My sister has gotten involved with the union," Becky said. "The workers feel they have to organize to get better working conditions."

Diane put down her meal tray--a chicken and rice dish with green beans. "I read that new safety regulations were passed by Congress as a result of the Triangle Shirtwaist Factory Fire."

Becky frowned. "Yes, but Congress is slow to act, and there's no knowing what they'll do. They only pass the minimum safety measures. Business lobbyists try to get them not to pass safety legislation.

"Now I'm worried that my brother may have to go to the Mexican border with the army."

Civil war in Mexico spilled over into the United States when American sailors were arrested at Tampico. The sailors were soon released, but the incident put the United States on alert.

Maxine described the incident. "Mexico is not a large country. Only this big on the map." She held her hands about three inches apart, not realizing that this helped her listeners not at all since they had nothing with which to compare it.

The nurses read of another border incident. President Wilson learned that a German ship, loaded with arms for Huerto, was headed for Vera Cruz. As Wilson favored a different contender for head of the country, he sent marines to seize the town. Nineteen Americans and over four hundred Mexicans died.

◆ ◆ ◆

Most countries of Europe joined the war in the fall of 1914. Eventually, the fighting spread to the air and the sea, and to European colonies in Africa, the Middle East, Asia, and even the South Pacific.

On one side of the conflict were the Central Powers: Austria-Hungary, Germany, Bulgaria, and Turkey. On the other, the Allies: France, Britain, Russia, Japan, the United States in 1917, and several smaller countries.

In August, Kaiser Wilhelm promised his German troops they would be home before the leaves fell. He underestimated the length of the war by over four years.

In the first six months of the conflict a million men died in the fighting, shocking military and political leaders. The world had seen nothing like it.

New artillery made the old strategies of attack obsolete, a point missed by the commanders. Troops were slaughtered in huge numbers. In the initial battles, German machine guns mowed down the French who carried rifles.

Americans heard about fighting around the Marne in France. The armies burrowed in for something called trench warfare. Attacks and counter attacks killed millions of young men to gain very little ground.

The nation had difficulty remaining neutral. U. S. exports were in danger. Germany threatened to sink U. S. merchant ships trading with her enemies.

When the *Lusitania*, a passenger liner carrying 1100 civilians, including 128 American citizens, was torpedoed and sunk by a German U-boat, a shocked President Wilson demanded reparation.

"What right has the Kaiser to disrupt our trade?" Maxine wondered.

Becky, from an Irish family, stiffened. "I don't see why the English think that Germany has no right to keep armaments away from the Allies. Anyway, those passengers were warned by the German embassy not to board a ship carrying armaments to the Allies. They were foolish to go."

"But England is our mother country."

"Oh, yes," Becky said, with a sneer. "We call it our mother country because most of us are from Ireland, Italy, Poland, Russia, Germany, Africa, and God knows where else."

Diane was torn. "It was a devastating tragedy. But it does seem Germany has a right to prevent contraband from going to Britain. The Allies have blockaded German ports so they can't get supplies. Can't the Germans do the same?"

The country remained divided. Many, especially in the east, favored England, except for the Irish, who found nothing about the English they liked. In the middle of the nation, citizens tracing their ancestry to Germany favored their home country.

◆ ◆ ◆

On her visit to Plainville in the summer of 1915, Diane met Doris, her new baby cousin. Aunt Elizabeth still took occasional nursing jobs, while Vicky, who had quit teaching, watched Doris for her. The child would later be good company for Vicky's own little girl.

"Drew and I aren't able to travel to the chautauquas for the inspirational speeches and the snappy bands as much as we used to, or go to the moving pictures," Elizabeth said, "but Doris more than makes up for that."

Diane joined her young friends and cousins for parties where they played Wist and Authors and danced to phonograph music. With Barbara accompanying on the piano, they sang "School Days," "Sweet Adeline," and "When You Wore a Tulip."

Despite the problems in Europe, their country was growing and self-confident. After all, their country had built a railroad across the continent, and the Panama Canal to connect the two coasts by water. In New York, they had built the Brooklyn Bridge.

Of course, Diane knew that two percent of the population held fifty percent of the wealth. Still, workers were unionizing and people worked to improve the lives of the most destitute. Optimism reigned.

A risqué joke circulating around the country amused the young people as they played card games in the parlor. Eric the Red told them President Wilson, whose wife had died, pursued a widow named Mrs. Edith Gault.

"Question: What did Mrs. Gault do when President Wilson proposed to her?"

"What did she do?"

"She fell out of bed."

"Oh, Eric, that's awful." Barbara playfully slapped her brother on the arm. "You shouldn't tell such a joke in mixed company."

"Who's mixed? Not me. Are you mixed?"

Diane's friends began their working lives, started families, planned homes. They read about humanitarian legislation to remedy the abuses of society, and efforts to pass prohibition of the demon alcohol, which seemed responsible for so much misery. Young Progressives, they believed the world would become a better place. As Diane's drudgery at the nursing school lessened, she felt happier too.

Scott Morris came down from Omaha to visit Matthew and Vicky McCall at their new house, a fashionable white two-story Colonial Revival. He stayed for the Independence Day celebration. Vicky had written that Diane would be back in Plainville that week.

Vicky and Diane had made up through apologetic letters. Now, Vicky, acting as matchmaker, tried various strategies to get Scott and Diane together. She invited them both for dinner.

Diane disliked the idea, but after all, it had been a year since she and Scott had had words. She did not want to hold a grudge. When the young couple showed them their new, roomy, two-story house, Diane admired the house and the latest in home furnishings.

Though the two guests contributed to the conversation, the atmosphere was not overly friendly.

Scott, eager to make amends for his insensitive statements about her father, said to Diane, "You must be pleased to be so near finishing nursing school."

"I still have a year to go."

"But you're two-thirds of the way through."

"That's one way to look at it."

Knowing she was well-informed, he decided to bring up the issue of the war in Europe. "Do you think the Kaiser will pay reparations for the sinking of the *Lusitania*?"

"It's hard to say."

"Some men in Omaha have joined the Canadian Army to fight with the Allies."

"They must be very committed."

"Yes, or they just want to travel. They must think war will be glorious."

She seemed to disagree. "They could be outraged at the treatment of martyred Belgium."

"Very likely. I look forward to seeing your Aunt Elizabeth and Drew Robinson at the Independence Day celebration. I hear your aunt has a child."

"Yes, a little girl."

"A new cousin. And you have nephews of your own."

"I do. Tommy, Amy's son, and Henry, Julia's boy."

He did not dare mention her father, a sensitive subject, or comment on the fact that his grandson was given his name. He had come to realize that Diane, having been neglected by her father for so long, was willing to believe the best of him.

"I also have a nephew," he said. "He keeps Vince and Maggie busy."

"Congratulations."

"I remember when I first met you at an Independence Day celebration."

"Did you?" Diane studied her nails.

"Yes, we rode the carousel." Scott felt again the twinge of jealously he had felt when Matthew sat with Diane. Though he had loathed her father, he could not help being intrigued by the athletic girl.

Vicky reddened, not eager for anyone to remember that Matthew had preferred to sit with Diane on the ride. "How about some apple pandowdy?"

Matthew, the most comfortable person at the table, smiled in anticipation. "Vicky makes the best apple pandowdy you've ever eaten."

Chapter Thirty-Two

In her last year at nursing school, Diane and her classmates wore black bands on their caps to indicate their status as head nurses. They now had extra responsibilities. They gave medications, stimulants and hypodermic injections. They took temperatures each morning, made drug lists, requisition lists, etc., wrote up charts, prepared surgical trays, prepared patients for surgery, made rounds with doctors and made sure that all doctors' orders were carried out.

They were in charge of cleanliness, readiness of supplies, and the comfort of the patients. They checked for bed sores. They passed on reports and complaints to the assistant superintendent.

A probationer was put into their ward under Diane's special care. She tried to give the girl meaningful work and to teach her as much as she could. A quick learner and indefatigable worker, Sylvia's sweet nature brightened up the ward.

Because Becky's brother and Diane's cousin served in the army, the two women followed events on the Mexican border. Early in 1916, Pancho Villa murdered sixteen American engineers who were traveling through Mexico. General Pershing, given permission by Mexico's new leader, pursued Villa with his five thousand-man army for three hundred miles through the heart of Mexico, more than the leader had in mind.

Diane later learned that Jack Hoffman was with the invading force. The conflict escalated, but neither side wanted war. By the end of the year, tensions had eased--another border incident squelched.

During the winter, Diane was surprised to hear from Aunt Elizabeth that her Uncle Robert suffered heart problems and was often unable to work. He had always seemed very healthy. Eric the Red, one of the few people who enjoyed Robert's trust, sometimes helped out at the bank.

Diane gleefully finished training in June, 1916, but it was difficult to say good-bye to Becky, Maxine, Sylvia and other nurses. Together they had struggled through three long years of difficult work and training.

For the first few days back in Plainville, Diane visited with Aunt Elizabeth, Drew and little Doris. The three adults sat in the living room as Doris played with blocks on the floor.

"It's a shame Alex went to France to work as an ambulance driver for the Allies," Elizabeth said. "You just missed him."

"Why did he go?" Diane felt intense disappointment at missing her brother.

Elizabeth shook her head in resignation. "He had to see what the war was like, I suppose. And he wanted to help. Along with the rest of the world, he detested how the Germans attacked the French and mistreated the Belgians as they passed through their country."

"I hope he doesn't get hurt." Diane had seen so little of her brothers through the years. Now both of them were off in different directions.

It was a presidential election year, and President Wilson ran for a second term on preparedness, the concept of being ready for war.

"Why do we need to be prepared if we're not going to war," Diane said over the dinner table, as they enjoyed roast beef raised on a nearby ranch.

Drew chuckled. "Some believe it means preparations to come to the side of the Allies, despite the campaign claims that Wilson kept us out of war."

Elizabeth sighed. "I suppose we'll be dragged in eventually on their side."

Drew smoothed his new, thin mustache. "We're pulling troops out of Mexico. I guess the aims Wilson had down there (whatever they were) dwarf in comparison to what might be coming up in Europe."

Elizabeth picked up Doris to hold on her lap. "At least Jack, your oldest cousin, is at the Mexican border, Diane, instead of driving an ambulance in France. I just don't understand how we could possibly fight a war in Europe. How could we even get enough troops over there?"

Diane thought. "We'd have to build extra ships to carry them over."

"But an army couldn't arrive soon enough to do any good. The men would have to be trained."

"I believe Wilson deserves another term," Drew said. "He's lowered tariffs, and put an income tax on high earners. He got us the Federal Reserve to avoid panics, and got rights for labor unions."

"Hasn't done much for women, has he? Not according to Alice Paul." Elizabeth referred to a leader of the women's movement.

"Well, he says he supports women's suffrage."

"Diane, you must visit Robert," Elizabeth said. "He's not been well lately."

"Yes, I must. Tomorrow I will." Diane was not eager to see her unpleasant uncle.

As Uncle Robert let Diane into the house the next day, he wheezed as though he had trouble getting his breath. Though he walked with a cane, he still moved with difficulty. "I expect I won't last long," he said.

"Oh, Uncle, how silly. You're young yet." Diane sat down in the parlor, surprised at how pale and thin Robert had become. It was a shock to see the strong, proud man reduced to weakness.

The house looked cluttered. Dirty dishes covered the small tables in the living room. A cobweb hung from the ceiling.

"My heart's giving out. The doctor says I shouldn't work. Just stay home in bed. What kind of a life is that?"

He was very sad, and Diane felt tears flooding her eyes. How hard his position had become. "What will you do?"

"I don't want to go to one of those old people's homes. Couldn't you move back and look after me? It shouldn't be for very long. I'll pay you, of course."

Pained, Diane searched her heart. Though she didn't want to move back into the house where she'd been so lonely, she couldn't deny her relative in his time of need. Caring for people, no matter who they were, was what nurses did.

"All right, Uncle Robert. I'll go and get my things and move in today."

"Bless you, girl. You won't regret it."

Aunt Elizabeth protested loudly. "He should hire someone else. You'll be tempted to overwork. He'll take advantage of you."

Troubled, Diane threw her clothes in her bag. "He's not in a position to take advantage of anyone. The house is a mess. I've got to get right over there and start cleaning."

"Why you? You've barely had time to decide what you want to do."

"Because I owe him." Diane opened the door, bag in her hand. "He took me in, even when he didn't want to, when I had nowhere else to go. I should care for him now."

"Oh, Diane, I wanted to take all of you, but your mother wouldn't listen to me."

Diane stared at her, unbelieving. "You wanted to take me?"

"Of course I did."

Diane shook her head. "I didn't know, but it doesn't matter now. He needs help." She opened the door.

"He has children of his own. Why can't Rachel and Bob come?" Elizabeth called out to her as Diane hurried down the walk. Diane didn't respond.

At Uncle Robert's house, she took Rachel's old room on the second floor, instead of her room in the attic, in order to be available to her patient.

She tackled the housework first, making the dingy rooms sparkle again. Then she consulted Dr. Williams. He gave her little encouragement about Robert's health, but left instructions for his best care. Robert had been living on cold meat and bread. Diane's task entailed fixing vegetables, fruits, soups, and warm tempting dishes.

She knew a cheery atmosphere helped the sick, so she sang as she dusted and chatted to Robert about events around town. The smell of fresh herbs filled the air.

As a patient, Robert often complained about his health and his pain, though he tried not to antagonize Diane. But it was too late for her to feel any real affection for him. She had been hurt too often as a girl to care now whether he loved her or not. She nursed him only out of duty and compassion.

In the November election, women in Nebraska won limited suffrage, but Diane had no time to celebrate with her friends. Nursing Robert took up all her time, and she didn't like to leave him alone.

Bob, always unfriendly to her, arrived from Omaha for Christmas to see his father. She detested seeing him. It had been a relief when he moved to Omaha. Still, Diane helped to sooth the hurt feelings father and son had for each other.

"He's been looking forward to your visit," she told Bob as he entered the house.

"Is that a fact? He said he never wanted to see me again."

"Oh, he's over all that," she said in an attempt to placate him.

"He wanted me to stay here and work in the bank for the rest of my life."

"Well, he's given that up. He even brags sometimes about your job with the railroad."

When Bob indicated he might join the army, she could see that Robert worried.

"President Wilson might send you off to war," he said.

"If it's necessary to help the Allies, I want to go. Besides, it will be a great adventure." He spoke in a casual manner.

"But you'd be fighting the country of our ancestors."

Bob's lip curled. "Papa, we have nothing to do with Germany. Certainly not with defending Kaiser Bill."

Chapter Thirty-Three

Elizabeth decided that Diane needed to get out socially. She brought Doris over one night a week to sit with Robert while Diane attended women's club. Robert seemed to enjoy the antics of little Doris.

The women's group started a campaign to raise money for books at the new library. They drew up posters to leave around town and sent letters asking for donations from prosperous farmers. Diane volunteered to visit town businesses and ask for donations.

She visited the McCall lawyers first. Matthew pulled out his money. "We'll be happy to donate."

Scott Morris, visiting his friend at the time, said, "I'd like to contribute too."

"You don't even live here," Diane said, irritated at the necessity of soliciting in his presence. "I can't take your money."

"Sure you can." Scott smiled and held out his bills. "If you really want to help the library, you'll take whatever you can get."

"Don't be choosy, Diane," Matthew said. "Take his money. After all, we know his brother's Omaha paper makes lots of it. He might even settle here someday. Half the girls in town are crazy about him."

"It's hardly necessary to take money from outside the community."

Matthew raised his eyebrows. "What's got into you, Diane?"

Scott pushed the bills into her hand. "I seem to irritate her. Diane, it seems to me you're cutting off your nose to spite your face. If it will make you feel better, I'll read one of the books sometime when I visit Matthew."

"Thank you," Diane said stiffly and flounced out with his money. Why did Scott always oppose her? Did he have to stick his nose into Plainville affairs?

It was easy for Diane to get money from her uncle, blacksmith John Hoffman, and from publisher Drew Robinson, her uncle by marriage. How could they refuse their relative? Rex Jenkins, mayor and owner of the dry goods store, also gave generously. Miss Blue, now married to Mr. Muller, eagerly donated, as did Dr. Williams and his wife. When Diane visited Millie Smith at the general store, the woman stared at her.

"Of course I'll donate to the library. Even though you kept me away from Robert so long." She became tearful. "Now I hear he's sick. Because of you, I can't even visit him."

Distressed, Diane backed away. "Well, yes, he is. But you could visit him now that my Aunt Catherine's gone."

Millie looked scornful. "So now that he's almost dead, I can see him at his house."

"Well, I don't know that he's almost dead. But you're welcome to visit. I'm sure he would enjoy the company. He is a widower now." Diane quickly bought her supplies and left.

One evening Millie Smith did visit. She sat beside Robert's bed and the two cried together. He was overwhelmed to see her, and she was saddened to see him so wasted. Diane left them alone and tidied up the kitchen.

After that, Millie came regularly. She often brought little treats from the store and news about the townspeople. Her visits brightened his empty days. Diane was glad to see that Millie served as a tonic, but she didn't regret her role in keeping the two apart while Catherine was still alive. She felt she had been in the right.

It was obvious to all who saw him that Robert could not last long. Every day he grew weaker.

♦ ♦ ♦

At the *Gazette* office, Drew heard about Sonia Jones from an old friend, a fellow newsman who dropped by for a visit. The man told him about a woman in his community in the Sandhills who had come from Plainville. The man thought Drew would be interested in the former residents, who had moved to Little Antioch so Cal could work in the potash industry. The town had boomed as a result of the war need for potash.

The woman, Sonia Jones, had been charged with poisoning Cal to death. The jury found her innocent. Now Sonia appeared to be eyeing the field with the idea of marrying again. "She's one merry widow," the man concluded. "She says she wants a child."

Drew mentioned the story to Elizabeth that night. They decided to say nothing as the disclosure would probably depress Vicky and stoke painful memories if she heard about her mother.

Drew had other news that day. He told Elizabeth about President Wilson's efforts to force peace without victory in Europe--through negotiations. In response, Germany announced that any ships coming into the German-declared war zone would be sunk by their U-boats.

At the newspaper office later, Phil, Drew, and Elizabeth read the dispatches. "It's difficult to tell for sure," Phil said, frowning over one message, "but it sounds as though the Germans are involved in espionage in this country."

"Something like that happened a few weeks back," Drew said, examining the message. "It's becoming a pattern."

"Look at this one," Elizabeth said, holding baby Doris on her hip. "A German U-boat has sunk an unarmed American merchant ship without warning. Several crew members were killed."

"We can't keep taking that kind of treatment," Drew said, shaking his head. "But I hope we don't get into this war just to protect big manufacturers. I wonder why we have to ship armaments to either side. It's becoming very dangerous for shippers. And if it leads to us going to war, it would cost numerous American lives. Why should young men fight and die just to protect markets for munitions. It's like trading lives for money."

"Yes," Elizabeth said. "Couldn't we pass legislation prohibiting the sale of armaments?"

"Sounds simple, doesn't it?" Phil said. "But my guess is that businesses in other countries would just take up the slack and manufacture munitions, making them rich instead of businesses in America."

"Some country should make a stand," Elizabeth said.

After President Wilson learned of attempts by Germany to form a Mexico-German alliance, and after German U-boats sank three unarmed American merchantmen without warning, and with heavy loss of life, Wilson presented a war message to Congress on April second. His speech was greeted with thunderous applause. Four days later, Congress formally approved a declaration of war.

Robert did not live to see the United States at war with his ancestral land. He died quietly in his sleep three days earlier.

The whole county showed up for his funeral, though Diane heard one mourner whisper that he didn't see any wagon full of treasured worldly goods or bags of money following the hearse.

Robert would have been pleased to learn of the great number of people who attended and to learn that he was so well-respected, though he had no close friends.

Bob told everyone he was joining the army immediately. He had become enamored of the tan uniforms.

Mr. McCall reported to the two of them that Robert had left his house to Diane in his will. The rest of his estate, a considerable amount of money and shares in the bank, he left to be divided between Bob, Rachel, and Diane when they reached age thirty. If any of them died before then with no descendants or eligible spouses, their portion, and the house if Diane died, would revert to the other two.

Diane was left speechless.

Bob sputtered. "Why would he include Diane? She's only a niece." He stood with his hands on his hips, legs spread, as if to attack the will or its contents or even the attorney.

Mr. McCall gave him a bland look. "Perhaps he appreciated the fact that Diane nursed him and his wife all those years."

Bob mumbled something, his face fierce.

"She was his third child," Mr. McCall said. "Robert Hoffman obviously came to think of her that way."

"I never felt like his child," Diane said. "He never mellowed until his last few months."

"Sad, but true. He was sometimes a difficult man."

Diane nodded. *What an understatement.*

When McCall left them, Bob turned on Diane, his face filled with rage. "So you dominated the old man in his last illness. You got him to put you in his will when he didn't even like you. Well, you won't get away with it. I'll get even with you one way or another."

He stalked out of the house, slamming doors behind him.

Chapter Thirty-Four

"Why would Uncle Robert leave me the house and money?" Diane said to Aunt Elizabeth.

Elizabeth dressed Doris in her room. "Surely he left it to you to show his appreciation for nursing him and Catherine all those years. And why not? You did more for him in the end than his own children."

"I didn't do it to get myself in his will."

"Of course not. Diane, stop worrying about it. Everyone in town knows it is well-deserved. They're happy for you."

Diane felt confused. *What a strange situation to be in after all those years feeling like an unappreciated relative in Uncle Robert's House.*

That spring, Uncle John and Pamela heard from Jack Hoffman. Now an army lieutenant, he would soon be going with General Pershing's army to fight in France.

When Congress passed conscription legislation, which affected men aged twenty-one through thirty, many Plainville boys decided to join the services before they were drafted. Steven McCall became a sailor. Hansy Gephart and John's youngest boy, Samuel Hoffman, along with three Muller boys, joined the army. The idea of defending their country and going overseas filled them with excitement.

Some American soldiers marched down the Champs Elysees by July 4th, and then got their training in France. But most Americans trained in newly-built camps in the United States and thus reached the continent much later.

♦ ♦ ♦

"Guess what I'm wearing," Barbara said, twirling around, as she joined a sewing bee in her mother's home one rainy day. The children played about the house while the women worked at the dining room table.

They all looked her over. "You've done something," Lila said, "but I can't figure out what it is."

"She's wearing a brassiere instead of a corset," Leah told them. "I saw it when she brought it home."

Now the women stared. Thelma said, "I don't see much difference."

"That's just it," Barbara said. "It's much more comfortable. And you wear a girdle with it or not as you wish."

Vicky studied Barbara. "You are so brassy." Then, after a moment of thought, said, "I think I'll get one."

Diane laughed. "Leave it to Barbara to be the first to adopt the latest thing."

"Maybe she'll end up using one of those pessaries Margaret Sanger talked about on her speaking tour to Spokane." Thelma cast a teasing glance about the room. "Hilda Muller went to hear her speak at one of her stops along the way and told me about it."

"And why not?" Barbara plopped into a chair. "There's no reason why anyone should have to bear ten children. I read that Mrs. Sanger was jailed for opening a health clinic for women in New York when she got back. She's called for doctors to support her cause, but they haven't."

"Now that's not right." Leah shook her head.

The conversation turned from Sanger's tour to the war situation. Aunt Pamela had a suggestion.

"You young people should go to that "Kick the Kaiser" party they're having in Ash Grove."

Leah hunted for some thread in her sewing box. "The Red Cross is having a money raiser right here next week."

"I don't know whether to believe the posters or not," her mother said. "Last year, Germans were admired people, superior in science. Now the government calls them monsters."

"Have you seen some of the newsreels?" Lila said. "They've been monsters as they marched through little Belgium."

Thelma looked up from stitching on a waistcoat she had brought along. "And Belgium was a neutral country."

"The fighting seems to be a standoff," Diane said. "Neither side can gain enough ground to satisfy them, so the soldiers squat in the trenches to escape being hit by shells. When one side goes on the offensive, the enemy mows them down. It's an entirely different way of fighting."

"Our troops will make the difference," Vicky said. "We'll be sending thousands over there. Then what will the Kaiser do?"

Lila frowned. "What if they send their soldiers over here to invade us?"

"I didn't raise my sons to be soldiers." Pamela quoted the words of a popular song. She worried constantly about her four sons going across the ocean to fight.

"And I didn't marry Phil just to have him take off," Leah said in a hurt tone. A careful planner, she couldn't believe that events were ruining all her hopes for their married life. "Little Pam couldn't bear his leaving. He's a wonderful father." She got up to pace the floor.

"It will do no good to stomp around and act like a chicken with its head cut off," Aunt Pamela said. "If they have to go, there's little to be done. The draft riots during the Civil War didn't change anything."

"Keith and I just took our wedding vows," Barbara said, her voice breaking.

"Yes," her mother said, "and I'm afraid now you'll have to live up to them."

"I'm trying to talk Hiram out of going," Julia said. "His three children should make him exempt."

Diane asked Vicky, "Do you think Matthew will go?"

"Lord, I hope not." Vicky laughed. "I might hog-tie him to keep him here. The kids and I couldn't do without him."

"We should hog-tie all of them and keep them in the cellar." Barbara grinned. But her gayety hid her fear that Keith McCall would join the fighting.

"This war has destroyed all my beliefs about humanity. I thought we were slowly advancing and becoming morally advanced," Diane said with a doleful look.

Women were needed to fight the war and many women working as clerks and stenographers were eager to serve. Any Plainville telephone operator with a smattering of French applied to go overseas. Elma Black was quickly signed on.

Dozens of others applied to function as canteen workers, stenographers, and office workers who were recruited by the YMCA or the Red Cross. The numbers of applicants for those positions was huge, and many were not selected.

War required nurses, and those with qualifications were accepted by the American Red Cross, the organization authorized to send volunteer nurses to aid the forces. When Diane had trained for nursing, she had in mind caring for sick children, accident victims, women in labor, and the elderly. Despite her admiration for Clara Barton's work during the Civil War, she had not imagined working in crude wartime conditions or treating human-inflicted wounds.

Besides, she had looked forward to a new life in her home town. Now, instead of living among her friends and relatives, she'd be over there. But it would be selfish not to go.

Things had changed since nursing school days. Nurses were in demand, so Diane decided to volunteer. At twenty-five, she had reached the required age for nurses serving overseas with the Red Cross. Her application was accepted in a short time.

She began her preparations. The Red Cross recommended that nurses take matches, sugar, soap, candles, warm underclothing.

Aunt Elizabeth protested when Diane told her. "You can serve your country here as well as over there. You have a home here now. There'll be plenty of nursing work. Why should you go?"

Diane gave Drew, holding Doris, a playful look. "Is this the woman who traveled all over the country with the Red Cross to help in disasters?"

Elizabeth protested. "I didn't go overseas."

"I'm sure there will be plenty of disasters over there."

"If you must go, I suggest you stop off in Indianapolis to visit our relatives. My Spencer first cousin, Lucille Gilbert, would be disappointed if you didn't. Maybe she'll show you the house where my father and your grandfather grew up. Before he moved to Plainville, my father examined patients in a back room in that house."

"Can we help you in any way?" Drew said.

"I'd like to rent out Uncle Robert's house until I get back. Maybe you could take care of that."

"Of course. Anything else?"

"Look after little Doris. I'll miss all of you."

In Nebraska, thousands of acres of prairie lands were plowed up to fulfill the war demand for grain. Hans and Amy Shafer benefited from rising grain prices and put more of their land under the plow.

Herbert Hoover, in charge of increasing the food supply, talked of wheatless Mondays, and meatless Tuesdays. The Fuel Administration introduced daylight saving time and gasless days, and closed non-essential manufacturing plants in an effort to save coal. Before long, Ford automobile factories churned out tanks, steel helmets, and automobiles for the war effort. The whole country felt the effects of the European War.

As mayor, Rex Jenkins appointed Mr. McCall head of the Plainville Red Cross. McCall organized the community for its work. He headed campaigns for raising money, and planned to organize volunteers to roll bandages.

Organizations collected salvage donated by the population: clothing, rags, bottles, magazines, papers, tin foil.

♦ ♦ ♦

Diane boarded the train for her long journey across the country. When she reached Indianapolis, she telephoned Cousin Lucille Gilbert, who rushed to meet her, driving her flashy automobile.

"I'm so glad to see you. I met your mother when I was a small child. We went to Nebraska to visit my Spencer uncle and his family. Now, my dear, I'm throwing a party this evening so that you can meet other relatives and friends. One of the guests knows you. Her name is Maxine Davis and she was with you in nursing school. Her mother was a Gilbert."

"Maxine? Really? I knew she lived in Indianapolis, but didn't dream I'd get to see her. How kind of you to invite her."

"Everyone is eager to meet you."

At the party, Diane chatted with Lucille's friends and relatives. Their hostess had five children, and dozens of other more distant cousins milled about the house. Some were Gilberts who had married Spencers. Others were from Lucille's Spencer side of the family. The numbers and the intermarriages made it very confusing.

They all wanted to know about Hiram and Phil Spencer and she filled them in, adding that Hiram had married her sister, Julia Hoffman, and that Phil had married one of her cousins, Leah Hoffman.

Eventually, as always, the talk revolved around the war. Several young men would be leaving soon for basic training. One recent graduate from West Point, named Leonard Price, who sported a handsome handlebar mustache, seemed extremely knowledgeable. He had followed the war in Europe since 1914 and opined that the addition of the Americans would tip the balance in favor of France and England.

"But our troops aren't there," Lucille said. "Won't it take some time before we can move an army across the Atlantic Ocean?"

"We'll have to increase shipbuilding to produce enough ships to get them across," Leonard said with authority, "or get the British to ferry them over. They're the ones with the navy that rules the waves. Barge traffic on the Mississippi must be expanded. We'll be going into heavy production for war materials. We'll need additional coal for factories making munitions. And to train the soldiers and sailors, we'll have to build many more camps than we have now."

He turned toward Diane. "We'll need nurses. There's talk of an army nurse corps. I must congratulate you, Miss Hoffman, for volunteering with the Red Cross so early in the conflict."

Diane reddened. "Fortunately, I'm old enough and free of obligation at this time. I want to help."

"Tell us, how long was your training? I'm ignorant of such things."

"Three years to become registered as a nurse. But many women who nurse are unregistered, Mr. Price."

"Please call me Len. Have you much experience?"

"I nursed my aunt before nursing school, and my uncle afterward, during their long illnesses. I sometimes accompanied my aunt on her short nursing visits. Other than that, I have no experience, no hospital experience. I just recently finished my training."

"Sounds like useful practice to me," a Spencer relative said. "Will there be a shortage of trained medical personnel for the war, do you think?"

"I couldn't tell you, but I have heard that colored nurses were rejected though they've applied, and that the services refused to enlist female doctors. If a bad shortage develops they might have to reconsider those options."

Diane heard murmurs about the room. Considering the prejudice in the population against professional women in any field, and against colored people in general, she knew at least some of the guests agreed that the military acted properly.

"In the meantime, I've heard of volunteer groups that have utilized women doctors and colored nurses."

"I hear you're from Plainfield, Nebraska. Where is it exactly?" Len asked.

Diane laughed. "It's a small town south and west of Omaha."

When her friend from nursing school arrived, Diane learned that Maxine would soon be going to nurse in France for the Red Cross. They were both to leave from New York City.

"Maybe we'll arrive at Grand Central Station. It's only about four years old. I'll be happy to travel with you," Maxine said. "It will be much more interesting to go overseas together."

"I'm happy too. It will be more fun."

"I don't know where we'll be stationed, but I have an aunt living in Paris. If we get time, we might visit her for relief."

"That's wonderful. I suspect we'll need it."

◆ ◆ ◆

The next day, while the women shared a late breakfast, Lucille told them about Margaret Sanger, who had recently attempted to open a women's clinic in New York so women could get health care and learn about limiting their families.

"I thought you nurses would be interested. Elizabeth and I talked about women's lack of information to prevent pregnancy in this country. In Europe, such information is common knowledge."

Diane spread jam on her bread. "Why is it not available here?"

"The foolish Comstock Laws and over-zealous religious fanatics. Women's lives are endangered by such laws. A woman who already has several children should not have to keep having them. It's not good for children either; the more children a woman has, the less time she can devote to each one, even if she can somehow manage to keep them all fed."

"Surely keeping them fed is the father's responsibility," Maxine said.

"Theoretically, yes. But men often spend their wages, when they have them, for liquor. Women have no legal control over the family finances."

"Poverty also keeps women from gaining information about limiting their families," Diane said. "Middle class women get the information from their doctors and midwives, and consequently have fewer children. Many poor women never see a doctor. They need access to information too."

They shook their heads over the injustice Margaret Sanger faced for trying to improve and save women's and children's lives.

Lucille mentioned that Charles Beard had published a controversial book, *An Economic Interpretation of the Constitution of the United States*. His wife, Mary Beard, a friend of Lucille's, was now working with her husband on another history.

Unfortunately, Charles Beard had supported fired faculty members who opposed the war, though he supported it. In protest, he had resigned his position at Columbia University and went into public service.

"There's no sympathy for war opponents in this country," Lucille commented. "But people shouldn't be fired for their views."

The others agreed, but with less emphasis. The Espionage Act made it a crime to interfere with the draft or to encourage "disloyal" acts, and they were reluctant to say anything.

Eugene Debs, the head of the Communist Party, was sentenced to prison for ten years merely for speaking out about the war. As a result, dissenters were cautious in voicing their views about anything the government did.

Too soon, the young nurses left the comfort of friends and family to embark on their mission across the sea. Though somewhat nervous, they determined to bravely face hardship and danger for the sake of their country and the young men who needed their nursing skills.

By the time they boarded the ship, they had received smallpox, typhoid, and paratyphoid vaccinations and obtained passports. They were issued supplies from the Red Cross: a hat, an outdoor uniform, a coat, cape, gloves, shirtwaists, woolen underclothing, pajamas, a sleeping bag, a blanket roll, a woolen blanket, three pairs of shoes, and one pair of rubber boots.

On board ship, the nurses cheered in November when they heard about suffrage victories for women in Rhode Island and New York. Two more states where women could vote. Surely it would not be long before women gained national suffrage.

Weary after the long voyage and the earlier train journey, they arrived at their hospital late at night. A nurse named Hazel complained bitterly about all their discomforts, but quieted down when they commandeered an empty house nearby to sleep in until their tents arrived. The nurses tumbled into bed immediately, and rose at dawn to begin the first of their frequent fourteen-to eighteen-hour days.

Chapter Thirty-Five

It was a grim year for the Allies. In October, 1917, the combined forces of Germany, Austria, and Hungary in a massive offensive shoved into the north of Italy and killed thousands. In the North Sea, the Germans sank British ships left and right. And in November, when the Bolsheviks seized power in Russia, they signed an armistice with Germany.

As a result of the armistice, Field Marshall Erich von Ludendorff transferred thousands of German troops to join the battle in France. It was believed the German commander planned a massive offensive in the spring to win the war before more American forces arrived to fight on the Western Front.

At the end of 1917, Diane and Maxine were stationed in a small French town behind the front line. Their living quarters were in an old building next to the hospital.

Diane heard that Elma Black, from Plainville, reached France in March 1918 with other telephone operators. Clerical and stenographic workers followed that summer. Part of the Signal Corps, the young women were housed and fed by the YWCA. Each Signal Corps house was served by a live-in secretary who chaperoned the residents and enforced rules established by the Y.

In the spring, Diane and Maxine traveled to Paris to attend a party given by Karen Davis. Maxine's aunt welcomed several nurses and other young working women, and invited them to visit whenever they could arrange it. French and American servicemen were expected at the party.

"Cousin William will be coming for dinner with some friends," Maxine announced as the nurses visited in a sitting room of the large house.

Bridget had recently arrived in France. "I'm looking forward to the home cooked meal," she said. "Sometimes our food at the hospital is not very creative. Of course, compared to my home in New York, all food tastes good."

"What's wrong with New York food?" Hazel asked as she examined their surroundings.

Bridget looked embarrassed. "It's only that my large family seldom dines on much. They're very poor. I'm only here because an aunt of mine paid for my training."

Diane spied Elma Black among the women guests and the two exchanged greetings. "Tell us about your work," Diane said.

"The hours are long when something is about to happen on the battle field. Still, it's pretty exciting to handle calls from President Wilson to Clemenceau or Lloyd George. One time General Pershing called up and asked me for the time."

The women laughed. "Do you suppose he's not paid enough to buy a watch?" Maxine said.

"I hope you gave him the right time," Diane said, "especially if the troops were waiting for some command."

"Maybe he wanted to avoid keeping his young French mistress waiting," Hazel said, patting her hair. The others stared at her. "It's true. I got it from one of the officers in the hospital. He's thirty years older than she is."

"Of course," Elma said, ignoring the interruption, "there's a lot of military control over the telephone system."

"Are you part of the military?"

"I think so. We wear uniforms and work under army officers. And we didn't sign any contracts which we would have done otherwise. Some officers are big pains. You want to tell them to go to hell. Others couldn't be more polite.

"But we're constantly working with supervisors looking over our shoulders and it's stressful. Bell Telephone has a notion of scientific management.

Speed and efficiency, they tell us, are essential. We are expected to handle a substantial volume of calls."

Another Hello Girl spoke up. "We have to get back to the YWCA house by a certain time. The opera never concludes before 11:30 so this is a problem. We don't mind the requirement that two or more of us go on an outing. We'd probably do that anyway. But I feel like Cinderella with no prince due to the hour of expiration on our passes."

"We can't date civilians or enlisted men," Elma said.

"We can't either." Hazel frowned and indicated Bridget with a nod of her head. "But she does a lot of kidding and flirting with an orderly named Lewis."

Bridget blushed. "I'm just being polite."

"And our bathroom is shared by fifty women," the Hello Girl said.

"Now that's a big problem." They all agreed.

♦ ♦ ♦

When Scott and Matthew, along with other young officers in uniform, entered the room, Diane greeted them in surprise.

"I can't believe it. What were the chances of you Nebraska men meeting here? And you're officers already."

"Ninety-day wonders," Matthew said with a grin. "Scott and I corresponded and arranged to meet in Paris this week for the party. Gosh, it's good to see you, Diane."

"Have you heard from Vicky lately?"

"The family is fine, but you'll probably hear more from her than I do. We'll be on the move, I imagine. We've found it takes at least a month for letters to get across the Atlantic."

Len Price went to Diane. "It was such a pleasure to meet you in Indianapolis. I look forward to seeing you again. May I sit by you?"

Diane, blushing slightly, made way for him on the settee. "Of course."

As Scott watched this exchange, his brow furrowed. *Where did Len get his nerve? He barely knew Diane, whereas he and Matthew were her childhood friends.*

He compared Diane, petite and pretty, with other women he had known and spent time with in Omaha and in college. He remembered more beautiful women, but her face, lively and intelligent, had a hold on him. He supposed it always would. If her expression wore sadness over the horrors she had seen, her smile was genuine. They had all dealt with the shock of war.

He had been intrigued since the Independence Day Celebration in Plainville. She was fourteen then, and he almost seventeen. Though often quiet, she had always seemed older and wiser than her age.

♦ ♦ ♦

At dinner, the discussion turned to Scott's unusual company of colored men. "I volunteered for this assignment," he said. "It's my belief that coloreds should have the same opportunity to serve their country as others."

"But what can they do?" Will said.

"Why, they can do anything you and I can do. Unfortunately the higher-ups don't believe it. They've sent us to build roads, bridges and dams and unload trains and ships. Perhaps the policy is to train the men for the ordeal of trench warfare. Building a dam gives the men practice digging in the mud," Scott said dryly. "The soldiers grumble that they could do that back in the states. They came here to fight Germans."

"Well, I hope they get to go to the front if that's what they want," Matthew said.

"There's opposition to them serving. And plenty of prejudice against them, especially among men from the South. Why, when they went south to train, those damn Southerners pushed colored lawyers off the street. They had to be moved to a New England camp to train. There's concern about the others fighting with them. The talk now is sending them to fight with the French. A colored company beside a French company."

"I admire your open-mindedness," Diane said politely, though Scott sensed a slight coolness.

"Well, I didn't stop being a Progressive just because there's a war on."

He surveyed the group, wanting them to understand his men. "About ten percent of colored men are officers. The colonel recruited for our National Guard Regiment in Harlem and tried to get leaders to sign up so we'd have more black officers. Few of them were willing to leave their careers and sign up for three years. Still, we have black lawyers, engineers, ballplayers, and all the professions in our midst.

"One thing the coloreds excel at is making music. They've organized a 60-man band headed by a famous man who played in Carnegie Hall. Their performances have wowed the French. They love them. They usually open with the 'Marseillaise' played in a completely different jazzy manner. Maybe you'll be lucky enough to see them perform."

"I hope we can," Diane said, sipping her wine.

"Why not come to the performance tomorrow. They're traveling east to an American rest and recreation resort near the Swiss Alps and playing in towns along the way. This performance is not far from your hospital. You could take the train. Better come soon. This may be your last chance. If we get to the front, they won't be available to perform. They have the option of permanently playing at a rest resort for the other servicemen, but they want to be in combat, to show what they can do."

"I suppose I could," Diane said.

Scott, encouraged, told her time and place and particulars. He asked Len to move aside so that he could make plans with Diane. Without waiting for a reply, he pulled up a chair and seated himself beside her, and Len was forced to move away.

Before long, several nurses indicated an interest in attending the performance. Those stationed in the area formed a group to attend, but it was understood by the others that Scott and Diane were together.

"I'll be too far away to come to the performance," Len said with a disappointed look. "Do you nurses get much time off?"

"No," Maxine told him. "Only occasionally."

A nurse asked, "Are we having trouble getting troops to fight this war?"

"I couldn't say," Len said, "but I do know that thousands of immigrants gain immediate citizenship by joining the services."

"And about one third of people living in the United States are immigrants or children of immigrants," Scott told them, "and I've heard that twenty percent of the troops are foreign-born."

"What do you hear from Alex?" Matthew said to Diane. "I know your brother was driving an ambulance for the Allies before we got into it."

"They're going to train him to fly an airplane. Imagine that. He wrote that they figured anybody who could drive an ambulance could handle an airplane. But I'm sure it's very dangerous."

Scott tended to agree, but he refrained from saying so.

"I have no idea where he is now or what has happened to him," she said, "and I don't know how to find out."

Scott wanted to erase the fear and anxiety from her eyes. "Perhaps I could make some inquiries," he said.

Faint hope appeared on her face. "Could you? If you can find out anything, I'll be very grateful."

He smiled. *Well, a kiss would be a tantalizing reward if I discover where he is, but I suppose that's out of the question.*

When the men left the dinner party, they went to find French women. General Pershing made sure the troops were furnished with prophylactics. Whatever his own beliefs, he knew venereal disease would hamper their availability as soldiers.

Matthew and Scott abstained. "I've got Vicky at home," Matthew said. Scott wanted to start seeking information about Alex.

For the first time, Diane saw Scott as a good man with ideals. She knew he had an interest in progressive causes, but she had assumed that was for journalistic purposes. She remembered that he and his brother saved a hungry thief from probable death at the hands of the authorities in San Francisco.

Her mind went back to the dance in Omaha when he had led her, in her confused state, skillfully about the dance floor, his touch awakening her interest for the first time.

At the musical program the next day, Scott helped seat the nurses, and then sat down beside Diane. She did not fail to notice that his knee, seemingly by accident, rested lightly against hers. She supposed it would be an overreaction to move hers, though the intimate contact left her unsettled.

The performance by the regimental band exceeded all expectations. Diane had heard nothing like it. Though Uncle John played his horn with the Plainville Band, their music was totally different.

The French school gymnasium rocked and rang with cheery tunes. The young people heard ragtime for the first time and, along with the French audience, gave the performers a standing ovation. Maxine and the other nurses talked about the performance for days.

Young officers offered to help Scott escort the nurses to their lodgings. As the young people exited the train and walked to the hospital grounds in the quiet dark, Scott took Diane's hand, ostensibly to guide her, an action Diane found foolish since she often walked around Plainville in the dark, and patrolled dark hallways in nursing school, but she did not resist. His hand felt warm and comforting.

"Thanks for coming," he said, squeezing her hand before he left,

◆ ◆ ◆

The next day, Scott made some inquiries from other officers. He learned that newsmen and fliers frequented Cira's or Harry's Restaurants in Paris or the Chatham Hotel Bar or even the Crillon Hotel Bar, where General Pershing had first stayed when he arrived in France.

At the first opportunity, Scott took the train to the city on army business. When his work was finished, he sought out fliers at the bars and restaurants, searching the dim interiors filled with cigarette smoke.

Hours later, he was about to give up. Yes, the pilots and newsmen knew Alex Hoffman, but they didn't know his whereabouts at the moment. When he went back to the Chatham for the third time, to his delight he finally found Alex.

"Good Lord, Scott. What a coincidence meeting you here." Alex shook his hand.

"Yes, isn't it?" Scott put on a poker face. "Your sister is worried about you. I saw her at a dinner party here in Paris. You know she is nursing for the Red Cross?"

"Yes, very spunky of Diane. Say, maybe you could get this letter to her." Alex pulled out an envelope from his pocket. "I've been trying to decide the best way to send it since I don't know where she's located."

"I'd be happy to deliver it to her." Scott reached for the envelope. "I'll be in her area on the way back to my base. Her hospital is not far from where we're camped at the moment."

"I'd be much obliged."

"How did you get to be an airman?" Scott took a seat beside Alex.

Alex laughed. "I drove an ambulance in 1916 for the French in the American Field Service. When I finished my contract, and we got into it, I signed up with the U.S. Air Service.

"I trained with the French at Tours for a time and now I'm in a muddy, miserable, newly-built American field. The food is even worse than the grounds. I will say the officers get better food than the troops.

"We've been flying patrols, but we can't cross our lines because we haven't any guns yet. Can you believe it? What the hell are we supposed to do if we meet any Germans? Invite them for beer?"

Scott laughed, and ordered a drink. "We've had the same trouble. It seems we're always waiting for supplies."

"A few of us got this jaunt to Paris for a couple of days. I'm enjoying it while I can."

"Flying must be exciting though."

"Flying is exciting. Some of the planes go forty miles an hour. They say we'll go to gunnery school next. Rumors are we'll be flying against the Boche in May with guns. They made most of us first lieutenants too."

"It's certainly more exciting than facing the Germans on the ground with the infantry. As an ambulance driver, I helped stack up plenty of dead and horribly wounded bodies near the trenches. Flying may be dangerous, but probably no more so than fighting on the front lines."

◆ ◆ ◆

The chief nurse called Diane off the ward. "There's a good-looking young captain with sandy hair here to see you," she said, a gleam in her eyes.

Diane joined Scott in the anteroom.

"You look pert and professional with that Red Cross band around your arm and nurse's cap on your head."

"Thank you. I certainly didn't expect to see you so soon." She gave him her hand.

He held it for several seconds as he examined her face. "I tracked down Alex in Paris and he's fine. He likes flying. He gave me this letter for you. Write to him at the address on the letter." He handed her the envelope.

"Why, that's wonderful." Surprised, she took the letter.

After a moment, he said, "I've wanted to tell you that I'm sorry I spoke harshly against your papa. I don't really know him at all. You must be well-acquainted with him by now."

Diane was silent. After several years away from his children, Thomas Hoffman finally came to meet them, but after that meeting he never came back. And despite her papa's offer to help her with training expenses, he did not follow through. Fortunately, she got by without his extra help. But she saw no reason to inform Scott about those hurts. It would reinforce his poor opinion of her papa.

"Thank you for delivering the letter. How can I ever thank you?"

"You could kiss me." He gave her a disarming grin.

His words startled her, but that didn't stop him. He suddenly put his hands about her waist and pulled her to him. Before she could protest, he kissed her on the lips, a slow, sensual, searing kiss, not at all timid. As he stroked her back, her pulse raced.

When he released her, he said, "couldn't you write to me? I would enjoy hearing from you."

Flustered, she said, "I...I suppose I could."

"Then I'll send my mailing instructions and look forward to hearing from you. Good-bye, Diane."

He touched her check and left quickly, leaving her confused and aroused.

♦ ♦ ♦

Nursing in France was like nothing the women had dealt with before. Shells and shrapnel ripped open the flesh, causing many deep wounds.

Because of the trench-dirt on the soldiers' skin and uniforms, all wounds were subject to infection from bits of soil driven into them.

The doctors also complained that the patients were sent to the hospital too late, sometimes hours after they were wounded, when gangrene and infections had set in.

After a great battle, the nurses heard the whistle blow three times, often in the middle of the night. In ambulance trains or in trucks the wounded arrived. During the rush, the nurses and orderlies administered morphine to ease the worst pain until the doctors could operate.

Bridget told the others about finding one boy with a bandage around his head. As she removed it, a great mass of tissue spilled out--part of his brain. No one was around to consult, so she pushed the mass back into his skull. Only later did she realize that he had been dead.

As the surgical patients were brought in, the wounds were hurriedly fluoroscoped. To guide the surgeons, the nurses and orderlies marked in indelible pencil the places where shell fragments or bullets were lodged.

The stretchers were carried into the operating room. Nurses cut away the patient's clothing, usually caked with mud, from around the wound. As the nurses gave him chloroform or ether, they cleaned the wound with gasoline and dabbed with iodine before the doctors operated.

A sickening odor of blood and vomit filled the air.

Nurses washed the men's bloodied bodies and cleaned and dressed wounds again and again.

The worst trial for the nurses was tending to the patients suffering from mustard gas. Little could be done for them. Sometimes they poured oil over the burnt skin, which seemed to ease the pain. And they washed their eyes to sooth them.

Treatment for shell shock concentrated on getting the patient well enough to go back into battle.

German prisoners were brought in. The nurses found the officers arrogant, but they got along fine with the regular German soldiers, who were often put to work as they recovered, helping the patients. One, in particular, seemed to have exceptional skill in soothing and settling the wounded.

Once, their hospital came under fire during a raid. Hazel became almost hysterical, but the gentle German helped to quiet her. Though the bombing did only minor damage, one nurse was wounded. Still, as they hurried to help their patients, the nurses had little time to worry about the noise overhead.

During a rush, no matter how hard the nurses, doctors, and orderlies worked, they could not catch up. More patients came. After long hours of constant pressure, when the numbers finally began to decrease, the hospital staff took rest periods.

"Nobody told us when we signed up that we'd become slaves over here," Hazel grumped as the nurses took a hasty meal break.

"Why did you sign up, Hazel?" Maxine gave her a bland look. "Was it because of the cute outfits?"

"Cute? That's a laugh. When I get home I'll never wear gray or white again. No, I signed up because the papers said the Germans were so cruel. Nothing was said about the patient/nurse ratio being way higher than they told us in nursing school."

The others hooted. "Forget about the nursing school ratio," Diane told her. "This is war. Horrible war. The worst the world has ever seen."

How would the sainted Clara Barton have stood up under these conditions," Hazel wondered aloud.

Between rushes, the nurses relaxed a little. Despite the fact that nurses were prohibited from dating enlisted men, Lewis talked Bridget into taking a walk with him on several occasions. Though they were careful to hide their trysts by meeting in town, the others worried that they would be seen and reported by someone.

"Our Little Red Riding Hood is headed for trouble with that orderly," Hazel said, referring to the red scarf Bridget draped around her neck to brighten up her outfit.

"Please don't say anything. I'm sure there's no harm." Diane said.

"Do I look like a tattletale?"

Maxine always left the hospital with Bridget, who browsed in the shops as the two lovers spent time together. "Bridget thinks it is a silly rule and she is determined to keep seeing Lewis," Maxine told the others. "I don't really blame her. I'd do the same myself if any of the orderlies appealed to me."

"I hope they don't reassign him," Hazel said. "He's the best orderly we have. Some of them practically refuse to take orders from women. Lazy bums. Too good to scrub floors. But nobody minds if *we* do it.

Chapter Thirty-Six

In Plainville, Drew Robinson studied a press release from the government. He knew many newspaper publishers ran the press releases without editing. He seldom did. They were filled with statements designed to promote patriotism, but they also produced fear and unnecessary suspicion.

People started to look warily at their German neighbors, people they had known and worked with for years. In some states, laws were passed banning the teaching of German, and speaking it was looked upon with wariness. Some were even naming their sauerkraut 'liberty' cabbage.

The Germans were not the only ones suspected. Posters everywhere urged people to report to the Justice Department anyone "who spreads pessimistic stories, divulges confidential military information, cries for peace, or belittles our effort to win the war."

A Vigilance Patrol spied on neighbors, investigated 'slackers,' and 'food hoarders,' and demanded to know why people didn't buy Liberty Bonds. Drew had no idea who was in the League in Plainville, but the Four-Minute government men who spoke after the local films questioned him whenever he and Elizabeth attended.

They wanted to know why he didn't run the releases. "Our boys are dying in Belleau Wood," they told him in June, 1917. The next year it was somewhere else. Sometimes, he put them off by saying there was no space in the paper that week. Other times, he felt he had no choice but to print them.

Mr. McCall had told him that the Illinois Bar Association had declared that lawyers who defended draft resisters were "unpatriotic" and "unprofessional." College faculty and professional people were being fired for criticizing the government.

Though President Wilson said the war was being fought to make the world safe for democracy, it seemed to Drew that freedom was disappearing for Americans.

Elizabeth and Doris entered the newspaper office. "I see you have another press release. Are you going to run it?"

"This one isn't so offensive. I suppose I will." He picked up Doris and gave her a kiss, while she giggled.

When he let her down, she said, "Papa, store."

"So you and Mama have been to the store."

"Yes," Elizabeth said. "We left our order. They'll be delivering it this afternoon. My, how the prices have gone up. Bella Johnston and Jane Reed were complaining to Millie Smith about how some people still speak German around here and sometimes keep to themselves. And they wonder what the Germans are hatching up. And so on. Can you imagine? Most of the Germans in Plainville settled here years ago." She shook her head in disgust.

"I'm afraid it might get worse before it gets better. How did Millie react?"

"Well, they are customers. What can she say? It's something you have to keep in mind when you're getting out the paper."

"Too true." Drew glanced at the dispatches on his desk. He picked one up. "University of Nebraska faculty members are accused of failing to support the war."

"What nonsense," Elizabeth said. "Didn't General Pershing go to college there?"

Drew picked up another dispatch. "There have been scattered reports of a dangerous Spanish influenza, so called because the papers in neutral Spain have been running the story. It's likely the warring nations are afraid of starting a panic if they allow information to be printed."

"So much for freedom of the press."

They walked slowly down the street to the hotel restaurant with little Doris between them. She hugged her Teddy bear, named after the former president. As they finished their meal, Rex Jenkins joined them.

205

"Too bad you wouldn't head the Red Cross, Drew. I've had a devil of a time getting someone to volunteer."

Drew winced. "I'm sorry. With Phil gone, I wouldn't have the time. And little Doris--"

"Yes, yes, I understand. But I had to appoint a responsible person. I've been asking people around the county as to who they thought might be a good candidate. I soon learned I had to be careful what I said. Seems the Mullers and the Hoffmans are related to everyone in town. If you say one unflattering word, you're likely to find that you're speaking to a cousin or an in-law, or some other shirttail relative."

The Robinsons chuckled. "With John's children and Mullers marrying now, they include many extended families," Elizabeth said. "There will be even more. The beautiful Barbara Hoffman and Keith McCall recently married."

"I finally got old man McCall to agree to serve as Chairman. The Red Cross will be busy everywhere before this war is over. We're mobilizing like crazy."

"We've never been in a war like this," Drew said. "No one remembers the Civil War, but my father told me about it. Over fifty years ago, he served in that bloody war. It was fought with rifles and cannon. Now they're using machine guns, tanks, and airplanes."

♦ ♦ ♦

When Drew came home one late afternoon from a business trip to the county seat, Elizabeth sat staring into space as Doris napped. She ached in mind and body. Most of the young men in Plainville had joined the service.

"So they've all left?" Drew said.

"Yes. We've had the big parade, the town band playing martial music, the patriotic speeches. I'm sure you didn't mind missing all that nonsense. I've written up a news piece about it. Now our boys must join the bloody frenzy of nationalism that has overrun Europe.

"The train took them all away, their eyes gleaming with the lust of adventure. Along with Alex, dozens of young men have left for the glorious pleasure of fighting the 'vile Huns.'

"You should have seen them, joshing, pushing each other, singing, laughing. They believe they'll be home in a few months. Like the Germans who were promised by the Kaiser in 1914 that they'd be home 'before the leaves fall.' They don't even realize they're marching off to their deaths."

Drew wanted to lighten her mood. "Well, Lizzy, they won't all die. Alex and the others feel they have to respond to the butchery that went on in Belgium." He sat down and put an arm around her.

"My third cousins, Hiram and Phil Spencer, have left their families to fight in France."

"Hiram feels he should go where Phil goes. They've always stuck together."

"Several Muller boys have gone."

"Well, there are so many of them."

"Three McCall boys have gone: Matthew, Keith, and Steven."

"The draft would have--"

"John Hoffman's three sons are all off in the service now: Jack, Eric the Red, and young Sam. Only Frank Hoffman is left. He doesn't want to leave Lila and the four children.

"Do you suppose the Hoffmans will have trouble because of their German ancestry?" Elizabeth worried.

"They might. I've heard that Ken Bischoff enlisted under a false name because of the anger against those of German heritage."

Elizabeth shook her head. "Who knows what hell our boys might endure. Maggie writes that Scott Morris joined a colored unit as officer."

"Have you heard anything about Bob Hoffman, Robert's son?"

"He signed up early," Elizabeth said. "You can bet he'll be lining up for metals as soon as the fighting is over. He wrote to Frank, still complaining that Diane should not have been included in his father's will. I think the man is crazy."

"He'll never get over that. Our young doctor has gone too. You're going to be busy looking after the people right here, Lizzy. McCall needs you to help organize and train Red Cross workers."

Tears filled her eyes. "Pamela is devastated. Three sons gone, and Phil, her son-in-law, too."

"At least Thelma and James out on the farm will be needed at home to raise crops. Anyway, they have children. He's not likely to be drafted. I'll miss Phil at the *Gazette.* But we'll get by somehow."

She looked at him and smiled through her tears. "You're ever the optimist, aren't you?"

"Think of the song, "Keep the Home Fires Burning." And look ahead. Remember "When Johnny Comes Marching Home." That's all we can do."

She stood up. "You're right, of course. I'll start dinner. Doris will be waking up soon. She seemed to enjoy the parade and all the commotion."

"I'll get her. Maybe we're lucky we don't have children old enough to fight."

She gave him a wistful smile. "If you and Frances had not delayed having a family you might be sending a son off to the slaughter too."

Elizabeth and Drew found disturbing reports of influenza outbreaks and deaths tucked away in the back pages of the *Omaha Bee* and the *Denver Post.*

"It's a strange thing," Elizabeth said. "On the front page the authorities keep reporting that the influenza outbreaks are nothing to worry about. But look at the number of deaths reported in the back, especially at the training camps. Something is not right."

Drew stared at her. "Do you suppose that they are trying to avoid panic? Keeping the news optimistic? We're practically ordered what to print these days. If it's negative about the war, we'll be jailed."

Elizabeth stood in agitation. "You're right. I'll bet it's an epidemic, and that this influenza is especially dangerous. I've already seen two patients die, Drew. Old Dr. Mason could do nothing for them."

"What can we do?"

"Well, it's already too late to keep it out of Plainville. But we can protect Doris. I've been exposed." She thought. "I know. I'll ask Vicky if Doris can stay with her and her children until the sickness is gone. Doris knows Vicky and she'll be all right there."

"Is it really necessary?" He'd miss seeing Doris every day and hearing her prattle.

"If it's a real epidemic, yes. The sooner, the better. I might expose you too. Perhaps you should stay at the newspaper office."

"Oh, no, my dear. I'm not going to hide away in the newspaper rooms. If there's nursing to be done, I can help. Maybe I should buy supplies in case we get too sick to go out."

"A good idea. I'll make a list. We'll start preparing right away, and take food over to Vicky. We'll gather nursing supplies for my patients too. Talk to the druggist about ordering more."

"Should we warn people?"

"Yes. You can take Doris over to Vicky as soon as I pack her things. Tell Vicky to keep the children at home until the influenza has run its course. Write an article for the *Gazette*. Tell people to stay away from public gatherings and to stay home if they get sick. Talk to the mayor and the council about closing school, shops, theater. I'll see Dr. Mason and McCall about getting volunteers to nurse the sick."

With a heavy heart Drew took the bundle of clothes and his small daughter's hand for her stay with Vicky McCall. He wondered how this epidemic affected the rest of the country.

◆ ◆ ◆

Rex Jenkins protested when Drew talked to him. "There's nothing in the Omaha papers about an epidemic."

"No, but deaths are increasing all over. Elizabeth has lost two patients from influenza right here in Plainville."

"As mayor, I don't dare go out on a limb and tell people to stay home on your say so."

"If you don't, you risk subjecting everybody in town to a dangerous disease."

"Look, Drew. I respect Elizabeth's opinion, but I have to take this to the city council."

"How long will that take?"

"We don't even meet for three days."

Disappointed, Drew hesitated. Then he decided. "Call a meeting today, Rex. This is important. Tell them it's my advice. As for me, I'm getting out an extra paper today to warn people, and we're putting Doris in Vicky's house where she won't be exposed."

Chapter Thirty-Seven

Both of the Spencer men were sick that morning. Hiram felt feverish, but decided to try to get through the day. Phil's face was flushed, but he made no complaint.

As the brothers went through drills, Phil suddenly collapsed on the field. Hiram called the drill instructor for help. By the time they got Phil to the camp hospital, Hiram could barely walk himself. The elderly nurse assigned beds for them in the crowded ward and walked away. She did not come to their bedside again all day.

They lay side by side on camp cots, feverish, head and limbs aching. They were in a huge building filled with hundreds of coughing, wheezing, vomiting soldiers. Some called out for help. Others were delirious.

Within a few hours, Hiram, sitting up on his cot, had watched several purplish-blue patients die right before his eyes. Because of the color, one man called out in panic that it was the Black Death, but another said that the doctors had denied that. It was influenza.

"Influenza doesn't kill people."

"Apparently, this variety does."

No doctors came to examine them. They heard that most doctors were sick or had died of the disease, and so had the nurses. A few old and middle-aged doctors and nurses kept working, but because of the huge number of patients, had little time to help them.

When Hiram spoke to Phil, he got no answer. Was he asleep? It would accomplish nothing to call for help. Others around him were getting no response when they did. He tried to get up to see if Phil was all right. But he was too weak to stand.

He heard men coming through the ward collecting the dead. The vacated beds were immediately filled with more patients. When the men with the death carts came to Phil's cot, they rolled him into a sheet and loaded him onto their cart, already crowded with bodies.

"No, no, he's not dead. He's my brother." Hiram, screaming, managed to stand and stagger over to Phil's cot, almost falling. The orderlies unrolled the sheet and allowed Hiram to see Phil. He felt for a pulse, checked for a breath, touched his skin for the warmth of life. It was no use. His brother was blue, quiet, and cold.

Stunned, he fell back onto his own cot as the orderlies hauled his dead brother away.

♦ ♦ ♦

Later, the doctor told Hiram that Phil had suffered from the more serious case of the disease. It affected his lungs. Hiram escaped with a milder form.

When he recovered somewhat, Hiram wrote a letter to Leah. The pen balked as he fought for the words to tell Leah that her husband and Pam's father had died a miserable death before even leaving the country. Tear smudges covered the first few drafts.

Only a year apart in age, the two brothers had been almost inseparable all their lives. Their parents had died when they were still in their teens, and their shared life on the road had brought them together as nothing else could.

Back with his company, Hiram joined training with the rest of his transport group. He and Phil were selected for transport because they had driven trucks now and then in Nebraska. In addition to the usual drilling, they practiced driving trucks in the dark around the base.

Those who did especially well in the practice, and had good eyes, such as Hiram, became corporals and did the driving. The others were made tailgate riders, some with the rank of private first class and the others as plain buck privates.

When their training was complete, the men filed into troop trains. They headed for the coast where they would board ships to carry them across the Atlantic to join the fighting in France or Russia. Around them, men of various nationalities spoke in several different languages.

Mike, a talkative soldier, figured they would be going to French seaports to drive supplies inland. "We'll probably never see the front," he said.

Others bragged that if they did, it would not bother them. They'd come to fight Germans and had practice with guns and bullets at home. The boys from Chicago and Texas were the biggest braggarts.

George thought they would be going to Russia, to help put down the Bolsheviks, and set up a democratic form of government.

Hiram wasn't the only grief-stricken man on the train. Many had lost friends to the influenza. Others had just recovered from the disease. Some brought the infection into the rail cars.

But the majority laughed with excitement. They burst into the songs of the day as the crowded train swept along: "Over There;" "Pack up Your Troubles in Your Own Kit Bag," "Smile, Smile, Smile;" "Madelon."

The train picked up additional soldiers along the way. At every stop for refueling and watering, men got out and mingled with workers and other civilians to escape the stuffy air in the cars. And they unintentionally left a dangerous disease.

At one stop, they all stood quietly as a funeral for an influenza victim passed on a nearby street.

Within a few hours, men on the train developed symptoms of influenza: They coughed, sweated with fever, bled from the nose and ears. A few collapsed. Others became delirious. The soldiers shrank from them.

Hiram believed he was immune to the disease since he had just recovered from it. He carried water to the sick soldiers and tried to help.

By the time the train reached the port of embarkation, one-quarter of the men were taken directly to the base hospital, quickly followed by hundreds more. A young officer, impressed by his new rank, told Hiram that around 10 percent of the sick died within a few days.

"Why were we put on these infected trains?" Hiram said in astonishment.

"Of course, it's only influenza."

"But it's obviously deadly and very infectious."

"Well, some of them could have died from other things."

"Young, healthy men?" Hiram raised his voice.

"Good lord, man, they're screaming for soldiers over there to fight the Germans."

"But they've just wasted hundreds, and all those who died in the camps too." What an unnecessary tragedy.

"We have to send men overseas." The officer became defensive. "General Pershing is calling for them."

Then he said in a reasonable voice, "I've heard, though, that some courageous official is delaying the next draft call because of the influenza at the training camps. At least we won't be infecting any more new recruits for a time."

"Why didn't we hear about the contagion before we went to the camps?" Hiram felt great resentment. Did his brother have to die?

"The influenza seems to have started in the camps. No one knew it was there. Anyway, the newspapers aren't publishing the worst of it because of the fear of panic."

Hiram wondered how the civilian population could help knowing about such a dreadful epidemic. Surely it must be swarming over the whole country by now.

At the dock, thousands of young men from around the nation were put onto the ship with Hiram. Seasickness hit some of them right away. They threw up all over the ship. Within forty-eight hours many became deathly ill from influenza. It had boarded the ship with them.

When they caught influenza, more men threw up. The sailors constantly swabbed the decks, so Hiram, George, and Mike slept there, wanting to avoid the smell of blood and vomit in the sleeping rooms. The stench became almost unbearable.

The sick bay became overwhelmed by sick soldiers and sailors, stacked one on top of the other in bunks, coughing, bleeding, delirious.

Nurses and doctors worked constantly tending the sick. Groans and cries echoed during the night. Pools of blood from the patients lay on the floor.

Finally, with all space taken in sick bay and in makeshift sick bays in additional rooms, the nurses began to lay the sick out on the deck, where the waves washed over them during storms.

As the orderlies collected bodies, and the burials began at sea, Hiram thought of his brother, buried in the ground, surely a better resting place than the frigid ocean.

Chapter Thirty-Eight

A member of a free society from the informal west, Hiram found it difficult to adjust to the regimentation and the rank system in the army. Officers slept in luxurious separate quarters, only six to a cabin, served by orderlies, who were enlisted men, often black men. It seemed to him that some of the officers treated the men with contempt.

As the soldiers recovered, they did calisthenics on deck and practiced drills for abandoning ship. In the event of a sinking, the survivors would have to depend on life jackets and rafts.

Food on board consisted of stew and yellow corn meal. But the meals were usually late. Once Hiram joined the line for breakfast and when he finished eating, it was time to line up again for the next meal.

The ship developed mechanical problems. It dropped out of the convoy and they were all alone on the ocean. The men worried about the possibility of being attacked by German submarines, but the ship was soon repaired, and the ship joined the convoy, zigging and zagging to avoid becoming a target for U-boats.

Meanwhile, even those who escaped influenza grumbled in the steerage quarters in the hold of the ship.

"If the ship goes down, what chance will we have of getting out of here," Mike said. "They treat us like steer being led to slaughter."

"Meat for the guns," said another man. "Get ready for it."

When they finally arrived in France, ambulances collected the soldiers who were too sick to walk. The rest were marched toward camp. True to army custom, they were not told where they were going.

Children accompanied them, laughing and shouting greetings. Hiram chuckled when one soldier remarked, "even the kids here speak French."

None of them knew where the front was, but they were all reluctant to show their ignorance in front of the others. As they left the town and dusk fell, they feared the Germans would sweep out of the hills and machine-gun them as they marched. They did not carry rifles.

At the camp, they looked forward to a good night's sleep on solid ground in clean-smelling air. Instead, they were set to work moving goods in large bags: flour, sugar, rice. They toiled all night. In the morning, they were fed bread and oatmeal. Finally, they were allowed to rest.

Within a few days, they were loaded into railway box cars, forty to a car. That worked all right during the day, but at night, they struggled to find room to stretch out. Hiram woke up in the morning with a booted foot in front of his eyes, and an arm thrown over his legs.

The food stored in the car for their meals was canned tomatoes and canned beans, a menu they would see often. The train chugged along slowly for several days. Hiram assumed the delay was a result of heavy wartime rail traffic.

Along the way, they were offered coffee by bright young Red Cross women at a railway station, a very welcome treat. The workers seemed friendly and perky. But one looked tired.

After all the soldiers were served, Hiram spoke to her. "Are you all right?"

She looked at him in surprise. "I'm just a little tired. I had dance duty last night at the canteen. How good of you to ask."

"Dance Duty?"

"Yes. I danced with servicemen for seven hours straight. We're supposed to be friendly and fair to all the men. I like dancing, but...." She rolled her eyes.

Hiram shook his head. "I'm sorry."

Among all the tragedies of the war, he found it a shame that such a pleasant activity as dancing had become a grueling chore for the young woman.

◆ ◆ ◆

When they detrained, they first spent the night in pup tents in a forest. Shells passed overhead, though they were not under attack.

Hiram prayed to live. He thought of his children. He missed holding them and feeling their soft chubby little bodies against his. He wrote to Julia every few days and mourned their separation. He longed to see his brown-haired wife bustling about the hotel, winking at him if she caught his eye while he worked on maintenance and improvements.

No reason was given for their stay in the forest. Hiram figured no one knew what to do with them at that time. Eventually they were taken to a crude truck park with a number of small shacks containing several bunks.

When the men discussed the war that had been fought for four years, with little change in the French front line, Hiram joked, with only a little irony, "I wonder where the front line will be in 1950."

The first convoy soon went out with shells for battles. Mike, something of a braggart, claimed they had been under fire, but others said not. Hiram, miserable and despondent over Phil's death, depressed by conditions in the army, looked forward to his turn in the convoy as a welcome change, something to get his mind off the filthy absurdity with which they lived.

Chapter Thirty-Nine

Alex wrote to Diane at the Red Cross hospital about his service as a pilot. It gave him the excitement he craved. "I intend to fight with my squadron and survive this great adventure," he wrote.

When Scott's letter arrived, Diane tore it open at once.

>Dear lovely Diane,
>
>Thank you for allowing me to write to you. Please write back. It will brighten my days.
>
>I'm sure your work is as difficult as ours is. We men expected to serve in this war either by choice or by conscription. But since you volunteered for it, you should be doubly appreciated.
>
>I won't tell you a lot about the fighting. Nursing the troops has given you some idea of the horror of this war.
>
>I recall when I met you at the Independence Day Celebration in Plainville. You wore a pink dress which complimented your fine coloring and figure. I was intrigued even then.
>
>At your oldest sister's wedding, I think I fell in love with the pretty young woman you had become. I wanted to talk to you and apologize for my rudeness in San Francisco when we first saw you. In the end, I admired the way you rescued a wagon load of supplies from a thief by jumping into the wagon bed and attacking the driver.
>
>Later, I thought you and Matthew were courting. I never had a chance to tell you how much I regretted my words. By now, I hope you have forgiven me all my sins

against you. Our misunderstandings seem petty compared to this war. If I get a chance, may I visit you at your hospital? Perhaps we could take a walk.

Your friend and admirer,
Scott Morris

Diane read the letter with something like amazement. Who could have known? She had seen him at Julia's wedding, but he had seemed aloof, distant. He was correct that she often paired with Matthew.

"An interesting letter?" Maxine said, as she put down her news from her family.

"An old friend." Diane folded the letter and stuck it in her pocket to read again later. Suddenly, she definitely thought of him as an old friend, despite their differences in the past.

"Oh," Maxine said, "I see. I believe you're blushing."

"I've bad news from home," Bridget said, with a worried expression. "Two more of my brothers are in the fighting."

"I'm sorry," Diane said. "How long can it go on? How many men do they need?"

"At least the immigrants can become American citizens by joining up," Maxine told her. "They will like that--no paperwork, no waiting, just instant citizenship."

Diane nodded. "Now we'll all be Americans together."

Just then, their head nurse, Bonnie Grell, told Bridget, with some satisfaction, that she was to report immediately to the chief nurse. Bridget looked at the others with apprehension. Was it about Lewis? Appalled, the nurses watched her hurry off to the main floor office.

"I'll bet Bonnie told the chief nurse about Lewis and Bridget," Maxine said. "Why on earth did we have to arrive in the same place as her? That little witch always panders to higher-ups."

"Why does she do it?" Diane said.

"She's still mad that Maxine doesn't get her invited to parties in Paris," Hazel said.

"My aunt doesn't invite her because I can't stand her," Maxine said.

Nurses working on the main floor passed the word to nurses working on other floors that loud voices were coming from the chief's office. Alarmed by their thoughts, they carried on their work, waiting for news. What punishment would Bridget face if she'd been observed with an enlisted man?

Chapter Forty

Finally, Bridget reappeared on the ward, her eyes red and swollen. "Lewis is being sent to another hospital. I'm on probation for a time, it seems. Because they're so short of nurses, I'm allowed to stay if I 'behave myself,'" she said bitterly.

Diane put her arms around her. "I'm so glad you're not leaving us. You'll still be able to write to him."

"Yes, I can write to him. Now he and I will have to endure separation, along with thousands of others who have had to endure it in this miserable war."

"I'll miss him," Hazel said with a wistful look. "He was such a good, happy worker."

♦ ♦ ♦

Diane wrote to Scott at the first opportunity:

> Dear Scott,
> Your letter surprised me. I thought of you as a cold person. I am glad to discover that this is not true. I would like to be your friend.
> You are correct that being near this war is depressing because of the sight of so many dead and injured men, not diseased or accident victims, but deliberately maimed by their fellow man. It is a mystery that such things could happen in this modern day and age.
> Getting supplies is difficult. Sometimes we have barely enough food to feed the patients. We carry water from

a nearby creek to do laundry and bathe the troops, though we also have orderlies--French civilians, and other Red Cross volunteers--to help.

I hungered for news about Alex. He is well, and I thank you again for your help in locating my brother.

If you are in this area, I would be happy to see you, and take a walk if supervisor will allow it.

Your friend,
Diane Hoffman

Scott visited Diane again. As they sat in the anteroom, she thanked him once more for getting in touch with her brother.

"I know you must have gone to some trouble. It was very thoughtful of you."

He shrugged. "I was glad to help. He seems pleased to be flying. What do you hear from Plainville?"

"I'm worried about my relatives. Aunt Elizabeth writes that many people have influenza and are quite sick with it."

"It's hit the army too. Hundreds are unable to report because of the illness. It's a new, stronger strain, some say."

"As if we didn't have enough tragedy at this time."

He wanted to get the visit on a lighter note. "It's a beautiful day. Can you take a walk through the woods at the edge of town?"

"Yes, I have permission. It would be good to get away. Let me get my wrap, just in case."

When she returned, she wore a dark gray cape over her shoulders and had removed her nurse's cap for a straw hat with a brim. He took her arm and guided her toward the cool trees. The scent of summer flowers filled the warm air, but in the woods, it was cool and smelled of lush green growth, slightly musty.

"You're very pretty in that uniform," he said, smiling down at her.

Smiling back, she said, "I'll bet you say that to all the girls."

"No, only the pretty ones."

She laughed, seeming to relax a little. "You always were exacting."

"And you were always pretty. I've admired and loved you for some time. See how well we know each other?"

She gave him a tentative smile as she looked up at him. "You're always ready with an answer, aren't you?"

He found a smooth spot under a tree and sat down, gently pulling her down beside him.

She sighed. "This peaceful scene is certainly a contrast to all the battles raging in the land. When will the war ever stop. It feels as though I've been here for years. The only reason I'm with you today is because there's a lull in the fighting on the nearest front."

"There's talk of an armistice, but it's probably just that--talk."

"How much longer can it possibly go on? Millions slaughtered around the world, farms and land destroyed...."

He took her hand. "What will you do when it's over?"

"Go back to Plainville. I'll probably do private nursing. There's speculation about building veterans' hospitals for all the wounded. That's something to think about. How about you?"

"Home to Nebraska, of course, but I'm planning my own newspaper somewhere. I've been with Vince long enough. I need to strike out on my own."

"I'm sure you'll be a success. You're so energetic and clever."

Her words pleased him. She was not one to flatter needlessly. "I've got a question for you. Let's see if you have the correct answer." He took a deep breath. "Will you marry me?"

She said nothing.

He laughed, slightly nervous. "It's not a difficult question. A simple yes will do."

"Oh, Scott, I'd love to marry you. You do me a great honor. But I'll probably always want to nurse. I've trained for it so long and hard. And I've admired Aunt Elizabeth."

Relieved, he said, "And I'll probably always want to be a journalist. Where's the problem?"

"We don't actually know each other--"

"We've known each other since before the San Francisco earthquake. We know what we've been doing since then. You know my brother's family and my sister, and I know most of your family. We have mutual friends. Why, you're half the reason I've kept coming to Plainville all these years."

He gave her no opportunity to respond, but put his arms about her small waist and kissed her, long, energetically, possessively. He pressed against her, and explored her lips, her mouth.

At last, with reluctance, he broke away. "I'll be very happy when we're married. I thought I might get off for a couple of days at a time, and we could manage it then. Would you be able to take release time?"

Things were moving faster than she could imagine. "It might be allowed under the circumstances," she said, tentatively.

"I've saved money to buy a newspaper of my own. Vince helped raise me and train me. But he doesn't need me anymore. Would you be willing to leave Plainville?"

"Yes, if necessary. But I own a house in Plainville," she said, getting into the spirit of his plans. "Uncle Robert left it to me. We could live there."

"That's very enticing, and I've always liked the lovely little town, but Drew Robinson already puts out an exceptional paper in Plainville." Scott took a lock of her hair and twirled it around his finger.

"I have to get back," he said with regret, touching her cheek. "I'll write to you and let you know how things are going. God, I'll miss you. I'd like to be with you forever."

"I feel the same way," she said, breathless.

With throbbing passion, he kissed her again in the woods before they headed back. A long wait would be intolerable.

Chapter Forty-One

Diane decided not to tell her friends at the hospital about her engagement yet. She had a hard time even believing it. She reeled to discover that Scott could be affectionate and tolerant. She had always thought him a fine specimen of the male sex, but as long as she considered him arrogant and judgmental, that counted for little. If he had been bow-legged and ugly, she could have at least pitied him and overlooked the faults she saw.

It felt like a dream. A beautiful Adonis choosing *her*. A man with a muscular, athletic body, beautiful sandy hair, a fine appearance with knowing, intelligent, green eyes, asking for her hand. A man with a respectable profession and progressive ideas.

She had waited forever for love such as this. She felt needed and treasured as she hadn't felt since her mother died.

She had thought she would never marry. After all, she was twenty-six years old, considered a spinster by most of society. She had imagined herself following in Aunt Elizabeth's footsteps, remaining unmarried into her thirties and beyond, and maybe never marrying. With four siblings, she too would have nephews and nieces to love. Still, Elizabeth had married eventually. Why not her? The love she and Scott felt almost made up for her lack of it as a teenager in Uncle Robert's house.

At dinner that evening, Maxine, who had met Scott at her aunt's house in Paris, said to the other nurses. "Diane got a visitor today. Scott's extremely personable." She turned toward Diane. "Is he the friend who's been writing to you?"

Diane evaded. "Yes, the men like to get letters in combat."

Bridget raised her eyebrows. "So, he visited you just to thank you for the letters?"

"Well, yes. I believe things are heating up for our men in the fighting. They've been in more skirmishes lately, and they're arriving by the thousands. We're certainly getting more American patients."

Hazel groaned. "No more rushes, please. Look at my hands. They're completely ruined."

"I have some good news," Diane told them. "In June, women over thirty in Great Britain won the right to vote."

"Over thirty? Well, hallelujah," Hazel scoffed. "The men can vote at twenty-one. Are men smarter than women at twenty-one? Just the opposite, I'd say."

"Well, it's better than nothing," Diane said. "Maybe women in America will gain the vote soon."

Maxine changed the subject. "I met some airmen at my aunt's Paris house last week. They're into battle in the air now, too."

"My brother trained as a pilot," Diane told them, in an offhand manner.

Surprised, Maxine said, "I remember now. What's his name?"

"Alex."

"Alex Hoffman. Of course. It was your brother. How amazing."

"It's a small world," Bridget said, as they all wondered at the coincidence.

"Alex is very handsome. I should have recognized that dark brown hair and those blue eyes," Maxine said.

"I'm glad you find him so agreeable," Diane said, with a broad smile.

"He's coming to see me when he gets a chance." Her eyes glowed with pleasure. "He mentioned Eddie Rickenbacker, an ace pilot. To become an ace, a pilot has to shoot down a number of planes, that is make kills," Maxine told the nurses who were following the discussion.

"President Teddy Roosevelt's son, poor Quentin Roosevelt, was shot down in July and killed. I've heard some reports that about half of the pilots don't make it. The odds of survival are lower than for the doughboys in the trenches."

Diane winced.

"Oh, I'm sorry I mentioned it," Maxine said.

Within a few days, Maxine and Alex arranged to meet at her aunt's house in Paris for a day of sightseeing. "He's traded flights with a fellow officer," Maxine told the nurses. "I can hardly wait to see him."

Chapter Forty-Two

In American communities, influenza hit the civilian population worse than it hit the servicemen. Most of the citizens in Plainville fell ill, even though the mayor had put the town in quarantine. They had been issued face masks, but those did not stop the epidemic.

So many people caught influenza that John Hoffman had no blacksmith business. He stayed home to help nurse the sick in his family. Beautiful Barbara, living at the house, contacted the influenza. When Lila and Frank and their children came down with it, Pamela sent John with a team of horses and a wagon to collect them so she could nurse them with the other sick children and grandchildren. She bustled about the house, her stout figure seemingly resistant to disease.

Leah and the new baby also came for care. Little Pam remained well. John rocked her and cared for his granddaughter until it was time to eat. Then he carried her upstairs to be nursed by her bedridden mother. Strangely, neither he nor Pamela contacted the disease. It usually attacked the young. Middle-aged adults appeared to be immune.

As a result of Elizabeth's precautions, Vicky McCall, her children and Doris escaped the influenza. By telephone, Elizabeth urged Vicky to stay at home and avoid social contact. Drew delivered food and supplies to Vicky's house and left them on the porch.

At the hotel, Julia, along with her children, Henry, Harvey, and Mary, escaped with light cases of the influenza. Amy and her children in the country avoided town and stayed well at the farm.

Elizabeth could not avoid the sick. From house to house she went, from dawn until dusk, nursing and fixing meals. In some houses the entire family lay in bed, unable to obtain food. Mr. McCall had posted bulletins printed by Drew, asking for the healthy to assist in such cases, but few volunteers showed up. They feared catching the disease. Several had died already. Others were nursing relatives.

Hannah Baker from the hotel, Mrs. McCall, Mrs. Millie Smith, and the former Miss Blue escaped the influenza and gave Elizabeth what help they could.

When the newsboys fell ill, Drew delivered the newspapers. If they were not picked up, he alerted Dr. Mason and Elizabeth. It meant someone was sick or dead inside.

Shop owners closed their doors. Classes were cancelled. Only the most courageous, with masks covering their faces, attended church services. The streets were empty. A fifty-year-old druggist kept the drug store open where people picked up what medications were said to help-- until he ran out of supplies.

Vicky received word that her mother had died from the disease. Sonia Jones had told a landlady about her daughter in Plainville, and the woman sent Sonia's few possessions to Vicky along with her remaining money. Her husband, Cal Jones, had died earlier of food poisoning, the landlady wrote.

Vicky McCall wept when she heard about Sonia's death. She had not missed her mother in a long time, but in the back of her mind, she had expected to see Sonia again. Now that would never be, and she felt the loss.

And in Plainville more people died.

♦ ♦ ♦

In France, Alex visited Maxine and Diane at the Red Cross hospital. The minute she saw him, Diane sensed that something bothered him. "What is it?" She asked him in the anteroom.

"Oh, girls," he sobbed. "Something terrible has happened."

Maxine took his hand. "Tell us."

"The pilot who took my place when we visited Paris, his plane crashed. He and the gunner were killed." His voice broke. "They were such nice fellows, both gone. It should have been me."

Diane took his other hand. "Alex, it is not your fault. You must not think that."

He nodded, his eyes moist. "I feel so guilty."

"Take a walk with Maxine. Get away for a time. Maybe you'll feel better." Diane led them to the door. "I'll tell them you're gone, Maxine."

Back on the hospital floor, Diane wondered how Alex or anyone ever got over such dreadful deaths.

Chapter Forty-Three

When Captain Scott Morris's soldiers joined the French, they were equipped with everything French except for their actual uniforms. The Americans were disappointed with the rifles, not nearly as good as the American Springfields.

Though somewhat skeptical about the chocolate soldiers, the French officers tolerated them. The troops, however, were happy to share their bread, wine, mud, and lice with the colored troops at their side. The French had fielded colored troops from their colonies in Africa--Senegalese and Sudanese warriors, much feared by the Germans for their fierceness.

In the spring, Scott Morris's regiment, including the members of the band, were moved up into the trenches. To get to the front they trudged through mud several feet deep. Each doughboy carried a canteen full of water each day for drinking and washing. Many of the men used coffee for shaving both because it was hot and because it was more abundant than plain water.

Scott was surprised to find the trenches as deep and elaborate as they were.

Slits dug into the ground, six feet deep and wide enough for two men to pass, the trenches were broken up by niches for rifles and machine gun nests and by steps leading to ground level. Along the front of the line, sandbags reinforced the trenches.

Behind the front line, additional trenches provided service areas wide enough to accommodate trucks bringing in supplies and ambulances carrying off wounded soldiers.

One French captain had a dugout deep underground with stairs leading to it. Inside, it looked like a neat little suite.

Scott was invited for a meal. Amazed, he watched the host officers linger over fine wine, rich sauces, delicious dinners cooked by French chefs. Even the enlisted men were issued a portion of wine each day. This didn't work with the doughboys. As they were not used to wine, they were issued extra sweets instead. Otherwise, they enjoyed well-cooked food by superb chefs.

The space between the opposing front lines was called 'no man's land.' Barbed wire and land mines discouraged casual fraternization. But each side sometimes sent out patrols at night to capture prisoners who might have vital information. When Americans later went along on patrols, they wore French uniforms so as not to alert the Germans to the presence of doughboys.

Some of the men from the colored regiment hailed from Puerto Rico. Scott remarked to fellow officers, "If Fritz captures one of our boys from Puerto Rico wearing a French uniform, who tells them in Spanish that he's an American soldier in a New York National Guard regiment, German Intelligence will have a devil of a time trying to figure it all out."

In May, after training in trench warfare with the French, the colored regiment was sent into action in Champaign where they were responsible for holding an entire sector without any help from the French. A long section of the line had been abandoned by French troops that had mutinied a few months earlier.

Only tree stumps remained over the leveled land, but, to the amazement of Scott and the men, nightingales sang among tree stumps.

The colonel of the regiment got the editor of a New York newspaper to feature the unusual colored regiment. People wanted President Wilson to know that black soldiers also were fighting for democracy. They hoped he would condemn the lynching of blacks going on in his own country.

Soon, reporters had a bona fide black hero to present to the country; a young private almost single-handedly repelled a raiding party of twenty-four Germans and was awarded the French Croix de Guerre. The report of the exploit was written up in several papers.

President Wilson, urged to speak out against the lynchings, finally did so in July, pleasing Scott and the rest of the regiment.

As the fighting continued, a lieutenant in Scott's company carefully checked every German prisoner and dead German, looking for a cousin. He would peer into their faces and remark to the others: "This one looks a lot like Uncle Fritz." "Could this one be my cousin? Do we look alike?" At night he would lament having to kill men who might be relatives.

Scott tried to imagine his distress--forced to fight his own people.

Their regiment was always with the French Fourth Army, even when they were part of the Second Battle of the Marne in the middle of the summer, when Paris was threatened for the second time.

The first scare happened in September of 1914, before America got into the conflict. French forces were greatly outnumbered at the front, some twenty-three miles east of Paris. Not enough trains or trucks were available to carry reinforcements, newly arrived in Paris from African colonies. As a remedy, General Gallieni had commandeered every taxi in Paris. At Invalides Square, each taxi loaded five soldiers and their equipment, and headed for the front. They tooled north through cheering crowds. The miracle of the Marne saved Paris.

This time, there were no taxis filled with soldiers to come to the rescue. Those in the field would do it themselves.

In preparation for the Allied defense of Paris, the roads were choked with troops, caissons of ammunition and supplies. French and American troops were massed, and tanks lumbered along the roads to the front.

While the French Fourth Army waited to hear of a German attack, nightly shelling harassed the boys from Gotham. Meanwhile, additional German raids across no man's land brought hero status to a few more men and more French awards.

During this lull, Scott managed to visit Diane. When she heard that he waited for her, she rushed to the anteroom of the hospital. They flew into each other's arms.

"I've been so worried," she said. "What's going on?"

"We're here to protect Paris. The Germans have moved their front closer to the city. We expect a German attack at any time."

"Oh, Scott." Her voice faltered.

"They likely won't get this far south. Besides, we intend to drive them back."

"I'm worried about you."

He delivered other news to divert her from her worries. "General Henry Gouraud has ordered the regimental band to perform at headquarters of the French Fourth Army on America's Independence Day. Could you get away for it, Diane?"

"I don't know. Won't the trains be crowded?"

"Probably. They'll be moving in supplies and troops. It's not far from here. Maybe you could find another way. I'll be going. It would cheer me to see you, and I'm sure you would enjoy it. The General planned the celebration to be held July Fourth for the benefit of the American troops under his command in the Fourth Army. It's to be in the city park."

"I'll see what I can do."

"Let's talk about life after the war. Have you thought about our wedding?" They sat down in chairs side by side.

He wondered if it was safe to marry while the war was on. Would it be fair to her? What if he were crippled? Maybe the war would be over before long. He could always hope.

"Our wedding? Are we getting married?" She teased with a smile.

"You vixen. You know we are. It grieves me that it can't happen right away. This moment. So we could lie in each other's arms."

"What a glorious thought."

"More than glorious. I think about it a lot." He caressed her face and shoulders.

For some time, they teased and talked and tarried, but Scott had to leave early. They finally parted with reluctance.

♦ ♦ ♦

When Diane mentioned the performance to the nurses, Maxine suggested that she rent or borrow a bicycle. "If you leave at dawn you can catch the performance."

"My God," Hazel turned from making up a bed. "Why do you want to go up there? I've heard the Germans might invade Paris at any time. Don't count on me going with you."

"Oh, you're going to miss her," Maxine said, so low that only Diane could hear. "I'd love to see that band again, but I'm on duty."

The head floor nurse, more lenient than most, expecting a rush at the hospital any day, felt nurses should get away while they could. She gave Diane her blessing.

Diane notified Scott that she would be coming. On the 4th of July, she left while it was still dark. She watched the pink morning light cover the countryside, gradually turning it green and bright. Birds called from the trees as she pedaled north. Sleepy little villages with orange-roofed houses stood around single church steeples.

Picturesque farm houses stood along the road. The residents were engaged in their morning chores, heading out to milk the cow and feed the pigs and chickens. How ironic that hundreds, perhaps thousands, of men would soon be engaged in a vicious battle in order to control a few miles of such peaceful territory.

Scott, in a pressed uniform, waited for her outside headquarters, smelling of soap on freshly washed skin, and polished boots. For the first time, she noticed his hungry gaze traveling over her. He reached for her hand, his eyes bright, and he escorted her to seats he had secured for them.

"You're going to love it," he said, exhibiting his pride in the regimental band. "I'm glad you could come. Was it a tiring ride?"

"No, no. Very beautiful. I enjoyed it. It's always a thrill to get away from the hospital and to see you."

He put his arm around her shoulders, smoothed her hair, took her hand, invaded her space. Comforted to be sitting beside him, basking in his attention, she stole glances at his strong features during the performance. Just being with Scott was worth the trip.

Five hundred French and American personnel, including Red Cross nurses, doctors, and ambulance drivers cheered the lively music. The French people, worn with sorrow and strain from four years of fighting, forgot their trials for a time.

General Gouraud, a popular officer who was left with a limp and only one arm as a result of previous battles, made a speech vowing his army, French and American, "would not fail in its duty to protect Paris." The General then asked to hear the drum major sing "Joan of Arc." He listened attentively, his face pensive.

After the celebration, Scott borrowed a car to drive Diane and the bicycle back to her hospital. He stopped for a time so that he and Diane could admire the silver summer moon. Scott pressed against her as her heart throbbed. His kiss left her lips burning.

At last he moved away. "I'll be thrilled when we can be together." He started the car again, knowing she was expected back.

On the way he talked about his men and some of their problems. He told her that though the black regimental band had entertained several weeks in the spring at a resort for resting doughboys near the Swiss Alps, none of them would ever be allowed to use the facilities. The army was strictly segregated.

◆ ◆ ◆

The Germans tried to cross the Marne and began an artillery barrage at midnight on July 14th all along the fifty-mile Allied front. Their fifth offensive of 1918, it would be their last. After days of fierce fighting over three weeks, the Germans lost all the gains they had made between May 27 and July 15.

In Scott's regiment, more blacks earned the Croix de Guerre, but the regiment suffered several casualties.

Afterward, Scott's company attacked several small towns. They dealt with constant anxiety and the threat of death from shells. Shell and shrapnel wounds usually meant death from infections.

In addition, they suffered injuries from grenades and poison gas. At the end of such battles, when Scott reported to the major, the man broke down into tears at the huge number of casualties.

They found German corpses strewn all over the fields, flies buzzing around their bloated bodies in the heat. Favorite souvenirs were German spiked helmets and belt buckles with their raised inscription--"Got Mit Uns" (God with Us). The soldiers were warned not to rifle the bodies, as the Boche mined their own dead in order to blow up souvenir hunters.

One evening, the firing lasted late into the night. As the sun came up they looked with incomprehension at hundreds of their fellow soldiers dead a few feet in front of them. Beyond the corpses lay dead German soldiers. As was the custom, the firing slacked off, aimed high, while each side ventured into no man's land. They needed to collect their dead and bring them back for burial.

On a beautiful, warm evening, Scott went into a field alone. *How long can it last, this constant butchering? Can't we just live in this lovely world without killing each other? Surely this war is a ghastly mistake.* Tears filled his eyes. But he quickly recovered. He had responsibilities, a job to do. He mustn't think of the larger picture. There was nothing he could do but help to end it soon.

In the following days, the officers heard of a huge planned Allied offensive against the Hindenburg Line.

General Ferdinand Foch, supreme commander of the Allied armies, planned an offensive all along the front for September. Twelve allied armies and a total of six million troops would attack at once.

The drive on the St. Mihiel salient on September 12th, was to be the first huge American-directed offensive of the war, a preliminary to the Meuse-Argonne battle on September 26th. General Pershing, having resisted all attempts by the British and the French to use doughboys to replace casualties in their armies, agreed to send his American army to the Meuse-Argonne a few days later, over sixty miles north.

Lieutenant Colonel George C. Marshall, in charge of operations for the American First Army, was ordered to draw up an operation plan for the Argonne assault. Aghast, Marshall nevertheless prepared a plan overnight for moving the troops in limited time that met with Pershing's approval.

As usual, Scott's regiment fought in the French Fourth Army, but they were next to Americans in the Expeditionary Force.

Tension filled the air. As Scott's troops marched in the dark on September 12th, they heard the big barrage starting. The artillery made a constant clatter and roar. They figured General Pershing had every cannon in France aimed at the Germans in the St. Mihiel salient. Doughboys for miles around could hear it.

The Germans, caught by surprise, faced two new tools of warfare--tanks and combat planes. The tanks rolled alongside the infantry, crashing into machine gun nests and destroying barbed wire and barricades erected by the Germans over their four-year occupation of the salient.

Thirty-two-year-old Lieutenant Colonel George S. Patton, commanding a brigade of light tanks, reportedly said, "American tanks do not surrender as long as one tank is able to go forward."

Scott mused that nobody mentioned what the tank crews had to say.

Hundreds of planes saw action in the skies in the first battle the American army fought under its own flag. The planes machine-gunned the opposing troops and signaled enemy positions for the American artillery.

Scott feared he would have to tell Diane about her brother's death in a downed plane. Right then, though, he battled to avoid his own death.

During the engagement, Scott's company mainly just held their position and went on patrols. One of his boys, a southerner named Joey, still struggled to hit a target.

The drive was surprisingly easy as the Germans were pulling back anyway. From the skies, Eddie Rickenbacker reported seeing them fleeing along the road. He swooped down to fire bullets over the leading horse teams.

In a few days, Scott and his men marched north at night toward the Meuse-Argonne. For the doughboys, it was the biggest battle of the war, something never seen in the world before, a vast horror.

The nurses dealt with terrible fears. Diane worried about Scott. Bridget's brother and Maxine's cousin, William, both served in the First Army and the women worried constantly about all three of them.

Everybody feared for Alex, flying planes above the battles and on patrols and reconnaissance.

Chapter Forty-Four

Only three roads led into the Meuse-Argonne area of assault. In the move to the front for the final Allied offensive a jumble of tanks, rolling kitchens, water wagons, ambulances, tanks, cannon, and ammunition containers filled the center of the roads, as rain and mud impeded their progress. Thousands of horses died along the way.

Scott examined the colored troops preparing in the trenches. Though they had often been in combat and were kept in ignorance of their destination, this time the doughboys knew they would be taking part in an offensive to break the Hindenburg Line. Just the name of the German line was enough to cause awed contemplation.

The plans called for the Yanks, with the French forces nearby, to initiate an attack on both flanks of the Argonne Forest and also to smash right through the middle of the 10-mile wooded area. The British, Belgian, Australian, and other units further north would also attack against the Hindenburg Line.

Scott's men left their packs behind to make their advance easier. They'd been issued extra rounds of ammunition, water, and enough rations to carry them through the following day: sardines, hard bread, and chocolate. They had also been issued spades for digging. With that, their bayonets, and grenades, they were ready to charge.

The area to be attacked was a stretch of low rolling hills, ravines, and dense woods, broken by well-defended trench lines and barbed wire. Crosses marked the graves of those who had failed to break the Hindenburg Line in the days preceding.

Their task was to take a hill and a village, both of them holding hidden machine gun nests, filled with Germans recognized as the toughest-minded troops of any army. At 5:30 A.M., machine guns blared against the Germans, an ear-splitting noise.

Next, Scott gave the command and the troops moved out at a fast walk. Twenty-five yards past the jump-off chalk line, they encountered the first German outposts. Bullets flew in both directions. Every few seconds a soldier crumpled, but the others kept going.

The mop-up company jumped off right behind them. They were to kill or capture any stragglers left behind in trenches or shell holes who would rise up and shoot the first advance in the back.

At one point, Scott and several of his men became pinned down by a machine gun. Shielded by a small rise, they were unable to move. If they advanced, all of them would be shot. They seemed doomed to miss the battle entirely, and they were badly needed.

Scott knew the German machine gunners were often the last to retreat since they had to cover everyone else. It was almost a suicidal position. If they could get past the nests, they could move ahead.

Something had to be done. Scott veered off to one side of the assault and, with his head down, squirmed on his arms and knees as bullets rained around him. He reached a small forested area and dashed though. He dropped down on his hands and knees again to cross an open area. He was then able to crawl up behind the machine gun and shoot the two men he found.

Later, Scott and others in his company became pinned down again by a machine gun. For an hour they were unable to move, enduring the whine of the shells and the stuttering of the machine guns. Their men could see them, but were unable to help. To everyone's surprise, Joey, a notoriously poor shot, ridiculed by the others, circled around on his stomach, came up behind the Germans and shot the three in the machine gun nest.

Joey grinned broadly at Scott as he joined the advance. "I done what you done. I'm a soldier now, ain't I, Captain?"

Scott couldn't help laughing. "You sure are, Joey."

Despite the personal danger, some men risked storming machine guns head-on to save their comrades. The wounded were carried off by stretcher-bearers, but the battle raged into the night, and the fighting lasted for days.

A few men deserted. Scott and some of his troops came upon a group of doughboys from the AEF sitting around a fire. They stood up and asked if Scott knew where their unit was. Giving them the benefit of the doubt, he dispatched a couple of his men to help them find their way.

Rumors flew about an armistice, about the Germans so affected by the British blockade that their soldiers ate bread made of grass. Those taken prisoner appeared malnourished. Once, slightly ahead of his men, Scott came upon a lone German soldier, a boy of about fifteen or sixteen. Each raised his gun to shoot.

Chapter Forty-Five

As Scott thought about the armistice coming soon, he found it impossible to shoot the young German in front of him. The boy also lowered his gun. He turned tail and scrambled off. Relieved, Scott hoped the child would grow old and tell the story of his confrontation with a Yank.

Scott's company, suffering heavy losses, was not relieved until early October and it took more days of ferocious combat before the Hindenburg Line was broken and nearby areas secured. The final push was led by Douglas MacArthur. Leading the Rainbow Division, so-called because the men came from several different states, McArthur stormed the last German stronghold. But fighting persisted in the Argonne until the day of the Armistice.

Scott was unable to get away to see Diane at all through September and October. He wrote hasty notes and cursed the conflict that kept him from seeing her. The days were filled with mud and blood and horror and terror.

In smaller skirmishes, they were a mere hundred yards or so away from the Germans. One night a German kept yelling, "Gott mit Uns, Gott mit Uns." Finally one of the boys yelled back, "We've got mittens too, you silly bastard. Shut up."

Eventually, they were sent to a quiet sector, but even there the Germans had a nasty habit of frequently sending over shells whenever they knew an American outfit was moving in. Injured in the leg, Scott was carted off to a hospital. But by then he and many of his men came down with influenza as well.

♦ ♦ ♦

In the transport service, Hiram Spencer drove Pierce Arrow or Packard trucks in convoys as German planes sporadically dropped bombs nearby. Cannon sometimes fired near them.

Cranked by hand, the trucks generally hauled ammunition to batteries of 75-millimeter field guns at the front. The famous rapid-firing French 75's gobbled up ammunition at a rate far greater than any other cannon. They were said to be able to fire thirty shells a minute.

On return trips, the unit sometimes picked up wounded at a dressing station and transported them to a field hospital. Because it was an extremely rough ride, they usually took only the lightly wounded. In addition, the cab was open and there was no heat for the injured.

Their food did not improve much. They often went hours without food or drink. One doughboy groused, "I suppose those Heinies in their U-boats sunk all the supply ships."

Another said, "Whose rump do we have to kiss to get some decent food?" Though they were behind the lines, conditions at the transportation base were crude.

An officer came by and told them to wash up. The troops watched the officer walk away. Then a private spoke up. "What's he talking about? We washed up last week."

Hot water was hard to get, so they sometimes bathed in a nearby creek to rid themselves of body lice.

Now and then they observed the delousing unit on its way to the front. It consisted of two large cylinders that were riveted to the chassis of steam-driven trucks. Fifteen minutes under steam pressure was enough to kill both lice and their nits from the clothing fed into the cylinders. These huge iron-wheeled machines traveled at a maximum of four miles an hour, and furnished sleeping quarters inside the cylinders for the men in the delousing unit.

"Those fellows must have the most sanitary sleeping quarters of any troops at the front," Hiram said. "I'd trade places with them any day."

Carol Albrecht Dare

◆ ◆ ◆

At the Meuse-Argonne front on September 25th, the transport trucks were unloaded in the early evening. Hiram received word that the trucks would have to remain where they were, perhaps for hours. They surmised the road was crowded with troop caissons and infantry marching forward. It looked as though a massive offensive was about to begin.

They were right. They waited. They paced beside their trucks. The hours dragged. Hiram chatted with Captain Harry Truman who commanded an artillery battery. Suddenly, in the dark morning, cannons burst all around them. The field exploded into flames and furious noise.

Hiram cringed to imagine the damage the cannon were doing, mangling human bodies and killing thousands. Though Hiram and his transport companions were in little danger, they were awed and horrified by the destructiveness of the attack.

Many hours later, when the traffic jam had cleared, the truck convoy started back to base. When they stopped along the way to pick up wounded. Hiram saw bodies all over the ground. One of them was Hansy Gephart from Plainville, not yet twenty years old. Hiram grieved for his sister-in-law. Amy loved her stepchildren as much as her own son.

He knew that some of the recently arrived doughboys had little training. Why were untrained boys sent into battle? He wondered what the newspapers reported at home. Did the civilian population know the number of casualties? The number killed?

Though normally an easygoing man, his resentment grew as he thought of the Kaiser and other world leaders who had let such carnage explode. His anger seethed at the idea of grafters and war profiteers who produced shoddy goods and bad food. Already miffed by the pompousness of some of the officers, he thought about the stupid mistakes they made which wasted time and labor and made life miserable for the troops.

He remembered the yarn going around the camps: A general briefed his officers on an assault they were about to make. Certain of victory, he brimmed with enthusiasm about the project. He admitted that, in round numbers, the fight would cost about a hundred thousand troops, but it would be well worth the price, and "we can afford it."

At this point, a junior officer, hence expendable, turned to one of his neighbors and muttered, "Generous son of a bitch, isn't he!"

Chapter Forty-Six

In the Red Cross hospital in France, Sylvia, from Diane's nursing school, arrived to join her old classmates. Diane and Maxine greeted her warmly. As Sylvia was the youngest of all the nurses, just twenty-five, and the sweetest, according to Maxine, they all tried to make her sojourn with them as pleasant as possible under the circumstances. With a smile for everyone, Sylvia breezed through the wards, giving special attention to the most desperate cases.

Diane heard from Aunt Elizabeth that Eric the Red had been wounded in the Compiegne fighting. It hurt to realize that her freckled partner in vegetable peddling had lost his left arm. She remembered him in her classroom through the years, and at normal school. Just her age, her cousin had been almost as close as a twin brother.

Her bitterness against the war increased when she read that Hansy Schaffer, Amy's stepson, had been killed. She knew how the news must have devastated Amy, who had raised the boy from early childhood.

Keith McCall, beautiful Barbara Hoffman's new husband, had also died in the fighting. When his widow got the message in Plainville, she left immediately for Washington, D.C. for a job as a stenographer in one of the many new agencies set up during the war. She longed to help her country in the war effort.

Aunt Elizabeth wrote about more deaths: Phil Spencer, dead from influenza in training camp, leaving his wife Leah and a new daughter; Lila, her old classmate, married to her cousin, Friendly Frank Hoffman, and their four children, all dead from influenza, despite Aunt Pamela's and Uncle John's nursing; Rachel, Uncle Robert's daughter in Oregon, and her husband, dead from influenza.

In France, the nurses heard frightening reports about the deadly influenza that infected the soldiers.

"The patients turn blue, their lungs turn black, and they die horrible deaths." Bridget, wide-eyed, told the other nurses what she'd heard. "How can I expose myself? My family depends on me to send money."

"Hazel says she's leaving," Maxine whispered. "She claims she did not sign up for a plague of influenza. What shall we do?" She looked at the others for guidance.

Diane too feared the deadly disease. Once exposed, a person had no way to fight it. No treatment was available. Already one ward of the hospital was quarantined for influenza patients. Young women had collapsed while working there and were sent to bed in a ward set aside for women. One had already died. A few older nurses cared for patients now.

The number of influenza patients increased every day. More quarantined wards were needed. Diane and her friends would have to care for them or abandon their chosen profession.

This ultimate service would test their commitment to aid the sick. With a bleak look, but with determination, Diane said, "it's our duty to care for patients, no matter what diseases they have. I'm frightened too, but we must work wherever we're assigned. Think of the soldiers. They go into battle because it's their duty. This is our duty."

♦ ♦ ♦

All the nurses volunteered to work in the quarantined ward, including Hazel, though she nursed with a stony expression on her face and fear in her eyes. Within days, several contacted the influenza, among them, young Sylvia, who became very ill. She begged the nurses to look after the other patients. She needed nothing, Sylvia said, as she died a miserable, painful death.

Diane had just started nursing in the quarantined ward when Scott was brought in, heavily sedated. "Oh, no, not Scott." She rushed to his bed.

The doctor arrived to tend to Scott's wound and leave instructions for his care. Diane sat by his bed well into the evening, hoping to find him awake so she could determine how ill he was. But he slept on, sedated, and she left him, to reappear early the next morning.

When he opened his eyes, he said, "I've gone to Heaven, and here's an angel."

Diane laughed, relieved to find him conscious. "No angel. No Heaven. Just a hospital. How do you feel, Scott?" She reached for a thermometer.

"Like I'd been hit by a tank, but it's worth it to see you, Diane. What's wrong with me?"

"You have an ugly wound in the thigh, and a touch of influenza. Open your mouth, please."

When she removed the thermometer, he said, "a touch of influenza?"

"Yes. If it were a bad case, your temperature would be higher. I need to look at your leg too."

"By all means. Look at both of them. And anything else you'd like to look at."

She blushed, glad to see he was well enough to banter. She moved his gown aside and studied the wound. "No need to call the doctor. The dressing is all right for now. I'll bring you some juice. Could you eat anything else?"

"No, not just yet. I think I could sleep again."

"Of course, Scott. Sleep. You'll likely be well in a few days. Rest is what you need." She tucked the covers around him. She too could use sleep. Perhaps it would cure her of her throbbing headache.

Chapter Forty-Seven

When Scott awoke, another nurse hovered close. "Where's Diane?" he wanted to know.

"I need to take your temperature," Maxine said, surprised at the quick question. "Diane is busy. She's reading to Leonard Price. He's recovering from a light case of influenza."

With the thermometer in his mouth, Scott groaned. *Good Lord, did the guy have to appear whenever he had a chance to see Diane?* He sank back on the bed, sulking.

Later, Diane came to him. "What have you been doing?" he said, in a slightly pouting voice.

She stared at him. "Why, working, of course. How do you feel today?"

"Jealous," he admitted. "Aren't we engaged?"

"Jealous? Heavens, Scott, I'm a nurse. I have to treat everybody."

"And read to them?"

She paused and eyed him carefully. "That's part of the treatment when we have the time."

"Then read to me, not him."

"I can't right now. We have to feed the patients. After the meal, I'll read to you," she said. "Just so you don't feel neglected and jealous. After all, you're the one I've been worrying about."

But Diane never returned to read to Scott. As he began to feel better, Maxine told him that Diane had collapsed from influenza.

A few days later, Scott had recovered enough to take a short walk to the women's isolation ward where Diane, delirious, lay. He touched her feverish face and took her hand. He spoke soothing words to her, though he had no idea whether or not she heard him or understood. He felt helpless. It seemed cruel that nurses contacted disease from their patients.

As from a great distance, Diane heard voices and saw human forms. She thought she heard Scott. It seemed that he held her hand, but she couldn't be certain. She felt cold and excruciating pain. When she moaned, nobody came to stop the pain.

She might die. She felt such misery that she hoped she would.

♦ ♦ ♦

In the men's ward, Bridget said to Leonard, "have you been to see Diane? She contacted the Spanish influenza."

"Yes, I heard," Leonard said. "Truthfully, I'm no good around sick people. I shouldn't visit her."

"You know you're immune to the influenza, since you've just had it."

"That's what they say." He made a helpless gesture.

Maxine, changing a bed nearby, thought that was a peculiar attitude for a man who had showed keen interest in Diane in the past and had received particular attention from her as a patient. If Diane recovered, Maxine intended to make sure that she heard about Len's callous remark.

Before Diane recovered, Scott was discharged from the hospital and sent back into action. He left a moving letter for her with Maxine, declaring his love and his fervent hope and prayer that she would recover.

♦ ♦ ♦

Bulgaria, Turkey, and Austria-Hungary all surrendered to the Allies between the end of September and the beginning of November. Because of the Allied blockade, Germany's starving civilian population demanded an end to the war. The government in disarray, the Kaiser abdicated and a new government took power. Desperate German delegates met with General Foch to sign an armistice.

Word of an armistice filtered through the American ranks. The newspapers reported the abdication and hints of an end to the fighting. The world waited.

General Pershing believed the Germans should be soundly defeated and ordered a general attack for November 11th. At 6:25 A.M., with some troops already over the top, officers received the news that the Armistice had been signed and that hostilities were to cease at 11:00 A.M. Word went forward, but too late to stop troops already in action. Both sides suffered needless deaths and injuries.

In some instances, officers, either for revenge against their men for some reason or hatred of the Germans or for an exaggerated sense of their commanding duties, sent their men into battle on the morning of the armistice, when they did not have to do so. They knew the armistice would begin at 11:00. Doughboys died as a result. Those officers earned the hostility of their comrades forever.

At 11:00 A.M., American artillery near Scott stopped firing. An aerie silence settled over the front. Scott's men looked toward some French artillerymen who were throwing their helmets in the air. An excited officer from another company ran toward them. "The war is over, the war is over," he shouted. "An armistice has been signed."

As the news sank in, civilians and soldiers on both sides reacted with relief and jubilation. Scott saw Germans stand up, shout wildly, and jump up and down for joy.

All along the front rockets and flares lit the sky. Troops blew off their grenades and fired ammunition to celebrate. Hundreds of American flags flew. Warm fires, previously prohibited, provided cozy heat for Scott's men for the first time in months. The men basked in blessed warmth.

What was it all for? Scott wondered. Over one hundred thousand American men killed and twice that number wounded or missing.

France and Germany suffered far greater losses. A total of over five million of the Allies and three million from the Central Powers died in battle or from wounds or disease. And that didn't even count the civilians.

He had read the preliminary numbers, and figured they were underestimates. With time to reflect, he shuttered at the carnage he had been a part of. What a grim time it had been.

For a few more days, the Allies stayed along the armistice line in order to give the Germans time to make an orderly retreat. Also, the Allies waited for supplies to come to the front in order to help civilians and to care for the numerous prisoners released by the Germans. If the war had lasted any longer, the Allies would have completely run out of munitions and materials.

When German wireless sent out locations of thousands of hidden mines, German prisoners were put to work removing them.

With all the medals they had earned, Scott and the colored American soldiers clearly deserved the honor of marching at the head of the French troops as they crossed the Rhine River into Mainx. In addition to the numerous citations they had won, they had spent more time in France than other American regiments.

♦ ♦ ♦

Because of the morning fighting, Diane's hospital experienced a rush throughout the day even as bells pealed to celebrate the end of the fighting. In addition, the influenza epidemic was just reaching its peak. No end of the misery was yet in sight.

Along with the patients, the nurses cheered the news of the Armistice. Despite the rush, the wards filled with happy remarks, gleeful laughter, hope for the future. Diane, slowly recovering from influenza, relieved along with the others, wept for the millions killed in the senseless slaughter. But soon they'd all be going home. She and Scott could build a life together.

The next morning the chief nurse called the nurses together.

"How soon can we leave for home?" Bridget said, in great excitement.

Miss Simmons gave her a sharp look. "I might have expected you to ask first," she said. "I'm afraid you'll all be needed for many more months."

"But why?" Bridget was unfazed.

"We'll be getting more Allied prisoners, just released by the Germans. Our badly wounded servicemen will need long-term care until they recover enough for the trip home. Sick and injured civilians will continue to come to the Red Cross hospitals until their own facilities are replaced. I ask all of you to please consider staying for an indefinite period."

Though disappointed, the nurses accepted the news with resignation. At least the carnage had stopped. The alarming rushes were over.

Chapter Forty-Eight

In Plainville, church bells rang all over town on Armistice Day. The quarantine had been lifted and the recovered citizens lit prepared bonfires. Crowds gathered around the fires.

Eric the Red joined his father and mother for the celebration. Despite her many losses during the war and the epidemic, Pamela Hoffman put her grief aside to join her neighbors. She grabbed old Mr. Owen's hat and threw it into the fire. Everyone knew it was twenty years old anyway. He took the exuberant act in good grace, laughing along with the others.

Eric saw Elizabeth and Drew throw kisses and talk to Doris, Vicky, and Vicky's youngsters as they stood in the yard and watched the fire with excitement. Elizabeth thought it was still too much of a risk to take the children out.

"Thank God." Vicky stood with the youngest child in her arms. "Now Matthew can come home, and all the others too."

At the hotel, Julia Hoffman Spencer and Hannah Baker handed out cookies to add to the celebration. Sugar would surely become plentiful soon. Hiram would be coming home.

Eric saw Leah at her window, holding her child, watching the happy people filling the streets, the fire towering over the town. Though her husband, Phil, would not be returning, her brothers, Eric, Jack, and Sam survived, as well as many friends.

Eric danced in the street with the townspeople. Eager to prove that he could function with only one arm, he amazed his family and friends by lighting cigarettes with his right hand. At the hotel dining room he entertained the coffee drinkers by playing the harmonica with the help of a homemade holder or neck rack to position the instrument in front of his mouth. He knew his future livelihood depended upon his skill with his right arm. He received a paltry disability pension, but it wasn't much to live on, less than those of Civil War veterans.

He had applied to teach school, but some townspeople felt a one-armed man wouldn't be able to control the students. He determined to prove them wrong by the next year. Meanwhile, with remarkable dexterity, he took over the motor livery vacated by Friendly Frank's death. For those few jobs he could not handle with one arm, his father, nearby at the blacksmith shop, helped out.

Bob Hoffman, soon to be out of the army, wrote to Eric complaining bitterly about Diane inheriting his father's house and one third of his money. When Eric mentioned his letters to Elizabeth, she reminded him that Diane had nursed both Uncle Robert and Catherine for long periods in their final illnesses.

"Bob threatened her," Elizabeth said. "I'm uneasy about that."

♦ ♦ ♦

Restless, the troops in Europe waited to be sent home. One night Mike suggested to Hiram and George that they stroll into a nearby town for a drink.

George shook his head. "Some of the guys say there are toughs in the village who resent Americans."

Mike laughed off the idea. "Nonsense. We get along fine with the poilu."

After some discussion, Mike persuaded Hiram and George to go for a drink.

As the noisy bar was crowded with Frenchmen, the Americans shouted over the noise for service. A Frenchman, speaking in a combination of poor English and rudimentary French in order to be understood, said, "Wait your turn, buddy. You're just visitors here, you know."

"Visitors, hell. We saved your country." Mike stood up as though to confront the man.

"Saved us? We fought this war four long years before you even got organized, you swaggering Americans. We're ready to see your backs."

"Yes," his companion broke in. "You Yanks have overstayed your welcome. You're all three-fourths German anyway."

At this seeming insult, Mike's fist reached out and slammed into the speaker's jaw.

Chapter Forty-Nine

Pandemonium broke out. Hostile Frenchmen surrounded the three Americans. Hiram, dodging blows on his face and chest, grabbed Mike and George by the scruffs of their necks, pushed them forward, and fought his way out of the bar. "Good God, we've got to get out of here. The MPs will be here any second."

Mike, bleeding at the mouth, wiped his face on his shirt. "Stupid Frogs. No appreciation. We should have knocked them all out."

"Are you crazy? The three of us against a whole room full?" Hiram managed to squeeze the three of them in a doorway at the end of an alley. "Shut up," he said, "so we can hear what's going on."

The MPs searched the bar and the street but missed the alley. After a long anxious wait, the three bloodied Americans stumbled back to their camp.

Hiram, mystified, wiped his face with his handkerchief. *Does the human race never get its fill of violence?*

◆ ◆ ◆

A few weeks after the armistice, Maxine's aunt threw a party at her home in Paris for her niece and her friends. Diane hugged Alex in relief, overjoyed that her brother had survived. Though still struggling with the deaths of the airmen who had traded flights with him, he and Maxine sat together, talking quietly.

Airmen and officers from different services sipped wine, something the French always seemed to have on hand, and discussed their plans for a peaceful life back home.

Len tried to strike up a conversation with Diane, but Maxine had told her that the man had not bothered to visit her when she was sick. Now she avoided him. She heard that Scott had sat beside her bed for hours. As both of the men had had the influenza, they'd both had immunity and would not have caught it from her.

When she saw Scott arrive, she greeted him in the foyer, giddy with excitement. He kissed her passionately, moaning with pleasure.

"I was afraid I'd never see you again," she said, her eyes sparkling.

"Thank God you're all right. When I saw you last you were delirious." He continued to hold her and pet her hair.

"People will see us," she said, shying away.

"Who cares? We're engaged, aren't we?"

She sighed in pleasure. "I hope so. I've worried about you and longed to see you."

In a quiet corner, he told her about the record of his troops. Justifiably proud, he figured his colored regiment was under fire in France for a greater number of days than any other American regiment.

Their engagement as part of the Meuse-Argonne campaign earned the regiment the Croix de Guerre as well as 171 individual citations for the Croix de Guerre for its officers and men.

"This must have been the bloodiest war of all time," he remarked.

"It's been a war like no other. Surely the world has learned something from the chaos."

"Now we have to wait for our orders home. It should not be long. Shall we marry in Plainville? I'm stationed too far away to get to your hospital again for a wedding."

"Oh, I'm sorry to hear that. A Plainville wedding will be fine."

But back at work, Diane confided to several nurses at breakfast that Scott seemed to expect her to leave France as soon as he was ordered home.

"How can I leave now, when we're still needed here so desperately? I'm being tugged in opposite directions, like a yo-yo. I want to be with Scott, but I also want to stay here and finish our job."

"Good God," Hazel said, "why are you hesitating? If it was me, I'd be out of here so fast, you'd call me Miss Speedy."

Maxine considered. "If it was me, I'd probably leave to be with Alex, er, Scott. We don't all have to stay. You've done your duty for the Red Cross cause already, Diane."

♦ ♦ ♦

Scott did not have to wait until they met in Plainville to see Diane after all. In February, his regiment was scheduled to return to New York aboard a French superliner. He managed to wangle a pass to see her at the hospital. The train was packed, took hours, and the tedious trip tired him. Only the thought of being with Diane and giving her the happy news made it bearable.

In front of the hospital, Len stood smoking a cigarette.

"What are you doing here, Len?" Scott said. "I thought you had recovered."

"I am recovered. I'm about to visit Diane."

"Oh? I heard you didn't visit her while she was sick with influenza."

Len threw down his cigarette and stomped on it. "Well, not that it's any of your business, but she's well now."

Scott glared. "I consider it my business. Diane and I are engaged to be married. I've come a long way to visit her. So I'd appreciate it if you'd leave."

"I haven't heard anything about an engagement. Maybe she's changed her mind. I see no reason for me to leave."

Scott stepped close, his fists clenched. "Get lost," he said.

Len was no fool. The man who stood before him radiated hostility. "Well, since you've come such a long way." He stepped back, turned, and hurried off.

That should set Len straight. Scott entered the hospital. He flushed with eagerness. He and Diane could be together much sooner than either of them had expected. When she entered the foyer, he ached with longing for her, his need to touch her soft brown hair, to caress her face.

"Now you can quit the Red Cross and get passage over yourself," he said in great excitement after he had explained. "We can meet in New York and marry there."

She looked at him for a time. "Scott, I can't leave for some months. I'm badly needed here."

He shrugged off her concern. "They can get along without you. Whereas, I need you desperately."

She backed away. "My work is important. It's my duty to stay until the servicemen recover and civilians are properly cared for in their own facilities."

Stunned, he said, "what? You won't come home?"

She held firm. "When I'm no longer needed, I'll come home. I'm sorry. There's nothing I can do."

Overwhelmed with disappointment, he said coldly, "I've gone to some trouble to see you today. Too bad you feel duty toward everyone else." He turned to go. "I'll see you in Nebraska."

He left quickly, his disappointment fueling his anger.

Chapter Fifty

When they arrived in New York, Scott's regiment marched in a grand parade as the band played in front of cheering crowds. It culminated in Harlem where the honoring friends and families outdid themselves to show their pride and appreciation for their National Guard Regiment. The parade was followed by a dinner reception downtown. The next day the men were mustered out of the service at Camp Upton.

Scott enjoyed the festivities, but he felt empty inside. As the train carried him home to Nebraska, his anger began to fade. Why had he left Diane in such a cold rush? She had told him earlier how important her work was to her. She only asked for a little more time. And there was Len, always waiting for his chance with Diane.

Scott's mood grew darker as he passed through eastern cities, filled with smoke and soot due to all the new war industries.

But as the train left the pollution behind, his mood improved in the fresh countryside.

After all, Diane hadn't rejected him. She'd only said she had to stay for a time. He'd write a letter, apologizing. And he'd have time to make arrangements.

For several months, he helped out at his brother's newspaper, investigating opportunities to buy a paper of his own. His presence allowed Vince and Maggie to take a much-needed vacation. He wrote to Diane, apologizing for his impatience, pleading his eagerness to be with her. She wrote back, but it seemed to him that her letters were slightly cold, less passionate than before.

In early July, he persuaded his sister to travel to Plainville with him for the Independence Day celebration and to visit Matthew and Vicky. As Ann had lost close friends in the war, he wanted to give her something else to think about. He also planned to consult with Drew Robinson about starting a newspaper in a small town.

Drew welcomed Ann to the newspaper offices, listened to Scott's questions, asked some himself. Finally, he said, "Scott, it's occurred to me that your visit is providential. You've probably heard that Phil Spencer died in training camp of influenza."

"Yes, I'm sorry," Scott murmured.

"The thing is, I can't continue getting out a paper without help. As the town grows, we get more advertising business all the time. Have you any interest in becoming my partner?"

Scott gaped. The thought had never entered his mind, but he saw advantages. He had always liked and admired Drew and could benefit from his guidance.

He liked Plainville. Diane had a house here. But would she still want to marry him?

Drew went on. "Elizabeth says that you and Diane are engaged. If you settled here, you'd both be near family and friends. We'd miss you if you went off."

"Well..." Scott didn't know how to explain. He wasn't sure they were still engaged.

"Say, you and Ann are probably hungry. Let's go over to the hotel and get something to eat. We can discuss this further. Elizabeth and Doris are meeting me there later." Drew stood up and ushered them out the door.

Scott went along with the invitation. "We're expected for dinner at Matthew's and Vicky's house. But we can eat something light."

While they settled themselves at a table, Hiram Spencer brought wood inside and put it beside the fireplace. Recognizing Scott from as far back as the San Francisco earthquake, he hurried up to greet them. When Julia approached to take their order she said, "Look who's here. Scott and Ann Morris. It's wonderful to see you. Hiram and I have been wondering about you, Scott."

"And I've worried about all my friends in Plainville."

"I'm the luckiest woman in the world to have my Hiram back." She took the back of her husband's hand and stroked it, as though to prove how much she'd missed him. Obviously pleased, he patted her cheek. He'd spent months longing to be at home with his family.

"I wish you could see the children, but they're visiting Hannah in her new house today. Perhaps another time. We have a nice vegetable beef soup today."

She took their order and, after a few more comments, Hiram resumed his work.

♦ ♦ ♦

While Drew and Scott discussed details of journalism, Ann watched a young redheaded one-armed man at a nearby table entertain his friends by lighting a match with his right hand and managing a number of similar tasks. His left shirt sleeve was doubled over and neatly pinned so as not to dangle.

As Ann continued to watch, she recognized him from his sister's wedding. Called Eric the Red, he had attracted attention then by his unusual coloring and vibrant personality.

When he looked in their direction, she smiled at him in recognition.

After the three had finished a light meal, Eric approached their table. "Drew, you and Scott could probably talk about newspapers all day. But I sense that Ann is bored to death. Allow me to take her for a walk about town. It's a fine day."

Ann stood up immediately and joined him. Scott and Drew nodded absently and continued their discussion. On the street, Eric offered Ann his right arm.

"Where did you lose it?" She asked."

"Compiegne. Honestly I don't miss it much. Two arms can get you into double trouble." He grinned philosophically.

"How will you make a living?"

"Right now, I'm working at the auto livery, but I hope to get back to teaching next fall."

"I'm a teacher myself."

"Cousin Diane suggested I think about working full-time at the bank. She's part owner. I haven't decided yet."

"Sounds as though you have options."

"Yes, about work, anyway. I have connections. Finding a wife may be more difficult." He grinned at her, his eyes bright.

She smiled back. "Well, you'll just have to work harder at it."

"I'm willing to do that," he said with alacrity. He indicated a dwelling nearby. "Now this house belongs to Elizabeth Spencer Robinson, married to Drew. It was built by her father, Doctor Spencer. The house two blocks up on the corner belongs to my father, John Hoffman. He and my mother raised seven children there. But, of course, you were at Leah's wedding. This house…"

She listened, totally absorbed and fascinated, until they returned to the hotel.

Chapter Fifty-One

Bob Hoffman left the train in the nearest town and walked to Plainville long after dark. He let himself into his boyhood home and fumbled around in the dark. Settling down in the kitchen to a meal of cold chicken, bread, and cheese he had brought with him, he helped himself to water. He did not dare make a fire. The neighbors must not see lights.

Jack Hoffman had mentioned in his letter that Diane would be returning this day to her house. It stood empty and ready for her return. He'd been smart to foster a correspondence with Jack, even though he had not seen his oldest cousin in many years. He complained to Jack about Diane and how she had bullied his father to leave her his house and a third of his money.

He had planned this trip carefully. Since Rachel and her husband had died of influenza, he and Diane were due to divide Robert Hoffman's money. If Diane was gone, he would have it all, and the house. He alone should inherit everything his father had owned. It was only right.

He could strangle Diane with a scarf he'd purchased, and smother her with a pillow, if necessary, when she arrived, then sneak off in the dark. When he returned to Plainville on the train, he would talk to people at the depot and wave to everyone he saw. He would stop off at the hotel for a snack to make sure he was noticed by as many people as possible. Then he would go to her house and find the body, if it had not been discovered already, and alert the police. Who would suspect him? He might even invite someone to come to the house with him to make the find.

He dropped the remains of the chicken he'd brought on the floor, to make it look like an accidental choking death on a chicken bone. Even if it was not ruled accidental, he would not be a suspect. Everyone would have seen him arrive that day.

He anticipated some difficulties. Diane might stop off to see her Aunt Elizabeth first. He might even have to wait a day or so. But in the end she would come to the house.

If she came with someone, he could claim he needed shelter until he found a room. Then he would have to devise another plan. Still, he figured she would come to the house alone to savor her ill-gotten gains. How dare she seek to inherit what rightfully belonged to him?

He went over his plan in the dark and mused on his war experience as he waited for sleep on the living room sofa. By lying and by judicious politicking, he'd held a staff job far from the front. Even that had tried his patience. Glad to be out of the army, he planned to sell the house, collect the money, and get back to Omaha where he belonged, working as an executive for the railroad until he turned thirty, when he'd have it all.

◆ ◆ ◆

Diane, bone tired, tried to sleep on the train, but the noise and the commotion prevented that. As the train neared Plainville, she watched the prairie fields of grain ripening in the sun. It looked like a good crop if an August souther wind did not dry everything up. The farmers would be planning the harvest as soon as possible to avoid losing their crops.

She had mailed a letter to Scott in Omaha at their last stop. He had been so proud of his men. Because of his concern about segregation and other difficulties of the blacks, she had sent some money to the organization for colored people.

She had cried bitter tears when he left her in France. Had she been unreasonable? She didn't think so. She had warned him that nursing was of paramount importance to her. Apparently, he was unable to tolerate her work after all. He had conveniently forgotten her commitment to her profession. Still, when he wrote to apologize, she began to hope they might work things out.

She looked forward to seeing what was left of her relatives. So many had died from the war, from the influenza. But her sisters and brothers,

Aunt Elizabeth and her family, and Vicky thrived, as well as her cousins: Thelma, Leah, Eric, and Jack. Barbara worked in Washington, D.C., as a stenographer.

She was eager to see all of them, but first she wanted to visit her house, to remember Catherine and Rachel, and to enjoy the quiet and the peace she had never found there.

By late afternoon, she left the train depot and walked to the house she now owned. She knew Elizabeth had prepared for her return. The renters had vacated.

Chapter Fifty-Two

At the hotel, Elizabeth arrived with little Doris and greeted Scott and Ann. "It's wonderful that you're visiting today, Scott. Diane is due today or tomorrow."

She must have seen the surprised look on Scott's face. After a moment, she said, "she probably planned to write to you in Omaha when she got home. You know how unpredictable the trains are these days, with all the servicemen coming back."

"Of course." Scott covered his embarrassment. Diane should have let him know. His ignorance about her whereabouts put him on the spot. "It's wonderful to see you. We're here for the Independence Day celebration. Matthew and Vicky are expecting us."

When they left the Robinsons at the hotel, Scott and Ann climbed the slight incline to their host's house, Eric strolling along on the other side of Ann. He seemed reluctant to leave the siblings, and Scott had no intention of questioning his presence. Ann's smiles told him she enjoyed Eric.

Vicky McCall came running out of the imposing house. "Did you see Diane? Mrs. Smith called that Diane's come in on the train. She saw her trudging up the hill."

He was sure he gave her a blank expression. "I suppose she walked up to the old Robert Hoffman house," Vicky said. "It's hers now, you know. She probably wanted some time alone."

Matthew urged them all inside, including Eric. "Vicky's been baking berry pies all day and cooking a pot roast. We're due for a fine meal." The smell of spices, browning meat, and onions drifted from the kitchen.

Scott fidgeted. "Do you mind if I run up to Diane's house before dinner? I'd like to know if she's there. She had no idea I'd be visiting, and I didn't realize she would be here."

"By all means, go." Vicky, her matchmaking instincts in high alert, spun him around and gave him a gentle push out the door. "We won't be eating for some time."

Scott sprinted to Diane's house.

♦ ♦ ♦

As Diane opened the door and surveyed the front room, she saw immediately that something was wrong. Remains of a meal were scattered on the low table beside the sofa. She heard footsteps in the kitchen. Suddenly, Bob stood in the doorway.

She frowned. "What are you doing here?"

"Diane," he gushed, walking toward her. "How good to see you. I'm here for a visit and had nowhere to stay. Surely you won't refuse me shelter in my old home."

She tried to hide her irritation. "How long is your visit?"

"Not long at all," he said.

"I'm surprised to see you. You never liked me, and never had much use for Plainville either."

"Ah, well. Things change, Diane. I'm glad to be out of that damn war and away from those stupid French."

"Are you working in Omaha again?"

"I plan to get my old job back." He moved close.

She took a step backward. "Well, Bob, I must ask you to go stay with Uncle John and Aunt Pamela or get a room at the hotel. It wouldn't do for cousins to share a house together. People would talk."

He gave her a cruel smile. "Of course, if that's what you want. Here, let me take your hat."

She lowered her head to remove her hat, her hands running over the large hat pin in the middle. Suddenly, he had his hands around her neck in a vise. "You little crook. Nobody cheats me out of my inheritance." His hands tightened. "I'm getting rid of you for good."

Panic seized her. She was at his mercy. He was much larger than she.

Controlling her terror, she realized what she had to do.

She was no soft female. Working long hours scrubbing, lifting, carrying at the hospital had strengthened her young muscles. She had one chance to escape him.

She rammed her knee into his thigh. She grabbed the hat pin from her hat and shoved it into his middle. He howled, and released his hold.

◆ ◆ ◆

As he approached the long porch in front of Diane's house, Scott heard angry talk, sounds of a struggle, and then a pitiful howl of pain.

He burst into the room. Bob was bent over, apparently in pain, Diane backing away. "He meant to kill me," she said in astonishment, holding a hand to her neck. Blood flowed from a cut made by Bob's fingernails.

"What? Are you all right, Diane?" He rushed to take her in his arms.

"Yes, yes. He tried to choke me. We need to call the police. He's dangerous."

"My God, you're right. You go call Chief Johnson. I'll watch him."

Diane hurried to the kitchen telephone. She screamed to the police chief on the line that Cousin Bob Hoffman had tried to kill her. He'd said so as he attempted to choke her. She'd stuck him with a hat pin.

When she returned, Bob showed signs of recovering, though blood oozed from his abdomen. Scott gave him a threatening look. "What did you do to him?" He asked Diane.

"I stuck him with a hat pin."

Scott stared at her, awed. "Why would he want to kill you?"

"So he could inherit Uncle Robert's money. With me dead, he would get it all, and this house."

Scott glared at Bob. "He's a monster."

"From the looks of things, he's been here a few days, waiting for me to arrive so he could get rid of me."

The police squad car, its spotlight blazing, braked to a squealing stop in front of the house. Chief Johnson and another officer rushed through the open door. Bob, still bent over and bleeding from his injury, protested that he had only planned to visit in his old home, that Diane had attacked him with a hat pin.

"She wants to inherit my money, the bitch."

"Suspicion of attempted murder," the chief announced as he handcuffed Bob and led him away. "I'll have the doctor look at that wound," he said as he handed Bob a handkerchief to stem the bleeding. "Then you're going to jail."

Since he knew both of them, he accepted Diane's accusation, especially when he noticed the scarf on the floor, the bleeding wound on her neck, the slight swelling which would turn into bruises, and Bob's injury the size of a pin. If it had been premeditated murder, she would have used a more deadly weapon. "You'll need to file a report," he told her.

Their departure left Scott and Diane in silence. She located tape, gauze and scissors and handed them to him so he could bind the wound on her neck.

"Are you sure you're all right?" Scott cut off gauze and applied it to her skin.

She nodded.

"I'm sorry I didn't understand your need to stay in France. It was no different than my going in the first place." He snipped off the end of the tape. "I didn't want to go to war, but I felt I must."

"Oh, Scott, it's all over. We can forget about the monstrous fighting and killing and get back to life as it was before."

"I'm afraid the country will never be that innocent again. Conditions are worse than ever. My trip across the country showed me that. The cities are covered with dirt and smoke from unregulated heavy industry, and the richest people have become even richer."

"We don't have to live in a city."

Relieved to find she was not holding a grudge against him, he took her in his arms. "In fact, I have good news for us, my dearest. Your uncle-in-law, Drew Robinson, has invited me to become his partner at the *Gazette*."

Her eyes lit up. "That's wonderful. We can live in Plainville."

"Drew and I have a few items to iron out. Still, we have the rest of our lives to see all your many relatives, even your papa.

She winced. "Oh, you're subtle. I know how you feel about *him*, but he's hopeless anyway. Let's not argue about my papa again. I have you now."

At that moment, through the open door, a crowd of their friends appeared. The police presence had brought half the town sprinting up to view the spectacle of Bob's arrest. From the comments of the observers, no one felt much surprise when Diane explained what had happened.

Vicky hugged Diane. "It's so good to see you, Diane. Come with us. We're having a little party at our house to welcome you and Scott back home."

Scott took Diane's hand and they joined the group.

Made in the USA
Middletown, DE
23 June 2015